WATER

THE ELEMENTALS BOOK THREE

L.B. GILBERT

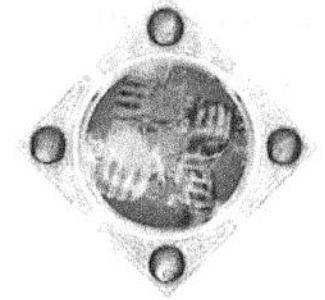

❀ Created with Vellum

CREDITS

Cover Design: Rebecca Hamilton
http://qualitybookworks.wordpress.com/

Logo Design: Juan Fernando Garcia
http://www.elblackbat.com/

Editor: Cynthia Shepp
http://www.cynthiashepp.com/

TITLES BY L.B. GILBERT

The Elementals Saga
Discordia, A Free Elementals Story
Fire
Air
Water
Earth

A Shifter's Claim
Kin Selection
Eat You Up*
Tooth and Nail
The When Witch and the Wolf

Charmed Legacy Cursed Angel Watchtowers
Forsaken

Writing As Lucy Leroux

The Singular Obsession Series
Making Her His
Confiscating Charlie, A Singular Obsession Novelette
Calen's Captive
Stolen Angel
The Roman's Woman
Save Me, A Singular Obsession Novella
Take Me, A Singular Obsession Prequel Novella
Trick's Trap
Peyton's Price

The Complete Spellbound Regency Series
The Hex, A Free Spellbound Regency Short
Cursed
Black Widow
Haunted

The Rogues and Rescuers Series
Codename Romeo
The Mercenary Next Door
Knight Takes Queen
The Millionaire's Mechanic
Burned Deep - Coming Soon

*As Lucy Leroux

PROLOGUE

Daniel Romero fingered his gun as the other agents rounded up the bikini-clad girls from the estate's pool. Technically, the danger was over. The raid had been aborted on arrival when their target—a ruthless drug lord nicknamed *the Reaper*—was found floating face-down in his jacuzzi.

The operation had shifted into recovery-and-interrogation mode. The coroner was on his way to pick up the body, which had been covered with a sheet while they questioned the witnesses. The Reaper had been having a pool party, so there were a lot of those.

And yet, no one saw a damn thing.

Daniel's eyes ran over the crowd. All it had taken was the wrong combination of booze and drugs to end the Reaper's brief reign of terror. How many of his *'friends'* would have jumped into the pool to save him?

Daniel turned, catching his partner's eye. "Do you believe this? There are almost fifty people here, and not one noticed the piece of shit drowning five feet away."

Ray Doyle scratched his nose. "They're all probably too high— including our guy. He must have passed out and went under just in time to fuck us over. Over a year of prep down the drain. What a letdown."

A girl in a skimpy leopard-print bikini passed in front of them, escorted to a shaded poolside table by one of their team.

"Okay, I take that back." Ray murmured, his eyes tracking leopard girl.

Daniel spared a moment to thank the manufacturers of mirrored sunglasses. The shades masked Ray's blatant interest in the teenager.

"C'mon, man. That's jailbait right there."

He didn't bother to mention his partner already had an age-appropriate girlfriend. Ray was just looking.

His partner scowled. "You think? Nah. She's got to be at least twenty."

Daniel scoffed. "Wishful thinking won't make it so."

Ray flipped open his notebook. "Well, standing here with our dicks in our hands won't prove it, either. I'm going to get her statement."

"Go ahead," Daniel sniped. "I'm sure she'll have lots of valuable intel."

"Oh, fuck off, man." Ray walked away.

Daniel watched him go with a sigh. His partner was used to his moods, but he'd have to buy him a beer later.

The crowd shifted. It was mainly women in bikinis, but there were a few men, presumably some of the Reaper's many lieutenants. He made a mental note to track them all in case one stepped up to take over what was left of the operation.

He tried to make himself move and pitch in, but couldn't summon the motivation. This raid had been their baby. It had taken months to plan. Daniel had personally overseen every detail of this joint DEA and ATF operation. He'd worked day and night for the last few weeks to make sure everything went off without a hitch and their people weren't faced with unnecessary danger. Now their scumbag was dead, any intel he knew about the larger drug network he was connected to went with him.

As if he would've talked. These guys were all the same. They kept their mouths shut, then continued to run their criminal empires from a jail cell.

Felix Desjardin, aka the Reaper, had risen through the ranks of the southeast US cartels like a rocket. He had no loyalty. Felix had jumped ship whenever a bigger opportunity had presented itself, leaving his old partners dead or in disarray. He'd started his own outfit, carving up a niche—and a few competitors—here on the gulf coast of Texas.

Desjardin was the main suspect in a string of high-profile murders. Most of the victims had been linked to the drug trade, but a few hadn't appeared to have had ties to the underworld at all. There had been an insurance adjuster from Nogales, as well as a social worker from Houston. Both had been community-oriented volunteer types. No one would have guessed a dark past if it hadn't been for Desjardin's M-O.

Felix didn't kill people. He sacrificed them. Each death scene had been elaborately decorated with weird satanic symbols, sprinkles of a specific mixture of herbs and esoteric flowers bits showered all over the place.

Daniel had been looking forward to bringing the asshole in and asking him what the fuck he thought he was doing.

The coroner better get here soon. The more time the body spent cooking in this sun, the more difficult it would be to determine the time of death. He was about to call over some agents to help him move one of the many oversized parasols over the corpse, when movement in the water caught his eye. Squinting, he frowned as a flash of white on dark skin shot by under the water at Olympic-level speed.

"Is there someone in the fucking pool?" he asked.

Wilkes, a junior agent, glanced up from his interview. "It's only the queen," he said, gesturing to the pool with his pen.

The what?

Wilkes shrugged.

Daniel sniffed. "Is it Desjardin's girlfriend?"

All their intel had said their man was unattached. A girlfriend would have meant the Reaper had to give up his harem of beach bunnies.

The uniformed servant Wilkes was interviewing piped up. "No, Serin's not his girlfriend. It's just what we call her. You'll understand when you meet her."

Unfucking-believable. "Get that woman out of the pool *now*," Daniel said.

Taking a deep breath, he snapped his shade clip back on his aviators. He waited at the end of the pool, his arms crossed, while Wilkes gestured frantically to the woman in the pool.

She took her sweet time, finishing her lap with languid grace. When she was done, she began to walk up the steps facing him.

Time slowed as a dark curly head rose from the crystalline blue-green water. Daniel blinked as she shook out her hair, a natural afro bouncing back in a way that defied the laws of physics.

The rest of her movement was equally hypnotic, and slightly alien like a CGI creation—the amateur ones before they got human movement right. People rarely moved with such grace, except maybe ballerinas and strippers. He was betting on the latter.

What was that about wishful thinking?

Water cascaded down the woman's body in sparkling rivulets that gleamed like mercury against lush dark curves. The striking contrast of the pristine white bikini against the cocoa-colored skin was almost indecent.

Daniel could feel his breath shortening, each inhalation punctuated by his distant heartbeat. One of the faceless uninformed staff rushed to the woman, holding out a diaphanous red robe that did nothing to conceal the over-the-top hourglass figure.

Wilkes led the woman toward the ornate French doors. Agents were conducting more interviews inside. She passed in front of Daniel, her blue eyes flickering over him with a little smile he found difficult to interpret. Their eyes met for a beat. The moment was enough to send a shooting thrill down to his gut.

Confidence and power trailed from her like an invisible cloak. He suddenly understood why they called her the queen.

"*Damn.*" He started and turned, surprised to see Ray standing next to him. Daniel gave himself a little shake, snapping out of his stupefied trance. What was wrong with him? He was on the job for fuck's sake.

Daniel cleared his throat. "What?"

Smirking, Ray mimed a little rolling motion with his hands before holding out his fingers as if he were presenting Daniel with something.

"What the hell are you doing?"

"I'm rolling your tongue back in your head for you," Ray said with a shit-eating grin.

"Shut up, man." Daniel signaled to a subordinate that they were going inside. "Let's go. We'll conduct the queen's interview ourselves."

But when they went inside, they found their witness had excused herself to clean up in the restroom. A few minutes later, they found it empty. They searched the house, which was crawling with agents and other law enforcement officers.

Her Highness had left the building.

1

SIX MONTHS LATER

Serin lifted her heel off the man's throat long enough to let him speak. "I'm sorry, but I didn't quite catch that."

"You bitch!"

She pressed her heel back down, cutting off the rest. "I thought you private mercenaries were supposed to be tough. I have to say—geriatric sharks have more fight in them."

Scanning the room, she took stock. The rest of the team was scattered around them. All were dressed in black, their many weapons useless and broken on the ground.

She removed her foot and knelt, taking care not to snag her crystal-encrusted skirt. "I think you might be overpaid," she whispered in his ear before smiling and hauling him up by the shirt collar. She shook him like a rag doll, pointing his head in the general direction of his employer.

"As I was explaining to your boss, Mr. Sayer over there—" Serin broke off to wave to the overweight oil executive.

The gag in the man's mouth prevented him from answering back.

"The oil company is in violation of an existing treaty we signed with the Agunte for water rights in this mountain."

"There are no fucking Indians in—"

She held up a hand. "The Agunte aren't an indigenous tribe. They're the squid-like creatures living in the aquifers surrounding the oil deposits your company illegally seized."

The merc blinked. "You're doing this for *squid*?"

"Squid-like creatures," she corrected. "They're sentient, highly intelligent creatures from an extremely far away land. They came here after centuries of war wiped out most of their kind. In exchange for a safe place to live, they kindly offered us what they could—a few seeds of a useful little plant from their home world. Humans extracted aspirin from it. That was centuries later, of course."

The merc grumbled something under his breath, but she heard him clearly.

Serin rolled her eyes, then slapped him like the little bitch he was. "I'm not crazy, nor am I delusional," she replied, turning to his boss. "It's so like a man to dismiss a woman as hysterical. But you know all about the treaty. The Agunte told you, over and over again."

She dropped the merc at Sayer's feet. "All the signs you ignored, the messages you received—their cries for help. You knew. Your staff knew. But the oil reserve was big enough for you to ignore them... even after the cries turned to screams."

Her face hardened. After moving to Sayer, she ripped off his gag.

"Please," he begged, his round face dripping sweat. "I have a family."

Serin put her hands on either side of his face. "So did the Agunte you killed."

The man whimpered, his mouth gaping and the scent of urine hitting her sensitive nose. He'd peed himself. She almost felt pity, but it wasn't just alien squid this man had killed. Plenty of humans had died as he bribed and killed his way to the top. For a cowardly little turd, he was ruthless.

Was being the operative word. She untied his hands, hauling him up by the neck, the feat of strength terrifying to the merc at her feet.

The other man scrambled up and out of the way as she dragged her mark to the exit.

"What are you going to do to him?" the mercenary asked.

"Normally, I would snap his neck. However, in this case, the Agunte have claimed the right of retribution."

She shifted her hold to minimize her contact with the Sayer's clothing. "Which, honestly, I'm happy to give them. He's so...sweaty."

She may have been an all-powerful Water Elemental, but her love of her medium didn't extend to disgusting acrid sweat.

The opening of the bore tunnel was just a few hundred yards away from the warehouse that stored the drilling equipment. The executive gibbered and pleaded, offering her bribe after bribe along the way.

"A million dollars," he shouted as Serin reached the edge of the aquifer. Gleaming turquoise water lapped the edges of the tunnel, a galaxy of bioluminescent patterns appearing on the surface.

There were stars, constellation patterns she didn't recognize, as well as occult symbols unique to T'Kaieri. The latter was formed in deference to her. The Agunte were speaking her language.

"What the hell is that?" a mystified voice asked. It was the merc. He'd followed them out.

Her nose wrinkled. "Have you seriously never looked in this hole?"

He shook his head. "Sayer told us to stay away. We were to secure the site from an unspecified threat... You, I guess."

She gave the merc the side-eye, still holding Sayer by the scruff. "So are we going to fight some more or what?"

The merc stilled, appearing to think about it. Then he shrugged. "I don't think they paid us enough to kill an entire species and fight off Superwoman. I'm going to pull my team back."

"Good," she said, although calling them back was redundant. She'd already taken care of the team.

With no hesitation, Serin let go of Sayer, dropping him straight into the hole where the Agunte were waiting.

He didn't even have time to scream. The star patterns disappeared, and the blue-green water turned black with blood.

The merc paled, then turned green. "Fuck," he said, gagging and clutching his throat.

Serin took a deep breath. "He's already gone. His suffering was brief. It was better than he deserved, trust me."

"All right then," the man muttered, backing up a step. Clearing his throat, he held out his hand. "I'm Reynolds."

She glanced at the hand before returning her attention to the pool. Reynolds pulled his hand back, holding it against his chest before giving her outfit a once-over. In his world, apparently, not too many women fought in silk and high heels. "I guess buying you dinner is out of the question."

Serin blinked. That hadn't happened in a while. In fact, she couldn't remember the last time a man of any species had asked her out. But then again, she didn't normally let anyone see her do her work and live.

Speaking of which...

The flat spelled stone heated the moment her fingers grasped it from the bottom of her bag. It was one of many, all with different purposes. This one altered memories—specifically those of small-to-medium-sized groups.

The spell on this memory charm was originally crafted by one of her ancestors, then perfected by Serin's mother, Dalasini. Her mother was skilled in spellcraft, but memory charms were her obsession.

By the time she withdrew the stone, it was hot as coal. But Serin didn't mind the burn. It was a nice contrast to the cold she'd felt in the ocean's depths.

Reynolds was still speaking. *Unbelievable.* He was describing the tacos at a local restaurant, still trying to convince her to go out with him.

She held up a hand. "I hate to interrupt, but there's a little something I have to take care of first."

"What is it?"

He almost seemed as if he wanted to be helpful. His expression soured when he caught sight of her fist swinging toward him, leveling him with the first punch.

Reynolds dropped like a stone at her feet.

"The bigger they come..." With a sigh, she knelt and heaved him up. Though she could bear his weight with no problem, the massive man sprawled awkwardly over her shoulder. She dumped him in the center of the warehouse, rounding up the other members of his team and piling them around him—a groaning mountain of muscles and steroids.

She kissed the hot stone before tossing it on top of the pile. There was an icy blue flash. As a group, the team of mercenaries fell asleep, a slumber too deep for snoring.

When they woke up, they wouldn't remember her or what had happened to their employer.

Serin was careful to wash all traces of herself away before walking back to the pit for a formal parting with the Agunte.

The water in the pit was clear now, luminescing in a kaleidoscope more psychedelic than any rave or high-end laser light show. The Agunte wanted to celebrate their victory with her. They beckoned her with their lights, inviting her to the warmth of their home deep under the ground.

"I'm sorry," she said with true regret. "Perhaps another time. Are you ready to close this entrance?"

A dance of squiggles lit up the water as they tried to convince her to join them one more time, but Serin stood firm. She had to leave. Jordan was waiting for her.

Yes, close it, they signaled. *And thank you.*

Putting her hand over her heart, she bowed formally. "Till we meet again. Now, for your own safety, you should depart to the deeper recesses of your home."

She knelt, then dipped her hand into the water. "It's time," she called, just in case there were any stragglers close to the surface.

Her voice reverberated through the aether. She sat at the water's edge, waiting for the telltale ripple that heralded the arrival of her sister.

Gia arrived in moments, the rustle of shifting earth the only sound.

"Thank you for coming so quickly."

"Damn, you've gotten better," Gia said, coming up beside her and offering her hand. "There was a time when you wouldn't have heard that."

Serin took it and stood. Gia embraced her, then bowed in turn to the Agunte.

Sharp senses were part of Serin's gift, but her sister was older—the senior Elemental. Gia could mask her arrival and departures with the greatest skill, far better than any witch, shifter, or other Elemental for that matter.

For the better part of a century, Gia could sneak up on Serin, scaring the crap out of her. *And then Gia would giggle like a two-year-old.*

Serin smiled at her sister, wishing for more time to dawdle.

"Remember when we used to paint the town red?" Gia asked, reading her mind and the nostalgic turn she'd taken.

"You mean when we used to rumble with an out-of-control black coven at dusk, then knock over a shifter bar in the evening?" she replied with a smile.

Gia grinned. "Then we'd have a nightcap with the wood fae, drinking all their best mead—the centuries-old stuff."

Serin sighed, the longing for those carefree days suddenly intense. Though they still saw each other and collaborated on cases regularly, there was less and less time for fun. "I wish we could relive old times, but..."

"I know, I know," Gia said with understanding. "Jordan is waiting."

"Yes." Neither spoke. They simply stood side by side, their arms touching.

Then Gia raised her hands, using her powers of Earth to shift the ground beneath them. Deep in the borehole, the soil responded to her call, moving and rolling like a wave until the opening was sealed.

Serin could have dynamited the hole shut, but she wanted to make sure the ground appeared undisturbed—as if the mining work had never even begun.

That had been her plan all along. Serin had spent most of yesterday afternoon laying the groundwork. She was framing Sayer for embezzlement—a crime he was guilty of, albeit on a much smaller scale.

According to the new and carefully hidden records, the reports on this area had been faked. There was no oil reserve for hundreds of miles. The employment records, progress updates, and payroll were a sham. Sayer pocketed the funds allocated by the company. At least, that was what they were going to think.

Gia knew her plan. It resembled many of the others she and Serin used in the past when their marks were human. Greed was one of the classics. When the relentless drive for profit ruled a company or organization, legal or illegal, their job was half-done for them.

"Where will you go next?" Serin asked, savoring the night's warmth before she had to make her way down to the sea.

"Home, for a time." Gia was the oldest Elemental, but her ties on this earth were as binding as Serin's. Though her immediate family was long gone, her blood lived on all over the world, but most was still concentrated deep in the heart of Mexico in the village she called home.

Like their sister Logan, Gia was blessed. Their homes were places of rest, where time with their families provided a respite from their work. For Serin, home was...different. She was a Water Elemental.

"I should go," she said.

Her sister stopped her with a hand to the shoulder. She pulled Serin into another warm embrace.

"It's date night, isn't it? What does Jordan have planned for you tonight?"

"Candlelight dinner, and a romantic drive up the coast to a new nightspot to dance under the stars."

"He always goes the extra mile, doesn't he?" Gia mused as they walked a few miles south, downhill away from the dig site.

Between the trees, crickets sang their nightly serenade.

"Like always," Serin replied, tasting the night air.

They reached the ravine at the base of the hill. Gia dug her hands into the earth, swirling it around the way a child splashed into the ocean. She felt for the ripple of water buried deep, tapping it and drawing it to the surface. The formerly dry stream bed became a torrent, one that would eventually reach the sea.

With one last embrace, Serin parted from her sister and went to meet her mate, wondering what dress she should wear. The red was Jordan's favorite, but she preferred the green.

Less than an hour later, she reached the Caislean Hotel in Cabos San Lucas, the beachfront five-star hotel Jordan had chosen for their stay in Baja California.

The room was a mess. The rosewood and teak coffee table and chairs were smashed to pieces. Cotton filler from the plush couch cushions littered the room, and there was broken glass everywhere.

An ominous splash of blood was in the center of the shards. A quick search revealed nothing was missing—nothing except her bonded mate, Jordan.

2

THREE WEEKS LATER

The roar of the ocean filled Serin's ears. She blinked against the bright sunlight, wondering why it was so much louder out here on the bluffs of T'Kaieri than it was on the beach itself.

Not a big hand-holder, Diana, her Fire Elemental sister, pressed against her side. The pressure was comforting, although Serin couldn't feel her heat. Not today.

"I'm so sorry about this," Diana murmured as the pallbearers brought the coffin down the winding path from the temple.

They were carrying Jordan's body.

After Serin discovered her bonded was missing, she had criss-crossed the globe in a frantic search. Failing to find even a trace of him, she came home to the island to discover their archives had been raided. Many dangerous artifacts had gone missing. The exact number was unknown. The archivists were still compiling a list under the direction of Diana's mate, world-renowned archeologist and scholar Alec Broussard.

Alec's presence made the islanders almost as anxious as the Fire

Elemental did. It was the first time a vampire had ever set foot on T'Kaieri.

The line of mourners broke as Uncle John approached. He'd found Jordan's body at his parents' house. There had been poison on the kitchen table, along with a note containing a single word—*sorry*.

The body had been prepared by John, Jordan's only living relative, according to his family's traditions. Jordan's body was going to interred in the ground instead of being buried at sea. It was a break of a millennia-old island tradition.

"Thank you," Serin replied in a low voice as the men marched past them.

Uncle John paused to touch her arm before skittering away. Diana raised a brow and jerked her head, silently asking if she should step back so the mourners could access Serin more easily.

Serin reached down, surreptitiously taking hold of the hem of Diana's shirt in an unmistakable *don't-go-anywhere* sign. The Fire Elemental's presence was an effective deterrent against the flood of funeral goers spilling into the valley. Her sister-in-arms made people nervous, something useful at times like this.

Even Serin's parents were giving them a wide berth. It wasn't that they disliked Diana, but the Fire Elemental didn't go out of her way to make people comfortable. She liked it better that way, with a few exceptions.

"Are you sure you don't want to wait for Gia to come back?" Diana asked as the elders continued their snail-paced shuffle to the open grave.

Serin shook her head, her eyes fixed on the plain ash coffin. "No, she and Logan have to keep on following leads and clearing cases."

Their mission hadn't ended just because Serin's bonded was dead. She was going to have to return to work herself sometime soon.

Her father stepped forward, beginning what promised to be a long prayer.

The service lasted an hour. Offerings of fruit and fresh flowers were laid at the bottom of the grave before the box was haltingly lowered by some of the younger islanders with the help of a few ropes.

Serin winced when one end of the coffin jerked and dropped a few inches. The men struggled to right the box.

Diana leaned closer. "Do they need help?" she whispered.

"They're fine," Serin lied as the box resumed its shaky descent.

As the deceased's bonded, her job was to stoically look on. Plus, there was every chance Diana stepping forward would cause the frail pallbearers to panic and drop the coffin altogether.

"Are you sure?" her sister whispered as the coffin careened again.

"They'll muddle through," Serin said bracingly. "Although, I think we'll go back to burial at sea after this."

"Might be wise."

Forcing her eyes to stay open, Serin couldn't stop from sighing in relief when the coffin finally touched down.

John nodded at her. She stepped forward, picking up a handful of soil from the edge of the grave as he'd instructed earlier.

With every eye on her, she opened her fist, letting the soil rain onto the lid of the box. Diana came forward, then repeated the gesture. Then both stepped back to allow John and the others to do the same as the island's few children began a solemn requiem.

The lengthy line of mourners filed past. One of the elders came forward, circling to Serin's far side to keep a small buffer between herself and her sister.

"You must be devastated," Elianne said, her withered hands covering Serin's own. "But you must be strong. She has a plan. Even Her chosen cannot always know what it is."

"Thank you," Serin said stiffly, squeezing Elianne's hand in return. The woman's thin lips parted as if she were about to launch into more platitudes, but Diana shifted her weight. A flicker of red lashes and Elianne excused herself, hobbling away with a little more speed than was typical.

The setting sun dipped below the horizon. People began to leave, returning to their homes for the evening meal.

Uncle John broke away from the crowd.

"Would you excuse me, my dear?" he said to Diana. "I would like to have a word with my niece-in-law."

Diana stayed where she was, glancing at Serin for confirmation.

She gave Diana the tiniest of nods. John waited for the Fire Elemental to walk away before offering his arm, one of the charming, old-world gestures that had endeared him to everyone on the island.

"Your sisters are very protective of you my dear. That's good. You need to lean on them now. I know how hard this must be. I can only imagine how it was, feeling him go like that."

Serin pressed her lips tighter, nodding as they stopped before the end of the bluff. Below them, the sea lapped at the rocks. It was far quieter now that the coffin was in the ground.

"He was a very devoted mate."

John patted her hand. "Yes, he was. I'm so sorry you had to experience that. I know how terrible it must have been for you." He trailed off, wiping his eyes.

"Yes," Serin whispered, refusing to say anything more.

An Elemental knew when their mate was in trouble. When Gia's mate Marco died, Gia said she'd felt the devastating blow halfway around the world. The same had happened to Logan when her werewolf had been hurt, though Connell had been lucky enough to survive his wounds.

"Yes, he was so in love with you. My heart will always be heavy when I think of all that might have been..." John's voice roughened. He blinked rapidly, turning to the sea. "I hope you don't mind my insisting on a burial. I understand your connection to the ocean, but I just wasn't comfortable with him out there, all alone. I'm afraid I'm one of those people who love the beach, but find these depths too vast and cold. I don't want him to feel lost wherever he is."

Wrapping her arms around her middle, she said nothing.

He twisted his head, checking over his shoulder to make sure they were alone. His cloudy yellow eyes were wide and red. "I know what people are saying about Jordan, trying to tie him to the thefts. They stop talking about it whenever I get too close, but I'm old, not deaf."

He broke off, swiping at his eyes. "Things look unbelievably bad, but I swear he would never take part in anything that would hurt you. Not willingly."

Serin took a shaky breath. "I will discover the truth. You have my word."

"I know you will," John said, hesitating. "You and your sisters are the most dogged and determined creatures I've ever met. It's simply that... Well, it seems much more likely now that Jordan *was* involved."

He turned away again. "I don't know what he got up to those last few months of his life. Someone must have threatened or black-mailed him. Whatever it was, I want you to know I don't blame you for not seeing it. I certainly didn't, and the boy lived with me for years after his parents passed on to their reward. *I* should have known he was in trouble."

He was being far too generous. She had been the one who'd lived with Jordan. For much of their union, he'd followed her all over the world on her missions, although that tapered off at the end.

"It's not your fault," she managed in a tight voice.

Everyone knew where the blame lay. It was just that everyone was too polite to say anything to her face.

John sighed, mopping his brow with a handkerchief. "Darling, I want to be here for you, but I'm afraid I can't be. This has been too painful. Jordan was the only family I had left. I'd hoped for grand-nephews and nieces in a few years, once you were finished with your service, but I suppose some things just aren't meant to be."

She kept her eyes on the surf. "No, I suppose not."

John smiled wistfully. "You two would have made beautiful chil-dren. You're so lovely, and Jordan was such a handsome young man."

"That he was." With his dark hair and sea-green eyes, Jordan Kincaid could have graced magazine covers or starred in Hollywood movies.

She had looked forward to seeing those eyes in the faces of her children, too...

John sniffed loudly. When he spoke next, his voice cracked. "I'm going to go away for a while, to clear my head. I'll leave in a few days, once the dust settles here."

She turned to him with parted lips. Uncle John had been a fixture here for so long she couldn't imagine this place without him.

"Where will you go?"

"I'm not sure. I think I'm simply going to take a walkabout as the Australians say." He shrugged through his tears. "I've been gathering moss here long enough."

Reaching out impulsively, Serin threw her arms around him, hugging him tight. "Don't stay away too long. You know we can't get along without you."

She let go and leaned back, jaw stiff. "When you return, I will have answers for you. Whoever drove Jordan to do what he did will pay."

A tear slipped down the older man's cheek. "I know you will, my dear. I know you will."

3

Serin tried to let the bickering of the elders wash over her like an ocean wave, but it was easier said than done.

Now that the funeral was over, the entire island of T'Kaieri was in an uproar over the missing artifacts. Some of the elders had only just discovered that the Elemental's ancient archive repository had been raided. Recriminations had been flying back and forth for hours, but at this moment, Noomi, the head archivist, was facing their collective wrath.

Since the artifacts had disappeared on her watch, they felt she should shoulder most of the blame—and she was. Willingly.

Mother save us from the inconveniently selfless.

Serin and her sisters didn't hold Noomi responsible. How could they? If anyone was to blame, it was them. Serin most of all...

It was difficult to believe they'd been burgled. T'Kaieri was an impregnable stronghold...to outsiders. But who could have foreseen deception from within? What did human detectives call it?

An inside job.

Breathing deeply, Serin stifled the rush of adrenaline and anger that came with the thought of being duped, but she betrayed her emotions by scowling at the elders. That was against her training as a Water of T'Kaieri. She'd been taught not to flinch in the face of tsunamis, but she couldn't stop from glaring daggers at the elder Wanat as he called for Noomi's removal.

The council was out for blood, and they didn't much care who got the ax as long as someone paid for the theft. But her sisters had already cleared Noomi.

Despite her exhaustion, Serin parted her lips, ready to defend the innocent archivist, but her sister Diana beat her to it.

"That's not fair," Diana cut in, her anger flaring as red hot as her hair. "Noomi has been nothing but honest throughout this entire affair."

The Fire Elemental's gift was sensitive enough to detect even the minutest fluctuations in body temperature. Combined with her background and years of training, she was like a human lie detector—a nearly infallible one, provided the right questions were being asked.

Diana was just getting going. "The junior archivists haven't lied either—and I would know. I've questioned them all about the missing artifacts. They are innocent of the theft. Place your blame elsewhere. Let Noomi and the others continue their inventory. We need to know how many things are missing."

"I thought your mate the vampire was doing that." Wanat sneered, his hook nose wrinkled as if he could smell Alec now. He turned to the others, muttering, "A vampire in the archives. What will this world come to next?"

"Alec *is* helping," Diana said. "And he's compiled quite a list already. But that archive is thousands of years old. It has more scrolls and antiquities than the fucking Smithsonian, so he needs all hands on deck if we're going to figure out what's missing."

"I agree that a detailed inventory is necessary, and I thank your mate for his help," Caimen, her father, interjected. "But the archive *is* thousands of years old, and it has never been violated before now. Someone needs to be held accountable, and Noomi was the one in charge."

"She was in charge of the archive's day-to-day running, not its security because you didn't fucking have any," Diana snapped. "It wasn't deemed necessary because who in their right mind would steal from us?"

Who indeed? Serin raised her head to find everyone but Diana staring at her. The mixture of pity and suspicion in those eyes was too much to bear. She murmured something unintelligible, then left the council chamber.

Outside, the warm night air of T'Kaieri burned her lungs. She walked a few meters to the left, to the tiny spring that ran from deep within Siba, the mountain peak that formed the heart of the island. Splashing inside, she let go of her corporeal form, letting the water carry her all the way down to the beach.

Her heart didn't calm until she was on the shore sitting on the lava rocks, her feet in the water at the island's only cove.

That was where Diana found her later. She sat down next to her, her presence silently comforting. "No one blames you."

Serin stared off at the horizon. "Everyone blames me—my father, my mother. All the elders. They say if I'd given up my position by now, Jordan wouldn't have done what he did."

Di put her arm around her, something Serin usually did to her, but only when she thought her sister needed it. The Fire Elemental wasn't a big toucher.

"You don't really believe he did it, do you?" Diana asked.

"Gia thinks he did. So does Logan."

The Earth and Air Elementals were still following leads, trying to trace their missing artifacts, but both had been blunt about their suspicions before they'd found the body. Once they had, his note only confirmed their suspicions.

"You don't buy it, though." Diana seemed certain.

"I don't know what to think."

Diana shifted, rocking them both slightly. "Yes, you do. You think he's innocent and his death was a frame-up."

Serin sighed. "I'm not sure. Jordan might have facilitated the theft.

He had the access and knowledge. He's been accompanying me on missions for years. Many of the missing artifacts are those I recovered recently. But if he did...then what John suspects may be true. Someone made him."

"If that's true, who would it be? Who could get to an Elemental's mate?"

It was an excellent question.

Serin picked up a stone, then sent it sailing over the water. It skipped over a dozen times before sinking. "I don't know. All I keep hearing is what John is repeating—that Jordan wouldn't leave me. That he loved me."

"He did love you."

Blinking, Serin turned to her sister. A corner of Diana's lips pulled down knowingly.

"I didn't talk to the man much, but the few times I was around him, he, well, he was being Jordan. Needy and a bit whiny, but demonstratively affectionate in a way that was weird to me before I met Alec." She put her hand on Serin's shoulder. "Jordan was always telling you he loved you. I would have known if he were lying."

That was true. But it didn't make her feel any better. There were so many things she could have said, but Serin chose the most expedient, the truth. "I wish I could say I was certain he'd been coerced, but I can't. I'm in the dark. I have been about this whole affair. I keep thinking I should have seen it coming, known he was in trouble and needed help."

"Well, there's a lot we haven't seen lately," Diana said with a tightening of her lips.

She was right. A black coven had risen in their midst, and they'd been none the wiser. The reason was disquieting.

Elementals were intricately tied to the world and what happened in it. The Mother had designed it that way. They were charged with keeping the balance, the ever-shifting dance between good and evil. Too much bad and the wheels that turned the world as they knew it began to slow and stop. It was their job to make sure that didn't happen. Through their actions, they kept Atabey, the Mother of them all, happy and healthy. She, in turn, gave life to the world.

Theoretically, an unbalance in the other direction was possible. Too much good and the balance would be threatened—in theory. Funnily enough, that hadn't ever been a problem for them. No, the ever-shifting tide was always in one direction.

"With the Mother falling asleep, it's going to get worse before it gets better," Serin said.

They had all noticed Her inattention. In years past—long before Serin's time—Atabey had fallen asleep. It was cyclical. These long, terrible periods were characterized by an uptick in natural disasters and violence.

Diana frowned. "That's not the Serin I know. Don't get me wrong, I'm as cynical as the next bitch, but now that we know there's a problem, we're going to fix it. Between the four of us, there's nothing we can't handle."

She leaned back with an involuntary yawn. "Listen to me being upbeat. I think we pulled a Freaky Friday personality swap. I don't know when I became such a fucking Pollyanna."

Serin couldn't resist a little smirk. "I think it was shortly after you met Alec."

Shrugging, her sister snorted. "You may be right," she admitted with a surprising lack of argument.

Diana tilted her head up, checking the angle of the moon in the way they were trained to tell time. "Speaking of Mister Fanged and Fabulous, I better go check on him to make sure he's eaten one of the blood bags we brought along. The last thing I need is for him to lose track of time... then realize he's hungry around the archivists."

"He won't eat one of them." Alec was old enough to resist the urge to snack.

"I know that, but they don't. And as much as I like Noomi, she's the only one of the lot with balls. If you even glance at one of the others cross-eyed, they run for cover."

"They only run from you, and only because you set that junior archivist's robes on fire."

Diana tsked. "It was his notepad. And he was the one who decided to try to put it out with his robe instead of stamping it out with his boot like a normal person."

Rising, Diana eyed Serin with a frown. "You're going to leave again the first chance you get, aren't you?"

It was more of a suggestion than a question.

"As soon as we have another viable lead, I am." It was that or stay in the bosom of her family. Serin didn't think she could take more of her parents' rigid and restrained comforting.

Her sister shook her head. "If I had to bite my tongue around those old council farts the way you do, I'd be out of here like a shot, too. But the elders made it clear—Alec can't stay unless I'm here with him, and we need him down in the archives now."

"Yes, they're not too trusting at the moment."

"They were like that before the theft. Renown scholar or not, there's no way they would have let a vampire have access under any circumstances if he wasn't my mate."

She had a point. "Thank Alec for his help again."

Serin had done so briefly, right after she arrived, but with the demands of the council and her extended family, there hadn't been time for a deep conference.

"Don't worry about him. He'd have given his right nut for access to the archive, and now he has it without begging or jumping through the Elder's endless hoops. He's as happy as a pig in muck."

That picture clashed with the mental image Serin had of the debonair and handsome vamp. "Thank him anyway. And if he finds something that needs to be checked out immediately…"

Something that would give her an enemy to take down and hopefully maim. She owed Jordan that much.

Diana held up a hand. "I know, I know. You have dibs."

4

The paintings that graced the walls of Serin's childhood home were snippets of an ever-shifting ocean. The white-washed walls of the central living room were the perfect backdrop for the stormy seascapes. Most her mother painted, but here and there one by her father was slipped in, almost indistinguishable in terms of style or execution. Nevertheless, Serin always knew which ones they were. She was the only one who could tell them apart.

The paintings were different each time she visited, despite being relentlessly the same. She used to love the stormy seascapes best, but they had lost something now. They were a pale imitation of the very real memories she had of being one with the raging sea, formless and far from any boat or landmass.

The newest picture dominated the living room wall. Serin traced a textured whitecap on the oil painting's surface. For a moment, the roar of churning sea filled her ears, but the antique grandfather clock chimed the hour and the noise ceased. She crossed the room, stepping over the stream that ran through the floor without looking, long years of muscle memory taking over. The reflected light bouncing off the water danced in greeting.

She loved this house, with its softly rounded walls and organic flow. The architecture was typical of the island. In appearance, the buildings were more reminiscent of Greek island architecture than the wooden cottages typical of this part of the world, but T'Kaieri was unique. The island developed its own distinctive culture and customs over the centuries, preserved by its self-imposed isolation.

Serin moved to the formal dining room, noting the four elaborate table settings complete with finger bowls. Her stomach tightened. Leaving a space for the dead was a part of island heritage, but only to honor those long dead. The spirits of the recently departed were too mercurial and confused to be acceptable company at her family's table. That meant her parents were expecting John.

Had he not told them he was leaving? Or had he delayed his departure? With or without him, this promised to be an uncomfortable meal.

So many questions floating in this room, unspoken. Why hadn't she known Jordan was in trouble?

Anger and suspicion warred with guilt, but she wasn't given time to dwell. Her parents walked in, still wearing their formal council robes.

"Serin, my child." Her mother floated in a cloud of orange-pink silk, a sunset in dress form.

Dalasini held out her arms, and Serin dutifully leaned down so her mother could embrace her. She bussed her mother's cheek before doing the same to her father. They sat as Joon, their long-time servant, brought in the dishes.

Dalasini helped Joon serve before dismissing her to join her own family. Her father delivered a brief prayer to the Mother before bowing his head. When he raised it, he picked up his fork.

"John will not be joining us," Caimen said when Serin hesitated, glancing at the empty setting. "This...situation...has been very hard on him. He wasn't feeling up to sharing our meal."

"Did he tell you he was leaving?"

"Yes. It's understandable under the circumstances."

They proceeded to eat. The silence stretched so long Serin was beginning to think she would escape unscathed, but she was wrong.

When the meal was over, Dalasini began by catching Serin's father's eye. He cleared his throat and began the long litany of prayers, an homage to their ancestors who carried the blessing of the Mother—the other Water Elementals of her line. There were four in Serin's lineage, which made her Elemental royalty to some. When she'd been chosen to serve, it had been a surprise to no one, except perhaps her own parents.

Caimen ended his speech with a prayer for Jordan's soul.

Taking a deep breath, Serin closed her eyes.

"Serin," her mother began.

"I'm not retiring."

"Why do you assume I was going to bring up retiring?" Dalasini asked.

She bit back a sigh. "Because it's what you always want to talk about whenever I come home."

"There are less than ten years left in your term," Caimen began.

"And you think I should give up my position. Let another take over so I can focus on building a family." She set down her napkin with care, resisting the urge to throw it on the table. "Because developing the next generation is as important as serving the Mother. I've heard all this before, back when starting a family was an option. But my bonded is gone and his killer is out there, so forgive me for not wishing to discuss retirement just now."

Her extensive training masked her true emotions. "Every Water Elemental chosen from this island serves for a hundred years, no more, no less. Abdicating my position even one day early would be an insult to the Mother and bring disgrace to our family."

Dalasini and Caimen shifted in their seats, exchanging another wordless glance.

"Under the circumstances, no one would judge you from stepping down before the term ends," her mother suggested softly. "You need time to mourn."

Serin's chin firmed. "What I need is to find out what happened to Jordan, and to find the missing artifacts."

Another pointed glance from her mother prodded her father to speak. "Of course," he said. "And I'm confident you will do all that quickly. You're a very talented girl. But if the rumors are true, then the Mother is falling asleep. If you step down now, there is time for a new Elemental to be chosen before the Mother is too deep in her slumber. You have to consider what is best for everyone."

So they were finally getting to it. They had urged her to step down before, but for more personal reasons, like settling down and starting a family. The suggestions had increased in regularity after being bonded to Jordan.

"Is that the council's official position?"

The skin around Caimen's eyes tightened. "I'm not speaking as the head of the council. I'm speaking as your father."

"Really? You could have fooled me."

Dalasini folded her hands tightly. "I don't know why you have to get so hostile whenever we speak to you about this. We only want what's best for you."

Serin's lips drew down. "You're contradicting yourself. You just admitted—finally—that it's not me you're concerned with, but the island's heritage."

She glanced at each in turn. "Giving up my position guarantees another girl from this island will be chosen next, and not some random outsider. At least that's how it's always worked in the past. I'm sure the council is concerned the Mother will be unable to honor our peculiar habit of picking our own successor if she's asleep. But all the signs point to her already slumbering, so it's quite a gamble to ask me to retire now. In fact, if you wish to guarantee that the next Water Elemental is an islander, we may have to wait another century for her to wake. The more prudent members of the council would agree...

unless, of course, they universally decide to condemn me for Jordan's crime."

Her mother's indrawn breath suggested she hadn't considered those arguments. Her father's face was stiff with irritation, but she couldn't tell if it was with her or his wife. "We don't even know if Jordan was responsible. And early retirement was only a suggestion—ours. Not the council's."

His face softened. "You and the other Elementals are the island's best hope for recovering its artifacts. Until those items are returned, or the people responsible are identified, there is no need to discuss this matter further."

"I still don't see why she has to be the one to investigate this now," her mother protested as her father rose from the table. "Others can handle it. Gia is very capable, for an Earth. Even the brash junior Elementals have proven to be up to the demands of the office, despite their questionable tastes in mates."

"*Dalasini.*" Her father's tone was repressive. Sighing, he turned to back to Serin. "The council's official position, as you put it, is to let you and the others do their job."

He threw his wife a pointed glance. "It's not as if the decision is ours to make in any case. The Mother selected Serin and the others as her servants. We are only here to preserve Her legacy and, by extension, yours."

There was a long silence. Caimen inclined his head in a formal parting. "I wish you well in your hunt."

He left the room, leaving a dejected Dalasini staring at her plate.

Serin waited for her mother to speak. Elemental lineages were usually matriarchal in nature, but in this house, Caimen always had final say. That didn't mean Dalasini didn't have more arguments up the sleeve of her diaphanous robe. She just needed time to decide on her approach.

It was taking longer than Serin would've guessed. "How is your research going? Any progress on that new spell?" she asked, trying to change the subject.

Dalasini had been working on a spell that selectively dulled traumatic memories for years. She didn't believe bad memories should be removed entirely. A person was shaped by their experiences, even the bad ones. Especially the bad ones.

Her mother had been trying to alter the intensity of such events, without removing them entirely. There were a few practitioners who worked as therapists in the human world who were eagerly following her progress. But her mother didn't want to discuss her work. She picked up her fork, proceeding to finish her meal in silence.

"Mother, please. Let's talk."

Her mother put her fork down before standing. "I'm afraid this isn't a good time. I'm going to the temple to pray. Please let me know when you're leaving so I can bid you goodbye. I assume it will be soon."

She swept out of the room, leaving Serin with a plateful of guilt. Closing her eyes, she rubbed her temples.

Being chosen as an Elemental was an honor, something almost every girl on the island coveted. It was a source of pride to the families as well, but her parents' reaction had been mixed at best. Dalasini's especially.

Serin had her ideas why, but it was conjecture on her part. Once she'd been bonded to Jordan, her parents' attitude shifted. Now that he was gone, they were shifting again.

She moved around the dining room, collecting plates so Joon wouldn't find them sitting here in the morning.

The sleeves of her gown kept getting in the way. She set the plates down, then wrapped her arms around herself. Like so many things on the island, her dress was about appearances. It was beautiful, but not functional.

Her sisters wore close-fitting tops and a lot of leather in the job. It was a style Serin eschewed out of habit. But those types of clothes were better for fighting. And they certainly made a statement. They said, *Don't fuck with me.*

The archive door was shut, presumably to prevent thieves and intruders from entering.

Too little, too late. She pushed it wide, closing it behind her. *I wonder who opens it for the archivists.* They were all practitioners, of course, but spells for super strength were onerous. *Maybe Alec opens it for them.* Vampires weren't as strong as Elementals, but they could manage the door. And Alec was a conscientious man, all things considered.

She found him down in the main reading room, a space he'd claimed as his own. The wooden table was littered with books and scrolls. Some were stacked so high the first things she saw was the top of his head. He was moving fast enough to make his hair flap in the resulting breeze.

Serin couldn't help but track the vampire's progress, her senses alert and battle ready.

Compared to her sisters Diana and Gia, Serin had always been viewed as the tolerant one. Being senior to Logan, most of the high-level vampire cases were thrown her way. She'd spent enough time around members of the major covens to be comfortable around vampires...after a fashion.

Nothing could ever prepare someone for the way vamps moved when they thought they were alone. Alec was darting all over the places, pausing intermittently to examine whatever scroll or paper he'd crossed the room to find. A human eye wouldn't have been able to track him at all, but she could see the faint traces of moisture most beings possessed streaking across the room, like a comet's trail.

She blinked, and the vampire was seated in one of the leather chairs situated between two large stacks of ledgers. His attention was fixed on the volume in front of him.

"Alec."

Blinking, he glanced up before breaking into a warm smile. Fire from the torches hit his fangs, making them gleam disconcertingly in the light. "Serin! I was hoping you would stop by. Diana said you were eager for a fresh lead."

Serin cocked her head at him, her mood lightening. "And you have something."

He nodded, standing in his seat to reach for a notepad he'd left atop a pile of scrolls. "The archivists and I have begun a list of the missing objects. I'm sure you've heard through the grapevine about the more concerning ones."

She nodded. "Yes, the gossip is everywhere."

The island was a fishbowl. People couldn't keep secrets here, so the news of which major artifacts had gone missing was known to all, even the island's children. Unfortunately, most of the objects were dark, imbued with an innate self-protection magic. Despite the fact most burned magic like shooting stars, they weren't trackable unless the tracker was very close.

Serin rubbed her face. "So which of the world-ending cursed objects do I have to worry about?"

The light in Alec's eyes was a little manic. "None."

She raised an eyebrow.

He beamed, waving a piece of parchment in the air. "Some of the items on the list are inert, meaning they don't possess magical properties. Given their age or the materials they were made of, I've surmised they were stolen for profit."

"Weren't all the artifacts stolen for profit?"

Alec's gaze softened. "Err...yes and no. Obviously, every item in this archive is priceless to a scholar like me and to the island's community at large, but to an outside observer, their value would be subjective."

He picked up the sketch of Feng Po Po's staff, the missing artifact that had caused Logan so much grief a few months ago. "Take this for example. It was the staff of a legendary Air Elemental, as well as a vicious weapon in the right hands. But what if a human had come across it?"

He broke off, flashing back to the table, then returned and handed her a familiar weapon.

Serin breathed out slowly. The Sai, a handheld trident weapon, felt like an extension of her hand. It was one of a pair, and part of the archive collection she'd personally collected herself. Out of everything Alec could have used to demonstrate, that he'd chosen this...

"Only one of the Sai was taken. I think the thief dropped the other one."

"Really?" Why would the thief have taken only one?

He nodded. "To a human, the staff and trident would still have had value because of their age and workmanship. Either would command a high price to the right buyer."

"So you think this was about...*money*?" As her bonded mate, Jordan had no need for that. The Mother supplied whatever they needed—jewels and precious metals, whatever was on hand in the soil beneath their feet.

Alec expelled a breath with a little too much force. "I can't speak to the thief's motive. But after compiling the list, I noticed a pattern. Yes, some powerful artifacts are missing. To the right practitioner or gifted Supernatural, they can do a lot of damage. But both Gia and Logan have their ear to the ground. Aside from the staff, there is no hint of them. No doubt the thief or thieves are laying low after the recovery of the staff of Feng Po Po. However, I have my own sources and they extend beyond the Supernatural community."

Serin was beginning to understand. "By that, you mean your background in archeology."

Alec was a known collector of rare artifacts.

He beamed at her like a professor rewarding a prize pupil. "According to Noomi, these objects aren't magical. Some of them are common, too—which, according to her definition, simply means they aren't one of a kind. Doesn't mean they aren't rare or expensive. Take this piece for example."

He dropped the pad for a ledger, pointing to the sketch. It was a figurine, a squat and ugly thing that vaguely resembled a toad. "The body is made entirely of jade. This indentation here is where the jewel is embedded. It's a diamond."

"A jade figurine could fetch a nice price, but jade isn't that precious. Diamonds are also common enough these days. They can even grow them in labs."

"Yes, but one this color and clarity is still beyond the scope of the current technology. It's *red*. A dark and clear red. And this stone is bigger than the Hope Diamond, the latter which is supposedly cursed by the way."

He shifted his weight, staring musingly at the ceiling. "I've never had the opportunity to test whether it was true, but there were some tantalizing hints. You see, the Hope Diamond has a very interesting history..."

Serin hadn't spent all that much time with the vampire, but she recognized the start of a lengthy lecture when she heard one.

"Alec," she interrupted. "*Focus.*"

His lips pressed together before he shrugged haplessly. "Right, of course. I surmised this artifact and the others on this list, the ones we consider innocuous, would be easier to trace than those imbued with magic. So I put out feelers to show interest in buying some of them—carefully. I didn't describe *these* objects exactly, just gave loose descriptions of similar artifacts, things that wouldn't be out of place in a collection as large as mine or the museums I'm a known patron of."

It was her turn to smile. "And you received an offer."

"Not exactly. It was a message from another collector, one I've competed with in the past. The man wanted to gloat about snagging a piece right out from under me."

He handed her a piece of paper, showing the aforementioned piece and an address. "Here are his details."

5

Daniel pulled his chair in to get a closer look at the footage. It was too grainy to be sure, but the female kicking the collective butt of an entire motorcycle gang did resemble his ghost—the woman who'd disappeared from the Reaper's compound.

He'd been searching for her ever since. Until today, he'd had nothing. Not until Ray had waved him over to watch some old security footage.

"Where the hell did you find this?" Daniel asked his partner.

"In the archives. It was part of an earlier investigation. The Devil's Hand was a motorcycle gang operating out of Detroit."

"Was?"

"Yup, was. They're defunct now. While they were operating, they were a nasty bunch—drugs, illegal gun sales, racketeering with a body count. We got wind of them three or four years ago. The FBI actually kicked their prelim case over to us. The group was originally flagged by their Behavioral Analysis Unit because of the bodies they were turning up. There were weird ritualistic aspects to the deaths."

Daniel rubbed his chin as the tiny figure on the screen headbutted a man three times her size. Then she tossed him over her shoulder like a sack of potatoes.

"Damn." Ray whistled. "Did you see that?"

Daniel resisted the urge to grab the screen to bring it up to his face. "We can't zoom this in?"

"Footage is from a liquor store down the street. It's aimed at their back-alley entrance. This is as good as it gets."

Daniel leaned back in his chair. "It's a start."

Ray sniffed. "You don't really think it's the same girl?"

"I do. Don't you?" Why else was his partner showing him the footage if he didn't agree?

"I just pulled it because Campbell said the suspect resembled the sketch you've been passing around. The entire office is aware of your hard-on for the woman in the white bikini. She pulled a Houdini under the noses of over two dozen law enforcement personnel. Her description is common knowledge around here. But, no, I don't think this is the same person. The girl we saw was way too soft for something like this. She was just window dressing for a drug dealer, nothing more."

The fight was over. Bikers littered the alley. The female was the last man standing, as it were.

Daniel squinted at the screen as the woman melted into the shadows at the far end of the alley. She didn't reappear. He reached over to rewind the footage, pausing on a frontal shot—the clearest picture he could get of her.

"I disagree," he said after a minute. "The woman on this video has been trained and trained well. I saw her use techniques from at least three different schools of martial arts in that fight. That kind of expertise doesn't come cheap. Someone invested a lot to turn this girl into a killing machine. I think we're dealing with a specialist."

"Seriously?" Ray asked skeptically. "Are you sure you're not reading too much into this?"

Daniel scowled. "Did we just watch the same video?"

"Of course we did. But you're jumping to the conclusion that the woman who did a vanishing act at the Reaper's is the same one here." Ray swiveled to face him. "I'm not convinced. Far from it. The woman in the white bikini was probably some hooker. The circumstances of her disappearance aren't a big mystery. She took advantage of someone's inattention to slip away—that's all. My guess is a local uni took a piss break and is too afraid to own up to it."

Daniel didn't buy that. He'd questioned every shield at the scene multiple times. As an experienced interrogator, he knew when someone was hiding something from him. None of the men present at the raid had even twitched. The woman had excused herself to go to the bathroom and then *poof!* She'd vanished, leaving the tap of the bathroom sink running.

"I'm going to search for more on the Devil's Hand," he said after a moment. "Maybe there's a list of their rivals in the files. The fighter's name, or at least her affiliation, might be there."

Ray shrugged. "Suit yourself, but I'd keep it on the down low. If you go off track now, you're gonna lose steam. We both know you want the D.C. job opening under Dallas Munroe next year."

The post in the nation's capital was Daniel's dream job. He had been lobbying for it for the better part of the year, ever since he'd heard the current department head was taking early retirement due to a health issue. The superstar Agent Dallas Munroe would be taking over, and Daniel was on the shortlist for Munroe's old spot.

He had a decent shot at it, but the competition was heavy. The shortlist was a who's who of the agency's rising stars. He was only one of many.

"You'd be better off fielding more grounders," Ray pointed out. "Keep that closure rate climbing. It's a numbers game."

"It's a not just a numbers game, and you know it. It's the big cases that make or break a career."

His partner snickered. "I know you pride yourself in sniffing out crime like some damn McGruff wannabe, but this girl isn't going to be a big score. She didn't even kill anyone in that alley. All of those guys are alive and doing hard time. They're scattered in various supermax prisons across the country."

Daniel picked up his sketch. "Which one is the closest?"

TINY, A THREE-HUNDRED-POUND BIKER, WAS A FORMER MEMBER OF THE Devil's Hand. He sneered at the sketch from the other side of the smeared bulletproof plastic.

"It's the same crazy bitch," he marveled before smacking his lips. "You finally caught her."

Daniel suppressed a smile. "Sorry, no. The girl who kicked your ass is still at large, but she is the reason I came to see you. Who is she?"

Tiny snorted. "Hell if I know. The bitch just showed up in the middle of the clubhouse one day—broke in and made it past two lookouts without any of us the wiser."

He wiped his nose, staring at the sketch as if he couldn't decide if he wanted to lick it or tear it up. "I've been telling my lawyer he needs to find her. *She's* the one who planted all those drugs and guns on us. When we tried to stop her, she went crazy, started beating us up with those fancy kicks and punches. But it was all her. I'm innocent of the charges they nailed me on. So are the other guys. The Devil's Hand was just a club, an excuse to mess around with our bikes, nothing more."

Daniel hid his skepticism. The FBI had been surveilling the Devil's Hand long enough for him to know they'd been guilty of everything convicted of and then some. But he knew why Tiny was making this claim.

When the local cops had come in response to an anonymous tip, all the guns and drugs had been laid out in the open. Hundreds of pounds of pot and heroin had been stacked on the pool table. The men themselves were laid out on the floor in a neat little row.

Combined with the earlier surveillance, the locals had been able to get convictions for almost everyone.

"I know the pot was yours at least," Daniel said. "There's footage of you getting it from a suspected cartel mule a week before. I also know it was well-hidden because a raid just a few days before failed to find anything. So tell me how a stranger knows your clubhouse layout well enough to have knowledge of your secret hiding places— the ones so good a squad of trained law enforcement missed them?"

Tiny scoffed. "I'm telling you none of that shit was ours."

Daniel waited. "If that's the story you want to stick to—fine. What do you have to tell me about the girl? Was she part of a rival club or perhaps contracted by one? Who was your biggest competition in Detroit?"

The tatted ex-biker pursed his lips. "I don't know what you're talking about. We were just a biker club. But I can tell you that girl didn't come searching for drugs or guns. Setting us up was an afterthought."

Daniel took out a notepad. "Then why did she target you? What was she in search of?

"Not what. *Who*." Tiny leaned forward. "She only had one question—where was Luthien?"

"Who is Luthien?" Daniel hadn't come across that name in the Devil's Hand files.

"He was a former member of the Hand. We had to kick him out."

Interesting. "Can I ask why?"

Tiny appeared to think over his answer. "I want to be clear...The Devil's hand didn't do anything illegal, but we sometimes get into disputes with folks in the area, especially in the beginning. Luthien joined us after we were established. He volunteered to go and handle some of these disputes. But we didn't like the way he did it. So we ran him out of town. End of story."

Hmm. Daniel had been over everything he could find on the club. Murder and mayhem had been par for the course. The stuff they'd been busted for wasn't unusual for a gang like theirs. But those ritualistic deaths—the ones that had gotten them flagged by FBI profilers in the first place—had been different and creepy as fuck. Reading between the lines, he now knew Luthien had been responsible.

"Does Luthien have a last name?"

"If it was mentioned, I never heard it. He was on the fringe. The only thing he ever talked about was his bike and getting laid."

"What did he look like?"

Tiny gave him an approximate description, although he couldn't pinpoint the man's age.

Daniel jotted it all down, but it was all so generic. "There's nothing else about Luthien? Nothing distinctive?"

The biker nodded as if something had just occurred to him. "He smelled funny."

"Define funny."

Tiny scratched his greasy head. "He smelled like those sticks you get in Chinatown."

Daniel stared blankly at the man.

"They're like spice sticks," Tiny said, gesturing with his hands. "You burn them to cover up pot smoke."

Daniel's brows rose. "You mean incense? Luthien smelled like incense?"

Tiny nodded. "Big time. Hey, what do I get for telling you all this?"

"What do you mean?" Daniel began to pack up, putting the sketch back in his bag.

"For providing you with information. Are you going to talk to the DA or something? Put in a good word for me?"

"For a single name and not the one I wanted? No, I'm not."

Tiny grew red in the face. "Hey, man, I helped you!"

Daniel stood to leave. "That remains to be seen." He turned to the door, but paused at the threshold. "And a little tip—the time to broker a deal for information is *before* you start talking."

A few hours later, he found out Tiny's information was good, up to a point. He found Luthien easily. The man was buried in Woodmere Cemetery. He'd died shortly after the Devil's Hand was shut down—a few days after they'd been visited by the woman in the white bikini.

Daniel threw himself into work after that, pouring over cold cases going back years. At first, he got nowhere. It took him a little while to make the obvious connection.

It wasn't enough to examine the old drug cases. They needed to include murder, and not just plain old murder at that.

The deaths he needed to investigate were labeled as weird or occult by the authorities who landed the cases. Ritualistic was a word that came up often. When he checked, he found two more blurry photographs of his suspect in disparate cases. More than one detective remembered her in the periphery of their murder cases, although they didn't have pictures or witness statements from her.

If he was right, the woman in the white bikini was a type of fixer. She didn't commit the initial crimes. She came in after and cleaned up the mess—by any means necessary.

Ray was wrong. This was a career-making case.

Daniel kept going through all the old case files, weeding out the flotsam, and came up with at least half a dozen likely sightings. When he put pins in the relevant cities of a map, he noticed something a little odd.

All the most likely cases were in cities near large bodies of water.

6

Serin tried to summon up the right degree of enthusiasm for the food. The large mahogany table was laid out with a sumptuous array of gourmet delicacies—succulent shrimp, lobster, oysters, and other shellfish. The sushi and sashimi alone were worth thousands of dollars. But seafood was a staple of the T'Kaierian diet. She'd grown up eating fresher and more delicate morsels than this.

The penthouse and its contents were as lavish as the spread.

"This is the rarest of all sushi. Fugu," Rainer Torsten said, winking at her as he brought the chopsticks to his lips. He popped the slice of raw fish into his mouth, closing his eyes as he chewed appreciatively.

In the week since she'd left T'Kaieri, she'd checked out Alec's lead. The ugly toad had been bought by another collector, one who did not care about the provenance of his prizes. She hadn't been able to learn much from him, other than he'd bought it from a new source —one recommended to him by Rainer Torsten.

The hovering waiter took the plate immediately when Rainer was finished. He was a mildly eccentric human billionaire and one of the country's most eligible bachelors. The event was a fundraiser at his lavish Manhattan penthouse.

Serin had resurrected one of her old covers to smooth her entry into Torsten's inner circle. Eileen Knight was a procurer for the British Museum of London. Serin couldn't blame Rainer for his interest. Eileen was a single woman. All her covers were.

His dark eyes flicked over her, taking in her low-cut red gown and matching heels before returning to her face. All things considered, she had to give him props for not lingering on her cleavage. Most of the other men at the ball had.

He picked up another slice, offering her the potentially poisonous sushi with a flirtatious grin.

"I assure you it's perfectly safe," Rainer assured her when she didn't let him feed her. "My sushi chef is the best in the States."

"But not the world?" she teased, a corner of her mouth turned up.

"He's an apprentice of one of Japan's premier sushi chefs. He's studied his craft for decades. This is a calculated risk, but you'll be quite safe as long as I'm here."

Serin wanted to laugh, but she had to admit Rainer was attractive. Mid-thirties at the oldest, he had made his fortune on Wall Street before leaving that rat's nest to become an angel investor. He'd made an even bigger fortune funding a few Silicon Valley start-ups, ones with very recognizable names, even to her.

Serin hadn't had much occasion to use computers or smartphones until recently. Electronics tended to get damaged around her, even when she didn't carry them with her through her medium. It was the humidity. Even the new ones made to be water resistant couldn't last around her for long.

Rainer's appreciative gaze swept over her again, his expression downright smitten. It was by design, of course. Getting a mark or unwitting informant to fall for her was part of her modus operandi. It facilitated her entry into the circles she was forced to travel on behalf of the Mother. Her way took a little longer than her sister Diana's *punch first, ask questions later* approach, but each Elemental played to their strengths. This was hers.

While necessary, a mark's interest in her was at best an annoyance. But she was almost enjoying flirting with Rainer.

No sooner had she realized that truth, guilt flared, tightening her throat. *This is about Jordan. Don't forget that.*

She bent her head and took the slice of sashimi from Rainer, chewing it with relish. Fugu poisoning deaths were rare these days. The number was in the dozens annually, but hundreds did have to seek medical attention for the blowfish toxin that made the sushi such a risk to eat.

Rainer beamed, waiting expectantly for her verdict.

"I prefer the sea urchin. That creamy umami that ends on a sharp note—it's my favorite."

He laughed. "You're a connoisseur. I appreciate that."

Serin pivoted, putting her hand behind her back and taking in the room. The other guests mingled, drinking champagne or eating tidbits from the many silver trays being passed around by the waitstaff.

"This is a beautiful apartment," she said, glancing at him coquettishly from the corner of her eye. "But I can't believe you keep a million-dollar collection out here in the open like this."

He paused, a corner of his mouth lifting. "The paintings are excellent quality but not that excellent."

"You know I wasn't talking about the paintings." Serin waved, indicating the priceless carved figures on the mantel. "Those are Aztec. And the bookends on the far shelf are Chinese fertility statues, very rare ones."

Those were just a few of the priceless artifacts hidden in plain sight.

Serin wandered to a set of Persian glyphs mounted on a nearby wall. Rainer followed her like a puppy. She rewarded him with a smile.

"No famous paintings hang on your walls," she said, pitching her voice to a throatier register than normal. "That's most likely why most people don't take note of the priceless artifacts all around them. The few who do notice must believe they're reproductions... or at best, real but inexpensive pieces. They have no idea this room is filled with antiquities worth millions of dollars."

He narrowed his eyes "You're very good. I thought your area of expertise was the Renaissance?"

"Well, like Da Vinci, I like to dabble," she said modestly.

Rainer shrugged. "I guess dangling the possibility of a private tour won't get me a dinner date now? Not when you can see the bulk of my collection in this room."

Serin crossed her arms. "I like that you live with your pieces, despite the risk. What if one of your guests bumped into a table and, God forbid, knocked over a Babylonian statue?"

He winked, gesturing at the slices of Fugu on the table. "Life is not worth living without a little risk." He leaned closer. "I keep my favorite treasures in the bedroom if you're interested."

It was the invitation she'd been waiting for, but Serin knew her craft well enough to play a little hard to get. "How long have we known each other? A week?"

"It's actually a hundred and eighty-seven hours." Rainer's eyes were dancing. "I used to be a math guy. I like precision."

"Don't get me wrong, I am curious, but what would your guests have to say if we disappeared now? This is a fundraiser for Columbia's medical school. Don't you have to mix and mingle? I thought events like these were all about drumming up more donations."

He paused, leaning against the back of the roomy leather sofa in the middle of the room. "Oh, I think the school's administrator has that aspect well in hand, but if you'd like to ensure it's a private viewing, you can come back in an hour or so...everyone should be gone by then."

Serin glided out to the nearby balcony, leaning against the rail.

She didn't have to strike a seductive pose. The setting and the dress did that for her.

"It's a tempting offer, but I have to make sure this doesn't get back to my employer. They sent me to study your collection—that's all. Anything more would be frowned on." She cast a questioning glance in the direction of the discreet security guard stationed across the room.

He leaned closer. "I promise we'll be completely alone."

She let her lips pull up into a slow smile. "Then I'll be here."

A few hours later, Serin tossed an unconscious Rainer on the bed, turning out the pockets of his thousand-dollar pants.

I should probably take these off now.

She was going to have to strip him before she left so he'd come to the conclusions she wanted him to draw. Normally, it wasn't an issue. Generally, her marks weren't the kind of men or women one had to feel pity for, but she could see Rainer's aura. He was a decent man, which made this aspect of her job distasteful this time around. *Later,* she told herself.

There was nothing in his pockets. *But there has to be a key fob.*

The state-of-the-art touchscreen had a fingerprint lock, but she'd hauled an unconscious Rainer to the desk, and that had only opened the top layer of the computer's operating system. She'd already searched all the papers in the desk. The name of Rainer's antiquities dealer wasn't on them.

The files in the top layer of the unlocked computer were just for show. The most Rainer could do there was browse the internet and store his photos. But long years of watching Gia at work with computers had taught her a fair amount about the new devices, and how humans like to hide their true valuables under more stringent— and hidden—security measures.

Hand on her chin, she spun on her heel, considering her surroundings. Rainer's investment materials weren't on the top layer of the computer. That meant he accessed the hidden layer every day for work.

And his most precious belongings are the artifacts that brought me here. One of them was hiding Rainer's secrets.

A systematic search of the antiquities in the apartment yielded fruit. She found the fob inside a small Grecian urn near the office entrance. Rainer must have found it convenient—a place to hide it in plain sight near his desk. The urn was tall enough that few people could reach inside, let alone see something lying on the bottom.

She removed the fob, then plugged it in. Her fingers flew across the keys, trying not to touch any of them for very long. Though he could afford it, she didn't want Rainer to have to replace it.

Unfortunately, all the effort didn't give her the name and address of the dealer. All she had was a nickname in the signature of an old email arranging the purchase of a Sumerian tablet.

Puck.

***

Daniel wanted to bang his head on his desk. Though the description of the woman in the white bikini was vague, the consistency across cases was enough for his supervisor to take him seriously. However, that acceptance came just as he hit a wall in his investigation.

Although he'd been able to scrounge more witness statements matching the description he was passing around, the fight with the Devil's Hand was the only actual footage of the woman. It was also the only evidence she was more than a bystander in any of the crimes he was investigating.

"Still at it?" Ray reeked of garlic. Daniel almost gagged, waving a file folder to get rid of the stench.

"How many times have I told you *not* to go to the Chinese place on the corner? Their stuff is toxic."

His partner put a hand over his face and huffed, checking his breath. "You're the only one who complains. I swear you have one those super sniffers."

Daniel shrugged, brushing the comment off. His coworkers claimed he had a sixth sense where dealers had hidden their stash because he found them faster than the dogs.

He gestured to the sticky note in Ray's hand. "What've you got?"

Ray flapped the note back and forth before sitting across from him. "I have the number of an embarrassed billionaire."

Daniel frowned. "I thought it was something good."

His partner was smirking now. "Oh, it is. My buddy Sal cashed out of the FBI. He does private security in Manhattan now. He's all hooked up there. Anyway, he has a buddy of his own who works for that hotshot investor Rainer Torsten. Turns out his boss is laying low and licking his wounds... after a beautiful woman roofied him to get into his computer."

"Would this beautiful girl be a stacked African-American with legs for days and a penchant for disappearing?"

"Yes and no. The physical description was spot on, but the woman's accent was British. She was posing as an antiquities dealer."

Interesting. The other guests at the Reaper's compound described her as an American. Apparently, his girl was a chameleon. "What did she get?"

"They haven't narrowed it down yet. The girl knew all about Torsten's antiquities, and she could put big price tags on all them. According to the security guy, she could put any of those in her pocket to sell on the black market, but everything was accounted for."

Daniel tapped his pen on his desk. "She could have swapped them for fakes."

"That's what I said, but apparently this Rainer is an expert—he says he could tell the difference. All she did was access his computer. His best guess is some competitor paid her to break into his files to find out what projects he was going to fund. Maybe they thought they could get rich investing in the same stuff."

There were too many holes in that explanation. "If that were true, why would she leave traces on his computer? She's too good for that. And why wouldn't she nick some antique to make it appear as if that was what she was after the whole time? Now the fancy investor gets to rethink his strategy. Wouldn't she assume he'll change what projects he chooses to fund?"

"You're still betting this girl is smart instead of just muscle behind a pretty face." Ray lifted a picture of the woman fighting in the alley from Daniel's desk. Her foot was poised inches from a biker's head.

He wasn't convinced. "I don't know. I think there's more to this Torsten situation. Any way you can get me a meeting with him?"

Ray stood. "I'll check with Sal and see if he can set it up." He started to walk away before doubling back. "I almost forgot the best part. Torsten has a clear memory of letting her into the apartment. Then she kissed him, and he was out. He thinks she may have worn drugged lipstick. Can you believe that?"

Daniel laughed. "It's like something out of a spy movie. Let me know when the meet is set. I want to see Torsten as soon as possible."

"What do you mean?" Daniel asked.

Rainer Torsten steepled his fingers under his chin, drumming them together. "You heard me."

He leaned back in the chair. Daniel was sitting across from the richest man he'd ever met, on the top floor of new office building downtown.

"I will see what I can do, but are you certain she can't profit from anything she found in your files?"

Torsten shook his blond head. "I'm between projects now. I had a few prospects under consideration, but none of them were truly viable. I am entertaining new offers, of course, but there's really nothing on the table that anyone could jump on for profit."

"And there was nothing else? No bank account numbers?"

"I have a keystroke program installed as a security measure. Eileen, as she called herself, ignored all my investment files."

Daniel blinked. "Then what was she after?"

"She zeroed in on some of my email correspondence. She stopped searching after reading some messages from an art dealer named Puck."

"An art dealer?" It sounded like a dead end, but his spider-sense was tingling. This was the right track. He was sure of it.

Daniel ended the meeting shortly afterward, texting Ray with a request to run Puck down.

His partner called him back right away. "Now we're chasing down art dealers?"

Daniel laughed. "It's who she's after, so it's who I'm after."

"So your meeting with the rich guy went well?"

He hailed a cab. "It did. And get this...Torsten doesn't want to press charges. In fact, he had a message."

"For who?"

"For the girl who called herself Eileen—my ass-kicking biker-beating suspect. He wanted me to tell her that he'd forgive everything if she would just change her mind about dinner."

7

Serin jumped back as the pipe swung through the air, the swooshing sound more like a flute than the hiss of a deadly weapon. It sliced through the drizzle of rain like a knife.

Pivoting, she feinted right, narrowly avoiding the second assailant's punch.

This is just my luck, running into a neo-Nazi parade while on the job.

"I don't have time for this."

Sprinting a few steps, she leapt, executing a parkour-perfect cat-back vault off the nearby wall, higher than most humans could jump without a big running start.

She landed on the burly human's back, grabbing his hair and punching down to break his nose.

He instantly crashed to the ground like a huge tree felled in the woods. Her feet landed lightly on either side of his head. Glaring at his slack-jawed accomplice, she repeated herself.

"I said, *I don't have time for this.*"

She advanced on the second overweight neo-Nazi, letting the unearthly glow of the Mother's gift show through her eyes. To him, it would appear as if they started glowing a brilliant azure, the color of the ocean around T'Kaieri.

In reality, this was the true color of her eyes. It had been since she'd been chosen. Gia called it a special quirk of the Mother's gift. It manifested a little differently in all her sisters. Serin had to make an effort to mute the luminescence of her eyes or risk complicating her day-to-day work among humans. Except when she needed to make a point...

The fat man dropped the pipe. He turned, running away as fast as his legs could carry him. Behind her, the other man groaned.

Turning her attention to him, she strolled over, her head craning to read all of his visible tattoos. Like the runner, this one was also a fan of the swastika, a sacred symbol perverted to another end.

"Care to tell me what you meant by jumping me just now?"

The man hissed, spitting at her. Since he was still lying on his back, the dollop of spit landed on his own face.

"You're the one who walked by our parade, you stupid cunt!"

He added several race-filled expletives. "People like you shouldn't even exist. You shouldn't get to breathe the same air as me."

Serin's face twisted. Perfect. Just perfect.

This hadn't happened for some time, but she had been around long enough to recognize the signs of a brewing race war. *You have to keep closer tabs on the humans*. It was just as her sisters said... they were cycling up faster and faster.

When Supernaturals fought, it was bloodier and a hell of a lot more dangerous, but their wars tended to burn out faster, lasting a few months at most—usually. Human conflicts could simmer and rage much longer. Sometimes it took decades to get to the boiling point, but once it did....

Whether the brewing resentments would erupt into a full-fledged race war had yet to be determined. *Damn*. This was going to complicate her operations in this country for years to come. The prospect was exhausting.

For now, the least she could do was take out the trash.

Serin picked up the still-swearing neo-Nazi by the collar. With a flick of her wrist, she launched him into space. He sailed several yards, landing in the open dumpster at the mouth of the alley. Clapping her hands together to dust them off, she continued to the end of the lane, this time avoiding the direction of the nazi parade route.

Keeping her hands in her pocket, Serin made her way down the block. Her skin itched to turn around and show the race-baiters they weren't as superior as they thought they were.

You don't have time. There was never enough time. It hurt her heart to admit, but some battles were not hers to fight. Her priority was to find Puck.

She'd already sent out feelers to contacts who had any sort of tie-in with the art world, both human and Sup. One of them, a Loki, said he had something. She was waiting impatiently to find out what that was. It was why she was in a damn alley, for the meeting.

Speaking of which...

There was a shift in the moisture in the air, a little change that told her she was not alone.

"It's about time, Loki."

She turned to find the fae posing, leaning against the wall in a black leather jacket and rolled-up blue jeans. He was wearing his favorite glamour, that of a rakishly handsome young man. The fae was gorgeous save for a crooked nose. He'd always said perfection was too much of a distraction for others.

Loki were a subclass of trickster fae. They were powerful shapeshifters who could look and sound like anyone they wanted. Some had the ability to create minor illusions, subtly subverting reality around them. A truly determined Loki would have been a terror. As it was, most were content to flit through life playing practical jokes and partying. Thankfully, they were rare.

"Why are you dressed like the Fonz?" she asked.

Loki was even wearing black sunglasses—at night no less.

His face fell, and he threw up his hands. "It's the fifties' greaser fashion. I'm going to a party later. It is Halloween, in case you've forgotten."

"I forgot." It was easy to do that when dealing with the supernatural every day. The fae didn't bother with costumes on All Hallows. "I take it this is a human party?"

"That it is. They're so cute in their little costumes. Besides, while the booze isn't all that good, it *is* plentiful." Loki pushed away from the wall, checking behind Serin to examine her handiwork. "Keeping busy, I see."

Serin glared at him. "You picked the meeting place."

Loki crossed his arms. "Yes, well, I distinctly remember naming the coffee shop around the corner, not the alley behind it."

"It wouldn't have made a difference. Do me a favor. The next time you insist on a face-to-face meeting, try to find a location that isn't less than a block away from a Neo-Nazi rally. Unless you did it on purpose, of course, to get your kicks."

They did have a history. Loki liked to attach himself to her cases, out of boredom no doubt. He was a bit of a nuisance at times, but he could be useful, too. And the trouble he caused was never more than she could handle...at least not yet anyway.

Loki was affronted. "I would never do that to you, my sweet Serin. You know that."

Behind them, a biker whimpered. Loki rushed him, delivering a swift kick to the man's gut before running back to Serin. "Please accept my sincerest apologies for this rabble. The humans are acting up again."

"Tell me something I don't know."

Loki winked and turned, holding up his hands. He waved, and the bikers turned into old tires. Their groans disappeared with them, but it was a shoddy illusion. It would only work for an hour or so, but a Loki's glamour was limited when applied to something as big as those men.

"What's the point of that?" she asked.

It wasn't as if they had to worry about the Nazis following. The only place these guys were headed to was the hospital.

"I just think they need to suffer a little longer for accosting your esteemed self. This way, no one will rush them to the ER straight off. Unless you think they need immediate attention, of course."

She scoffed. "I didn't do any permanent damage. Well, nothing more serious than a limp."

"They can fix that these days. The wonders of human surgery. It has advanced quite a bit in the last few decades." He held out his arm with chivalrous flair. "Let's get out of this weather."

Crossing her arms, she rested her weight on one hip.

"Yes, of course. The rain doesn't bother you." He sighed, giving her hair a longing glance. "Even with a glamour, mine frizzes in the drizzle, you know."

"You do that on purpose, to fit in."

Smiling, he batted his thick lashes at her. "And you're beyond that. That's why I love you. Tell me when are you going to leave that hopeless mate of yours and run off with me?"

Serin's shoulders stiffened. She narrowed her eyes at him before turning her back and walking away.

"Do you have the information I want, or not?" she hurled over her shoulder.

If Loki was surprised by her sudden temper, he didn't show it. He hustled to fall into step beside her.

"I do," he said. "But I'm afraid what I came across is quite sensitive."

Her baleful glare bounced off him. "Meaning?"

"Well, I didn't uncover the identity of your art dealer Puck, not exactly. There are, however, some rumblings. A few juicy rumors. But I can't share them with you."

Serin stopped short. "Why not?" The words came out hard and ice cold.

"It...err...is against policy."

"Policy?" The only rules Loki followed were his own...and the queen's.

The Fae Queen of Air and Darkness had ruled her people with an iron fist for hundreds of years, longer than Serin had been an Elemental. She doubted the queen had been whispering in Loki's ear. He wasn't a fan of court life, and he usually avoided it like the plague. Which meant this rule wasn't recent. And there would only be one reason for such a blanket policy.

"So Puck is fae," she confirmed. She had guessed as much from the name he chose to go by.

Loki shrugged. "I can neither confirm nor deny that, but perhaps if we continue, you might stumble upon a certain location that might prove helpful in your inquiries..."

Serin resumed walking. "I need an address."

They turned the corner, their legs striding in sync thanks to Loki's peculiar penchant for imitation.

"There isn't one to give, even if I was allowed to serve up one of my own to an Elemental."

"Denying me is against Covenant," she reminded him without heat.

Elementals were the ultimate authority in their world. Her request should have superseded the queen's, but Serin knew Loki well enough to realize he was dancing on a fine line.

"You did something to piss off the queen, didn't you?" It explained his reticence to give her real information outright. Loki wanted to help her, but he needed to be careful about it.

The queen wasn't their enemy, but she definitely wasn't a friend. Helping an Elemental would have been verboten, at least until Her Highness figured out how to make it benefit her.

Loki coughed. "Yes, well, sometimes the stiffs in court don't enjoy my little pranks."

A corner of Serin's mouth lifted. "What did you do?"

"There was a small matter of one of her favorite's being inconvenienced. Nothing serious. But it was a distraction from his normal duties."

She waited, meeting his eyes and lifting a brow.

"I dyed a certain part of his anatomy bright orange. The queen found it distracting."

An unwilling laugh escaped. "I take it this was one of her consorts?"

"Servicing the queen is an honor." His tone implied otherwise.

Concerned, Serin put her hand on his shoulder. "Were you ever forced to service her?"

Loki's eyes shone with crocodile tears. "You do care! But there's no need to worry, love. The queen only consorts with the highest echelons of fae, usually a member of her personal guard. I'm quite safe from her attentions. Besides, you know I only have eyes for you."

"Sure you do," she muttered.

A Loki's devotion was fervent and true...for the length of time they were proclaiming it. Nevertheless, while he was here, she couldn't afford to let his little games get in the way. "That's enough of that unless you want to find yourself in a dumpster, too—a full one this time. Your outfit would be ruined."

He hopped over a stray piece of trash on the sidewalk. "Not on All Hallows Eve, love. That would be too cruel. In any case, I can't tell you more about the Puck rumors, but should you happen to guess certain details, I can confirm. Hot or cold."

"So I have to play Twenty Questions to get intel that is little more than hearsay?"

"Right in one...as usual."

She exhaled, trying to control her impatience. "At least tell me what kind of fae Puck is."

"According to the scuttlebutt, he's the kind who likes acquiring things."

That could be anything from a gremlin to a leprechaun. "This is going to take forever, isn't it?"

Loki beamed at her. "Forever is a fluid term for our kind. Feel like getting that coffee now?"

"Fine. But none of that fluffy sugary crap you like. No whipped cream, or fancy leaves in foam. I take it black."

"I can be black like that." Loki snapped his fingers. "Just say the word."

Serin laughed despite herself. "I'd break you in half, and you know it."

Putting his hand where a heart would be on a human, he gave a theatrical sigh. "But what a way to go."

8

Serin parted the drizzling rain so she could see the street number of the darkened storefront. The windows of number thirty-seven were so crowded she couldn't see the room behind them—just like Loki described.

Once she 'guessed' the intel he was feeding her was not for Puck's location, but for one of his associates, Loki's tongue had loosened. He described how to find the obscure antique store buried in the diamond district, giving up the idea of going with her when she reminded him that he was all dressed up with better places to go.

Merde. Serin knew something was wrong as soon as she opened the door. The coppery metallic scent hit her like a rogue wave, out of place and overwhelming. A lot of blood had been spilled. It was too strong for a minor household accident. This pronounced a stench meant someone was dead.

Serin murmured a protective spell, a little extra shielding in case whoever was responsible was still around. Closing the door, she picked her way through the piles of bric-a-brac that filled the room.

The body was somewhere near the rear of the store. Like a shark, Serin could smell the minutest traces of blood and other signature olfactory cues. Not that she needed that degree of sensitivity to find this crime scene. Shutting out the overwhelming odor was more of an issue.

She edged around a precarious pile of old clocks and tiny cabinets. There was a thousand-dollar Waterbury lying on its side next to a hamburger phone. Everything was jumbled together in various states of disrepair as if the proprietor didn't have the time to organize or sort by value.

The owner of the shop was lying in the back of the room just beyond the threshold of his office. He'd been dead at least three or four hours, his slashed throat certainly the cause.

Frowning, Serin knelt to picked up the man's arm by the cuff of his sleeve. There was a matching gash on his wrist. She dropped it, then nudged the other hand with her foot. Another cut. Both deep, as if someone wanted to make sure this guy was drained dry. But all his blood was on the floor, so this wasn't the work of a vamp trying to disguise their kill.

The click of the gun cocking didn't register until she was rising to her feet. Pivoting slowly, Serin turned to see a man in a suit holding a pistol on her. His stance was wide, practiced law enforcement.

"If you're smart, you'll put your hands up and come quietly." He reached behind him, pulled out a shiny pair of silver handcuffs, and started advancing toward her. The man's face was familiar, but she couldn't place him.

Serin tilted her head. "You know, I could think of more entertaining uses for those."

Teasing a cop was atypical for her, but she was moving through these circles as Eileen and there wasn't much Eileen wouldn't dare.

The man responded by flushing, his blood coursing through his veins a little faster. She caught a blast of pheromones and then a little masculine sweat. He waved the cuffs again.

Behind him, she could see the distant red and blue lights of various police cruisers. It was getting closer, but they didn't turn on the sirens. He heard them anyway. "That's the backup I called for, so don't try any of those fancy fighting moves now," he said, his face hardening. Serin could sense his embarrassment, probably at becoming aroused.

Crap. That can't be a good sign. Where had this man seen her fight?

For a second, she debated pushing past him and making for the exit, but the uniformed officers were pouring in the front door now. They stomped like elephants, knocking and crashing things over.

Fighting her way out meant taking out half the squad.

The man gestured again, twitching his gun this time. "I said to put your hands up."

Her eyes flicked behind him. The back door was a dozen feet away, but it was completely blocked with piles of junk. Knocking them away would mean taking a bullet or two in the back unless she wanted to shift to her medium in front of the man.

Slowly, she raised her hands in the air.

I am going to kill Loki.

Whether he'd meant to or not, Serin had been set up. The body she'd stumbled on was the dealer she'd been searching for, but he'd been taken out just hours before she could question him about Puck.

And then there's this guy. She flicked an annoyed gaze at Agent Romero as he set a glass of water down in front of her. It was little more than a mouthful, but it was enough to drown him with had the circumstances been different.

She finally recognized him from the case down in Texas. That was almost a year ago. Apparently, her unexplained exit from the bathroom had put a bee in his bonnet. He'd been trying to track her ever since—not that he said as much. His partner was the big talker.

Blatantly, she eyed Romero up and down, ignoring the partner. He'd caught her attention back in Texas because there had been a trace of *otherness* to him. She'd felt it when their eyes met, but dismissed it just as quickly.

She should have examined him closer. Her first impression wasn't wrong exactly. Agent Romero was mostly human. But that something extra... It was shades of a hunter.

And I'm his prey. The idea made her smile.

"Something funny?" The other agent, Doyle something, slapped his hand over a photo of her fighting a bunch of bikers in a back alley. She'd done that enough times for her to not remember the city.

None of the grainy photos were from a close enough range to identify her, but that didn't stop Doyle from waving them in her face. "If these weren't damning enough, we've got you over a freshly dead body," he said, continuing a tirade she'd only half-listened to.

Serin leaned back in her chair, dismissing Doyle. This one was human through and through—swarthy, sweaty, and with the beginning of a middle-age paunch. He was a stark contrast to the lean and sculpted Romero, who was propped against the far wall with his arms crossed over his chest.

Romero said nothing, but his eyes hadn't left her face since they'd brought her in. It was like he was weighing her with his eyes, measuring her every breath.

"I had nothing to do with that man's death," she said.

Her comment was addressed to Romero. The hunter was the only one who mattered.

"See, that's not how we saw it," Ray replied, his mouth curling up in a sneer. He held up another photo, this time one of the body. "This poor old man was sliced and diced. Bled out all over the floor. And you were the only one in the room."

He slid it over to her with his index finger, nose wrinkled as if he smelled something foul. She glanced at the graphic photograph. The old art dealer had been alive when his throat was cut, judging from the arterial spray.

"I hope he didn't suffer," she said, knowing he had. "But I found him like that. He'd been dead for some time. Hours at least...I'm sure your forensics people can tell you exactly how long."

"And how would you know how long he'd been dead?" Doyle asked, leaning closer with a smirk.

Serin shrugged. "I watch old *Forensic Files* reruns. *CSI* too. That blood didn't look fresh to me. And I'm sure someone is checking that jacket you took off me for blood. It won't have any. Not a speck."

"The last time I checked, breaking and entering was a crime."

"I told you, the door was open. The killer probably didn't bother to close it after he did away with that poor old man." She knew how to pick a lock without leaving a trace. They had nothing.

"And what about this?" Doyle asked, indicating the other photos of the alley fight.

Cocking her head to the side, she smiled at Romero. "Do you always let your partner do all the talking?" she asked him.

Doyle banged his fist on the table, forcing her attention back to him. "Look at me, *bitch*. I'm the one asking the questions."

Serin raised one fine dark eyebrow, leaning forward in her chair. "I don't like that word," she murmured.

The room grew colder by several degrees.

"Like I give a shit." Doyle snapped. He didn't notice the temperature change, but across the room, Romero frowned and glanced at the air vent as if it were responsible.

"The entire Devil's Hand motorcycle gang wants to press charges against you," Doyle continued.

She doubted that. No district attorney worth a dime was about to bring a case on behalf of a bunch of killers and drug traffickers already in prison.

"I don't see why," she replied with flawless confusion. "The woman in these photos isn't me."

Serin pretended to study them more closely. "I can see a superficial resemblance, of course. We have similar hair, but this woman is much skinnier than I am." She added a wistful sigh, deciding to play on some tried and true feminine stereotypes. "I really need to lose five pounds."

Against the wall, Romero snorted. "Nice try, but every curve matches exactly."

Serin blinked, her laugh light. "Really now? You sound so certain. Just how closely have you studied this video and my body?"

Across from her, Doyle twisted to throw his partner a pointed glance of exasperation.

Romero glowered, but didn't answer. Serin realized with some surprise that she enjoyed baiting him.

You should be ashamed of yourself. Getting picked up by human law enforcement was a huge no-no. Avoiding government agencies was Elementals 101. Gia should have her stripped for this. But that thought didn't stop Serin from batting her eyelashes at Romero.

Doyle grunted. "Listen, lady, we know you. We both saw you at a crime scene in Texas."

"Well, my bathing suit was rather memorable," she said, acknowledging their first meeting. When had that been? Almost thirteen months ago...

Doyle pounced. "So you don't deny you knew the Reaper?"

The what? "I don't know anyone by that name. I was an invited guest of a man called Felix Desjardin—a very well-known art collector."

"So we're supposed to believe you were consorting with a known drug dealer for some sort of art deal?" Doyle was deadpan.

"That's what I do. I buy art for people who can pay—the hard-to-find pieces. I travel extensively for my work, from Texas to Paris, Rome to Afghanistan, and back again. I go where the art or antiques are."

"And do you always go to these places at the behest of criminals?"

Her fingers fluttered. "I don't ask my clients where they get their money, only if they have it."

"What did you buy for the Reaper?"

She tapped her chin. "If recollection serves, Felix asked me to acquire a fine Louis the Sixteenth writing desk for him. It was a bit ostentatious, but to each his own. I don't question my client's tastes."

"Really?" Doyle was dripping sarcasm now. "Did you by chance give him a taste of something else? Something that knocked him out like you did with Rainer Torsten? Is that why we found him face down in his jacuzzi?"

Gasping, Serin sat up straighter. "Rainer thinks I drugged him?"

She waited a calculated beat before frowning. "Well, I'm not surprised his memory is a bit off. He was drinking heavily the last time I saw him—he was in a celebratory mood, more so than I. But I'm crushed he believes I did something to him."

She paused, languorously tracing her collarbone and staring off into the distance as if lost in memories. "It was a memorable night. Well, for me, anyway." Straightening, she turned back to Doyle. "I should give him a call. I'd like to make sure he's all right."

"If that's what you want to use your last phone call for, go right ahead. But you're not fooling anyone. You're in a lot of trouble, girlie. We've got enough here to put you away for a very long time."

It was the *girlie* that did it.

Serin dropped her hapless facade. Ice infused her tone. "What you have is a whole lot of nothing. I'm an art dealer. I work with colorful characters at times. As long as they can pay for the things they want me to get them, I don't judge. My business is licensed and above board. I've never done anything illegal. Furthermore, I would bet my last dollar you didn't find any drugs in Rainer Torsten's system aside from alcohol. I won't make the same claim for Felix Desjardin. Word is the man liked to party. But he didn't do so with me. And this—"

She pushed the grainy picture of her fighting in the alley back at the agent. "This is some other woman."

Doyle narrowed his eyes. "How quickly you've forgotten the body at Charmed Antiques—Henry Hobbes, the owner."

"I haven't forgotten anything. I had an appointment with Mr. Hobbes. I was in search of an antique clock for another client, and he said he had one. It's why I thought nothing of entering when I found the door open. I was just about to call the police when you showed up. But I certainly didn't kill him. I'd never even met the man before. It was our first meeting."

Sprinkling truths in with the lies made for a better argument, but Doyle was a seasoned cop. "Maybe you killed him for the clock."

She tried not to roll her eyes. "I can afford to pay for my wares. It's better business practice."

The door opened, and a uniform poked her head in. She whispered something to Romero.

Stiffening, he turned to her. "How did your lawyer know where to find you? You haven't made any calls."

They hadn't charged her with anything either, so she wasn't in the system.

"A friend must have called them."

The agents wore identical frowns. Serin huffed in genuine exasperation. "Networking is part of my job. I make lots of connections, but you never know what you're walking into so whenever I'm meeting someone new, I tell a friend where I'm going." She shrugged. "A girl can't be too careful these days. My friend must have seen you take me in without cause."

The door burst open. Loki hurried in wearing a middle-aged Nordic goddess as a disguise, a well-known lawyer if her guess was right.

"Don't say another word." Loki turned to the agents. "You're questioning my client without her attorney. I've spoken with the officer in charge, and he's confirmed she isn't a suspect in the death of Henry Hobbs. There was no blood on the jacket they confiscated."

Loki, disguised as a female lawyer, showed them the jacket, still neatly wrapped in an evidence bag.

Turning to Serin, Loki patted her on the shoulder in a demonstration of comfort, but Serin could feel his anxiety transmitting through the small touch.

Serves him right. He'd gotten her into this mess.

Romero peeled himself off the wall. "We're not done questioning her. She's a suspect in dozens of other crimes."

Dozens? Damn, she'd been messy if it was dozens. That or Romero was a better hunter than she'd thought.

Loki smirked. "If you value your jobs, then yes, you are done. I've already contacted your superior to let him know we're willing to file harassment charges against you."

Doyle pointed a stubby finger at her. "That woman beat a gang of bikers to a body pulp. Seven ended up in the hospital." He proceeded to play the video on his cell phone.

Loki dismissed the video with a wave. "Please. That's obviously a fake. A woman alone couldn't take out that many men. Someone probably staged the whole thing to sell self-defense classes. That or it was shot for some budget web series. Have you even bothered to check YouTube?"

He poked Serin in the shoulder and she rose, taking her jacket out of the plastic wrapping and slipping it on. She nodded at the agents in turn, lingering on Romero a little longer than was strictly necessary.

"Well, gentlemen, thank you for an interesting evening. I would say let's do this again, but I find you both very unpleasant company. Well, Agent Doyle, anyway..."

She sashayed past them, deliberately slowing to swipe her finger along Romero's folded arm. It was as hard as corded steel, but it heated under her touch. Loki tugged her away, hurrying to a waiting sports car, one he no doubt 'borrowed'.

He threw the car in gear, snapping back into the handsome greaser after the first turn. "What was *that?* You were so *va-va-voom* with that cop. It was fucking hot."

Ignoring him, Serin waited until he pulled up to a light before twisting to punch him in the arm.

Loki yelped, holding his arm to his side. He pouted. "Is that a way to thank me for cleaning up after you with the humans?"

She glared at him. "I wouldn't have needed cleaning up after if you hadn't set me up."

"I didn't know someone was going to ice the old guy! I swear. I thought the intel I gave you was good."

"Well, someone killed him and then called the cops just in time for my unscheduled visit," she grumbled. "They must have been watching you. Hobbs died just after you took the bait and brought me his name."

The light changed, and Loki stepped on the gas. He was still sulking and rubbing his arm. "I haven't felt any eyes on me, and I'm pretty damn good at spotting that sort of thing."

She didn't doubt it. Lokis were known for pissing people off. Quick exits wouldn't be worth a damn if they were easily tracked. The careless among them didn't last.

"I guess Puck knows you're hunting for him, huh?"

"So it seems." Serin glowered out the window as the passing streets. Her ill humor brought the rain, the steady miserable drizzle opening into a downpour, something hard enough to clear the streets of people.

Loki peeked at her sideways, tsking. "Poor bastard doesn't know what he just started."

9

Loki grinned when he got the text. He hurriedly swallowed the last of his whipped-cream Frappuccino before waving goodbye to the cute barista behind the counter, then rushed out into the frigid autumn air.

He finally had a line on Puck.

Serin had told him to drop the whole thing now that her adversary was aware of his involvement. She said they wouldn't be able to trust any of his sources. The best they could expect was another trap. But Loki wasn't willing to accept that. Not only had he disappointed Serin, but he'd also been duped and used to mess with a friend. He lived by a code. Only *he* got to mess with his friends.

Loki had also learned Serin had lost her mate. He didn't know the details, but it explained why she'd been so distant and short-tempered. She was simultaneously grieving and out for bloody revenge.

Sending her into a trap, especially under those circumstances, was the grossest violation of his rules to live by. Crossing an Elemental was bad for anyone's health. More importantly, he liked Serin. Few other Supes of that caliber tolerated his company long.

But Loki was confident he could make it up to her. Since they had parted company a few weeks ago, he had pumped every source he had. He was going to find Puck, then he going to serve him up to Serin on a silver platter. Afterward, they'd go dancing. For someone so serious, the girl could cut a rug...

Today, he was in the east end of downtown Detroit. According to the latest rumors, Puck was a frequenter of a fae club in the area.

Dionysia was an old hotspot, but it was in a different spot each time. It ran on a circuit, shifting locations across the country at will. He hadn't been there in decades. It wasn't exactly select. The rougher elements of the fae always knew when and where to find it.

Loki zipped up to Midtown, the location for Dionysia for the past three or four months. He left the shiny Porsche he'd borrowed from a trust-fund brat parked in front of a fire hydrant before heading out on foot.

Dionysia didn't have valet service—a small consideration to those of his brethren who couldn't tolerate much iron in their presence.

As if those special snowflakes would ever step foot in Dionysia. Iron sensitivity was for upper-caste fae. Tricksters were immune. So were most goblins, which was what Loki believed Puck to be...

He was almost to Dionysia's door when his ears caught an out-of-place sound. It was the slide of a leather shoe—one perfectly in sync with his steps. He was being followed.

Loki turned around with exaggerated casualness. The car window next to him exploded with a loud bang.

Fuck. He dove for cover, tripping over his feet. Spinning through the air wildly, he nearly knocked over the human police officer from Serin's arrest.

Agent Romero pointed a gun at him. Horrified, Loki froze as the man pulled the trigger.

Romero winced as his shot was followed by a volley of return fire. Bullets flew, glass broke. In the distance, people screamed as random pedestrians ran away from the busy thoroughfare.

"I told you to get down," he hissed at the young man he'd just saved from getting his head blown off. He pulled the kid behind the rear of a nearby sedan, wondering how the hell this had gone south so fast.

After having to cut Eileen loose, he'd been forced to reevaluate the evidence against her.

Her ice-queen lawyer had been right. They didn't have anything concrete. Though he knew it was her in the photos, getting a jury to make the same determination would have been impossible. As for the murder of Harry Hobbes, the time of death was hours before they faced off over the body.

Ray had argued Eileen could have doubled back, but his gut told him otherwise. She hadn't killed the old man. But he hadn't been willing to let it go and move on. Too much weird shit had happened around the woman. And the way she'd left, touching his arm like that...

His arm had burned, sending streaks of electricity to his damn heart, jolting it like freaking cardiac paddles. He'd been hard for hours afterward. It had been both embarrassing and a bit painful.

Roy had a field day with that. He'd also given him shit for the *'every curve'* comment, deservedly so.

A bullet hit the windshield of the car he and the boy were crouching behind. It exploded, raining blunt shards all over them.

Daniel hugged the car's bumper, peeking out to aim at the black figure firing on them.

One. Two. Three. He breathed in time with his heart, calling on his training and something deeper for calm and focus.

Tunnel vision was sometimes a gift. Daniel was blind to his surroundings. All he could see was the masked man twenty yards or so away.

He fired, but the guy was too fast. Romero shook himself, his eyes were playing tricks. It was as if the gunman blinked out of existence, reappearing to his left where he had the partial cover. Firing resumed.

Daniel chanced another quick glance. Cold seeped through his gut as he saw the assailant drop the gun and pick up another one—a semiautomatic this time.

Not happening. Daniel fired again. This time, he didn't miss. His bullet passed through the man's palm, and the second weapons clattered to the floor.

The firing stopped as abruptly as it started.

He waited, wondering if the assailant was going to try to pick up the other gun despite the wound, but it stayed quiet. Daniel's shoulders dropped, and the noises of the outside world rushed in. The wail of sirens began.

"I think he ran off," he muttered, turning to check on the boy.

Fuck. The kid was gone. Streaks of an oily silver blue substance were left in his place.

Was it paint? It couldn't be blood, not unless it belonged to an alien.

Dismissing the weird mess, he poked his head out. No bullets came flying at it. The gunman had gone.

LOKI STUMBLED, HOLDING THE BALLED-UP REMAINS OF WHAT WAS ONCE a choice cashmere sweater to his midriff. He couldn't afford to leave a trail of fae blood while crawling up the stairs of the six-story condominium where Serin was staying.

No Jordan meant no hotels. Her former mate had always insisted on having their own space. The top floor suite of this place was an Elemental safe house, one he wasn't supposed to know about.

Loki dragged himself up the final flight of stairs, swearing a blue streak. Damn Elementals. Why couldn't they take quarters in places with lifts?

He knocked on the door before trying the knob with the last of his strength. It held fast. He swore under his breath.

"Hey, who's up there?"

Loki peeked over the wrought-iron railing. A pudgy man in brown overalls was huffing up the stairs. Thinking fast, he reached for his glamour. The ripple was weak. He couldn't hold the magic or this appearance for very long.

And I didn't get the hair right! Serin's hair was the most difficult thing to imitate. Loki desperately hoped this man was the super.

When the man finally reached his level, the stranger's mouth dropped open in surprise.

"Oh, hello there." He craned his neck, turning to scan the hall. "Did you see a young man up here?"

"No, I didn't, but I'm glad you came up." Loki summoned a weak smile. "I seem to have locked myself out. Do you have the key on you?"

Serin hid her knife in her pack as she passed the building's super. Murmuring a polite greeting, she jogged up the stairs, wondering why he appeared surprised to see her.

She liked the man, but she didn't want to get into another prolonged conversation about how she reminded him of his daughter and why the woman didn't call.

Serin knew the Elementals' inner sanctum had been breached before she got to her floor. The smell of Supe blood permeated the stairwell. A drop of it lay ominously on the floor in front of their door.

Suddenly, it didn't matter that she'd just been a pitched battle with a ghoul. Serin was running on full blast, ready for another fight.

She reached into her bag for the Sai Alec had handed her on T'Kaeri. On impulse, she'd taken it with her, tossing it in her pack along with her gear. It wasn't until today she realized there had been a reason.

The trident was one of a matched pair. The weapons were made of the strongest charm-infused Han Dynasty steel, and she'd always cast a covetous eye on them, wishing she could play with them.

Now the single trident would serve another purpose—with the right spell, she could track its stolen mate. It was another lead to the thief who killed Jordan.

The spell will still work, even if the Sai is covered in fae blood, she reminded herself as she pushed the door open.

Serin stopped short, taken aback at the vision behind the door. Loki was on the floor, his back to the couch. He was bleeding all over his cocoa skin—*her* skin.

Serin rushed to his side, crouching down to pull the bloody rags away from his stomach.

"*Shit*. What happened to you? And why did you take my form?" she added with a snap when she saw the wound wasn't fatal. At least, she hoped it wasn't.

"I needed to look like you, so your super would let me in." Loki's voice was weak. He was sweating, panting, as she probed his wound.

"Why do you have a bullet in you?" she asked, mystified.

"Cause I got *shot*," he cried as she pulled the skin to examine the wound.

Serin closed her eyes, putting her hand over the hole in his side.

"Please tell me you know some healing spells."

Her forehead puckered. "I do, but they're not going to help with a bullet inside you. We have to take it out first."

She considered calling Gia. Though she has some skill, her sister's healing ability was better than hers. The fae shuddered and he paled, grimacing.

No, there wasn't time. Loki was going to have make do with her skills.

"Brace yourself," she warned him. "This is going to hurt."

Serin parted her lips, calling on the Mother, twisting the aether with words. The long middle tip of the Sai burst into flames.

Loki started, then winced, holding his side as the movement jostled the wound. "How did you do that? You're a water talent."

Serin twisted her lips, examining the wound to plot her next step. "The older I get, the easier it is to borrow from my sisters. Now, hold still."

She blew out the flame, flipping the weapon over so the now-sterile tip was just over the bullet hole.

Loki held up his hands. "Wait, wait." He panted. "I—I don't suppose you have any fae painkillers around?"

"Do those exist?" There were plenty of drugs in the fae world, but all the ones she knew were hallucinogens and pleasure enhancers.

"Some booze then?"

She wrinkled her nose. "I don't think my sisters keep spirits around."

"What about Logan, the Air Elemental? She's young and down for whatever. And her mate goes everywhere with her. He's one of those crazy Colorado wolves. If they've been here, there must be something. Check the closet, *please*."

Serin measured the amount of blood soaking his sweater. His pulse was growing weaker.

"I'm sorry, but we don't have time." She patted his hand. "Brace yourself."

"*Wait.*" Loki reached behind him, fishing out a flask. Wiggling his fingers, he opened it one-handed and took a big swig.

"Absinthe," he panted before tensing. Exhaling loudly, he nodded. "Okay, I'm ready."

Shaking her head, Serin probed the wound with the tip of the Sai. She worked the bullet loose as Loki squirmed and swore.

Tossing it aside, she put her bare hands over the hole and began to chant. After several minutes, the flesh began to show signs of knitting together. She stopped, pulling back before his mouth and other orifices began to close too.

Relieved, she stood and helped him up. "Are you going to tell me how you got this now?"

Loki limped, settling on the couch with her help. "I thought I had a new line on Puck. He was supposed to be at Dyonisia tonight. I wanted to find him for you."

"Loki," she scolded. "I told you to stay out of it once that first body dropped. Puck doesn't want to be found. He is going to extreme lengths to make sure he can't be traced, not through you. I thought that was clear."

"I wasn't going to confront him, I swear. I was just going to check out the club. But I didn't even make it to Dyonisia. I was hit down the block."

Serin pulled a warm throw from an adjoining chair, then dropped it over Loki. "The spell is working. Rest now. You're going to need it."

She moved past him to the bedroom, digging in her drawers until she found a strap that accommodated both the Sai and a short blade.

"You're going to Dyonisia without me, aren't you?" he called after her.

Serin returned, strapping on the harness. "I am. Stay here. Heal. And please drop that glamour now. It's creeping me out."

"*Oh*. Right." Loki sighed, a shimmer passing over him. The other Serin disappeared, leaving the male greaser in her place.

Yawning, he snuffled under the wool throw.

"Oh, I almost forgot," he whispered, his voice slurring slightly with exhaustion. "You're never going to believe who saved me..."

10

Serin tightened her grip around the goblin's neck, shifting her hold a bit so he could breathe and talk.

"Why are you doing this?" Kerrick wheezed, kicking his legs in the air.

They were in the back storeroom of Dionysia, the noise of their confrontation disguised by the driving beat of the latest *blob* track. "I'm your friend! Haven't I been useful to you?"

"Once or twice in the past, you've provided some assistance," she acknowledged with equanimity.

Serin wasn't even out of breath, despite the fact the frequently flirtatious goblin outweighed her by at least two stone of muscle.

"Then why?" he asked, the pitch of his voice a hairsbreadth from a wail.

"Because I don't have time for your—*I'm-fae-so-I-can't-answer-a-direct-question* bullshit," she said, her jaw tight. "I want to know why Loki was almost gunned down in the street outside. Nothing happens around here that you don't know about."

"But why the strong-arm tactics?" He coughed, tapping her hand.

"I mean, I expect this from Diana—maybe Logan when she's on her period—but you're *Water*. You're the reasonable one."

"Period jokes? Really?" She shook him again. "Tell me another one and you'll see how reasonable I can be."

Serin may have been known for following the rules of engagement in their world, but that didn't make it safe to cross her. She adjusted her grip around Kerrick's neck, tightening it enough for his glamour to flicker. The overly groomed millennial with the perfect Van Dyke beard blinked out, revealing a pale green goblin with thin gold lips and bright pink hair.

"I wasn't joking about you!" he protested, his expression wounded.

Serin was unmoved. "And yet, as a woman, I'm still offended. Funny how that works…" She let him drop to the ground, leaning in close before smiling.

Kerrick's eyes widened as she let the ocean's cold blue shine through her eyes.

"Okay, okay, but I really don't know anything about the gun fight. Our kind doesn't deal in human weapons!"

"Then tell me what you do know. You've been the caretaker of Dionysia for decades. You know who is fucking who, and which of your clients came into money, all the normal gossip that runs in an institution like this. But you also hear the little whispers about those toying with the black—the ones who flirt with the edge and the ones who jump right off it with their eyes open."

Drawing her head back, she stared down at the goblin, her face a perfectly carved mask.

Kendrick winced. "I don't know anything about the gun attack. That's the truth—I swear on the covenant."

"Oh, I believe that," she said. "It must have caught you off guard. It certainly did Loki. But I think you felt the rumblings before that. You're this community's weather vane. When shit goes south in the royal court Dionysia serves as sanctuary for those too weak to face the storm on their own. You protect your own."

Serin put him down and loosened her grip. "It's why I've always liked you. But one of your people is putting profit over people. He goes by Puck and he traffics in stolen goods—artifacts that shouldn't be out in the world. One human is already dead. Loki came close to being the first fae to die. The person responsible is someone who drinks the drafts you pour and revels with the crowd you tend."

She crossed her arms. "It's true that talking to me is frowned upon by your regent, but Puck is the one violating the queen's chief edict regarding Elementals—he's making us get involved. We both know that is the last thing she would want."

The barkeep stepped back, rolling his shoulders as the glamour swept back over him. The human millennial returned, his eyes cast down. "I still don't know anything about the guns, but I might've heard something about someone new making money off objects of powers. However, it was just a rumor. Dionysia isn't the place for people to market those wares. My clientele doesn't have the scratch for the high-ticket stuff."

"Who'd you hear the rumor from?"

"An old dryad named Saz. Mind you, I don't think he's involved. Saz is an old barfly. He spends most of the week hugging the bar bench, nursing the same pint for hours on end. He was just repeating something he heard...and only because he's been searching for Eldertree stools for his place for a long time."

"All I want is a lead. Saz has nothing to fear if he's not involved." She bit her lip before sucking in a breath. "Thank you...and sorry for the rough handling."

"I get worse from the Dunkers when they've had one too many." Kerrick put his hand in his pockets, then kicked the floor. "Can I ask you something?"

She leaned against the shelf. "Depends on what it is."

"Is the other rumor I heard true? Is your mate dead?"

The Supernatural world was smaller than she thought, but Serin was struck by her lack of emotion. There wasn't a telltale shaft of pain, no tightening of her stomach. Just the coldness in her extremities that had been her constant companion since Jordan disappeared.

"Yes," she said hoarsely.

"*Oh.* Sorry." Kerrick rubbed the back of his head. "Hey, when this is all over—weeks or months—come back and I'll break out a bottle of Barda Rum. I've been saving for a couple of centuries. It should be coming into its own now."

Serin pushed her hair behind her ear. At least the goblin didn't hold a grudge, but if he'd already heard the news of her mate, it would explain his willingness to forgive and forget.

"We'll see. Are you expecting Saz tonight?"

Kerrick gestured for her to follow him to the door. That heavy bass of yet another *blob* song was making it vibrate. "If he's not, he'll be in tomorrow or the next day. He never stays away long."

He swung the door open, letting in an explosion of sound. It was a bit like being hit with a rogue wave. Every part of her body reacted as if struck, until it adjusted grudgingly like someone did after leaping into the ocean.

At least it adjusted up to a point. Her bones rattled, and she shot Kerrick a pointed glance.

"It's the new album," he shouted over the noise. He pointed to the pub's makeshift dance floor. An assortment of lower fae were slamming against each other to the beat. "Folks are celebrating. It's not often one of ours makes the top of the human charts."

Serin sighed and turned, narrowly missing being mowed down by a squat barrel-chested brownie. She corrected his course with a well-meaning shove and circled the floor, about to make her way to one of the darkened booths in the back to wait for her mark. She stopped dead when she saw Agent Romero.

He was standing at the bar talking to the relief bartender, a grizzled female centaur glamoured into the form of a voluptuous blonde.

How the hell had he gotten in here? The wards kept everyone but fae out. No shifters, no witches, and no vampires could come inside without an invitation. Elementals were the exception to fae wards, but only because the fae hadn't figured out how to keep them out yet.

Kerrick followed her line of sight, spotting the human seconds after she did. His mouth dropped open. "Is that what I think it is?" He grabbed her arm, hissing the question in her ear.

Serin shook off his hand. "It would appear so."

She gestured for him to follow her to the edge of the room, out of the detective's line of sight. "What happened? Have you given the task of warding the bar to a subordinate?"

"No! I always do it myself—I have since I took over the bar three centuries ago. There's no way in hell a human got past them."

She craned her neck to see the agent. He appeared to be enjoying his beer. "Well, apparently this one did."

When she turned back, Kerrick was watching her with suspicion. "Do you know him?"

"I do. He's a particularly persistent member of the human law enforcement. He's been popping up lately."

"A human cop? That's even worse." Kerrick was beside himself. "We need to get him out of here before he sees past Cincy's glamour. She's not that good at holding it for more than an hour or two. In fact, most of the patrons can't do any better. It's why they come here, so they don't have to."

Serin shook her head, still marveling that Romero had made it past the wards. "He really must have hunter blood in him."

"Really?" Kerrick slumped in relief. "Then that's settled. We can just contact the Court. One of the trappers will pick him up. He'll be conscripted into the Great Hunt, problem solved."

Serin scowled. "Don't even think about it. This guy's profile is too high. A top human cop can't just disappear without a shitstorm of scrutiny."

Not to mention the fact humans conscripted into the Great Hunt were essentially slaves. Elementals didn't interfere with the practice because most of the human predators started out by hunting their own kind. Agent Romero wasn't in that class.

The goblin scoffed. "Humans disappear all the time. The queen can have a changeling fashioned to replace him. No one will ever know the difference."

"The hell she will," Serin said. "Forget about it. We're not siccing fae bounty hunters on him. Loki's alive because of Romero."

Kerrick didn't care. "Lucky Loki, but the human has to go before anyone notices him. There are mountain trolls in here! You know how suspicious those bastards are. If they even get a whiff of him, they'll tear him apart."

Ugh. As much as she enjoyed teasing him, Serin didn't want to go to bat for this particular human. She was still annoyed at being dragged in for questioning.

"I'll take care of this," she said from behind gritted teeth.

Romero clapped a hand over his eyes, tears streaming.

"Sorry. Can I have a napkin or something?" he asked the gorgeous Playboy bunny behind the bar. "I don't know what's wrong with my eyes. Must be the smoke in here."

The blonde gave him a stiff smile and handed him the folded square of paper, dropping it on the bar in front of him to avoid touching him. Wiping his eyes, he turned around, wondering what her problem was. He was in plainclothes, and no one had ever made him as law enforcement in a bar.

Also, Daniel ordinarily did pretty well with female bartenders. He'd gone home with more than one in his day, but this girl was acting like he had the plague.

He sipped the beer she'd handed him moments before. Blinking, he glanced down at it in surprise.

At least the beer was good. It was nutty and had a hint of honey without being sweet. It must have been a new microbrew. He squinted at the vaguely Celtic design on the label, committing the name to memory so he could find it again before turning his attention back to the shifting crowd.

A cleared space in the center of the room served as a dance floor. There were more men than women in the melee, all dancing—if it could be called that. The raucous crowd behind him threw themselves around like they were being electrocuted. The beat they were moving to wasn't half bad. It was one of those heavy drum and bass tracks popular on the radio recently.

A massive figure broke away from the crowd, crashing into a barstool a few away from his. The ugly son of a bitch picked himself up with a gap-toothed grin, then went stumbling right back into the mix.

One thing was for damn sure. Daniel wasn't going to be a regular here, no matter how good the beer was.

"Is it always this...active?" he asked, swiveling toward the bartender. It was a Wednesday, for Pete's sake.

The woman shrugged, her head down.

Strike two. He was definitely off his game.

A particularly deep thrum in the soundtrack made his eardrum vibrate, and he winced.

Damn, he was getting old. A couple of years ago, he would have felt right at home in a place like this. It was strangely familiar, though he couldn't say why.

The decor was a weird mix of post-apocalyptic industrial and old-world pub. He polished off his beer and decided to order another when he saw his chatty blonde barkeep straighten suddenly. Her eyes flicked past his shoulder, widening as her whole body tensed.

Blinking fast to clear the continued stinging in his eyes, Romero spun around, his hand instinctively moving to the hidden holster under his jacket.

Despite the violence of the dance moves displayed on the floor, there wasn't a threat coming up behind him, nor was another behemoth about to barrel into him. It was the woman in the white bikini, only this time, she was dressed from head to toe in black leather.

She looked amazing. As usual, his brain short-circuited, and he stared open-mouthed at her like an idiot. He searched for something to say. *If you value your life...don't make a Catwoman joke.*

11

Daniel shook himself. He'd half expected to see his prime suspect here, but it wasn't supposed to go down like this.

She wasn't supposed to move in slow motion as if they were starring in their own personal chick flick, the part where the hero sees his dream girl across the room.

Eileen strode down the middle of the room toward him, cutting right through the fracas on the dance floor. But not even one of those raging dipsomaniacs so much as touched her. Instead, the crowd parted like she was Moses and it was the fucking Red Sea.

His breath caught as the light sparked off the red highlights in her dark hair. Her ridiculous curves shifted fluidly in their black leather casings. Unbidden, the image of a black panther stalking its prey flashed through his mind.

He forced himself to take his hand off his piece as she smirked, leaning with her elbows back on the bar.

"I think you're in the wrong place, Detective Romero."

Her throaty voice was low, but for some reason Daniel had no problem understanding her over the loud music. It was as if her voice could cut through the din—like it was wired directly to the nerve endings in his ear.

Daniel sipped his beer, adjusting his grip so his now-sweaty palms wouldn't drop the glass. "If you're here, Ms. Knight, then I'm in the right place. Especially since it's just steps away from where I got into a firefight earlier today," he said pointedly.

Her eyes widened. "A firefight, you say? What an exciting life you lead, Detective. But surely you don't think anyone here had something to do with that?"

She waved at the clientele as if they were all sitting down to a formal tea instead of moshing in a pit like maniacs.

He raised his drink in a silent toast. "Well, until I saw you here, I was thinking this place was a dead end. Now I know better."

It was no less than the truth. His skin was starting to itch, his cop sixth sense going crazy. The music didn't help. It was blending with the club's noises, confusing him. Was someone banging on a drum? That wasn't part of this song, was it?

No, it wasn't part of the recording. He couldn't make out who was doing it in the general gloom, but combined with the smokiness in the room, it was starting to give him a headache.

He spun around to surreptitiously rub his eyes. Oddly, looking at the hot bartender only made it worse.

Eileen leaned in closer. "I really think you should leave now, Detective, before the proprietor has you thrown out."

Daniel scowled. "It's agent, not detective. And this is a bar—a public space. I have every right to be here."

Her head drew back, her eyes flicking to the back of the room where a group of men was starting to push and shove each other. The beat changed, and the crowd swelled like a shifting sea.

"Actually, you don't," she corrected in her best English schoolmarm voice. "It's a private club. It is not open to the public. Under normal circumstances, you would have been stopped at the door, but the bouncer must have been taking a break."

Now he was irritated. "I'm conducting an investigation," he said.

"And this isn't some country club or posh society cabaret. I mean check out the people on the dance floor. They're just this side of—"

She poked him hard in the side. "I know the music is loud, but don't let that fool you. Some of these folks have excellent hearing. They don't like strangers, and they really don't like cops. Come back tomorrow with a warrant. Because that the only way anyone here will talk to you."

The woman had the gall to begin nudging him toward the door.

Daniel's head was spinning now, his eyes tearing, but he would be damned if he let his prime suspect give him the bum's rush.

"As much as I'm enjoying your hands on me, I'm not going anywhere so you can just stop that now."

"You're enjoying *this*?" She gave him another hard nudge, enough to make his shoes slide across the floor several feet. "You may not realize this now, but I'm trying to help you, Agent Romero."

Daniel sidestepped her grasp, wondering how the hell she'd propelled him so far. She hadn't even put her weight behind the move. Eileen Knight was half a head shorter than him, and weighed a buck twenty-five soaking wet. How was she *this* strong?

A group of four enormous, foul-smelling men broke away from the dance floor. He had a confused impression of horns and teeth. One of the men roared a bestial racket that made Daniel's ears vibrate. A wave of foul air rushed over him, stinking worse than that corpse flower he went to see at the botanical gardens last year.

"*I smell human.*"

"The hell you can," he snapped, holding his sleeve to his face to block out some of the stench. "What you smell is the very real and pressing need to shower."

Eileen laughed, seemingly unfazed by the fetid stink. "Now, boys, you don't really want to disturb my guest, do you?" she asked, standing in front of him as if she were going to somehow stop them.

The man in front of her grunted something that vaguely sounded like words, releasing another wave of that rotting stench.

Daniel couldn't help himself. Bending over, he gagged.

He held on to the legs of a barstool to keep from toppling over. "*Ugh*. This is worse than that time I pulled a three-month corpse out of a barrel. Seriously, what have you been eating?"

An unintelligible growl was the only response. It must have been Slavic—it was all guttural rumbles and clicks. Despite Daniel's supposed expertise in over half-a-dozen languages, he couldn't make a damn thing out.

Unbelievably, Eileen responded to him in kind. Daniel watched, fascinated, holding the cuff of his shirt over his nose as she slapped them down with an attitude a person had to be born with to get away with.

The entire bar crowd was watching them now. Most of them seemed strangely affected by Eileen's words. Some even backed away or hugged the wall, but the trio in front of them was unfazed.

"Serin, get him out of here," a man behind them hissed. "These are mountain trolls. They don't have enough brain cells between them to know not to mess with you."

Daniel pivoted to see that a young bearded man had joined the blonde behind the bar. Like her, he was model perfect and dressed like he was about to shoot the cover of *Hipster's Weekly*.

His head was really starting to pound now. It was also starting to play tricks on him.

"Do you hear hoofbeats?" he asked Eileen, spinning back around. It almost sounded like he was standing next to a mounted patrol in the park. But that made no sense at all. He was indoor for fuck's sake.

Behind him, the long rows of bottles behind the bar rattled. Daniel frowned. The female bartender was the only one anywhere near the bottles, but even if she'd bumped the bar, it shouldn't have rattled like that.

The blonde was staring at his scowling face like she'd forgotten to breathe. His lips parted to reassure her that everything was going to be fine, but the male bartender gave her a little shove. The girl dived behind him, effectively hiding from his view.

But not my ears...

Every time she moved, Daniel heard hoofbeats. "What kind of heels is that woman wearing?" he muttered under his breath.

The male bartender made a choking sound. "*Serin,*" the man pleaded.

Rapid movement made Daniel jerk back to the audience. A wave of unwashed flesh rushed forward, threatening to crash down on him and Eileen.

Daniel tensed, a split second from running in front of her, but a blinding pain forced him to his knees. Stunned, he stared down at the glass and liquid raining from his shoulders. It smelled like fermented honey. Had he been hit with a bottle of mead?

Darkness warred with his will to stay conscious. The scene receded as he slumped against the bar. The distant sounds of a fight roused him. He blinked, his hazy mind registering the full-blown battle raging around him.

Eileen was in the thick of things, landing a roundhouse kick that took down a man three times her size.

Daniel's last feeling before passing out was vindication. *I knew it was her in the alley.*

"Get off me, you rancid Yak turd," Kerrick swore, shoving away the last mountain troll still standing.

The troll stumbled closer, giving Serin the opportunity to deliver one last punch to the head, finally knocking it out.

"Hell," she huffed, breathing hard. "It's been forever since I fought any of these. I forgot how much it took to put one down—and how much they smell! I'm going to have to have this outfit dry-cleaned before I wear it again."

She raised an arm to smell where one of the trolls had caught hold of her sleeve. "Or maybe I'll just throw it out."

The bar was nearly empty now. Funny how a pitched battle between an Elemental and a trio of mountain trolls could do that.

Serin stepped back, nearly tripping on the prone figure of Agent Romero. "Son of a—what happened to him?"

She had been too busy with the trolls to check on him, but when he hadn't leapt into the fray, she'd assumed he'd been smart enough to stay out of it. Kneeling, she checked his pulse.

"Good," she said, relaxing. He was still breathing.

"What do you think happened to him?" Kerrick cried, retreating behind the bar. "I broke a bottle of my best mead over his head when Cincy's glamour started to break down."

"You did *what*?"

Serin grabbed the unconscious man's head, turning him to the light to check his injuries.

There was a bump on the back of his head. It was the size of an egg and growing. *Shit*. Agent Romero's blue and red aura was flaring white at the edges like a strobe light. She tensed, but her touch soothed him, slowing the flashing.

The blow to the head had been a shock to his system and he was going to have a hell of a headache when he woke, but, fortunately for him, Romero had a very hard head. He would recover.

She glared at Kerrick. "You could have killed him."

Dropping his glamour, the goblin ran a hand through his bright pink hair. "Better that I had. He's seen too much. Worse yet, he could understand some of it. He even heard Cincy's hooves against the wooden floor. That's too damn perceptive for a human. He's dangerous to let live—unless you've changed your mind about having him taken up for the Hunt."

Kerrick reached for Romero's shirt collar, hauling him up to a seated position. The agent's head lolled, smacking against the bar.

"For the Mother's sake, watch his head," Serin nudged the bartender out of the way. "I told you, I won't hand him over to the Seelie Court."

"But he can see through glamours!"

"*Almost*. He can almost see through them," she hedged. "And of all people, you know what being conscripted to the Great Hunt means—

what it does to a man, human or not. You're just freaking out cause it's your bar. If he'd walked into another tonight, you wouldn't be so trigger happy."

"Well, he didn't walk into another, did he? He walked into my place, and now look at it." He waved at the flotsam. "It's wrecked."

"So bill the mountain trolls—or better yet, bill me. I can afford the repairs, but Romero is out of bounds."

She reached down, grabbing the unconscious man's arms. After hauling him over her shoulder, she started heading out the front door.

Reasserting his glamour, Kerrick followed her, leaving Cincy to start on the mess inside.

"I'm obviously not going to bill *you*," he muttered, trailing her sullenly.

Inhaling deeply to find a smidgen of patience, she rearranged Romero so she could reach into her pocket. After fishing out a few gold galleons, she tossed them at the goblin. "I picked those up off the coast of Ecuador. Take them to a dealer for the historical value. You'll get more from that than if you make a deal for the metal alone. It's more than enough to cover the damages."

He fingered the coins, jiggling them before grimacing and slipping them into his pocket. "*Bollocks*. You make it hard to argue with you Serin."

She set her charge down in the alley by the dumpster, taking care not to jostle his head any more than she had too.

"If he remembers—" Kerrick began.

"He won't." She rifled through her bag, retrieving a small knotted string from her bag. Squinting at it, she glanced at Romero, weighing it in her hands.

"What is that?"

"A memory charm."

"C'mon, Serin. Every dime-store practitioner has a drawer full of those. They never work."

"This one was made by an expert in the craft."

"Who?"

"My mother." She fingered the string, then undid two of the knots. There was no need to erase more than a day's worth of the man's memories. Going back to just before the firefight would do.

Kneeling, Serin tied the string to the man's wrist. It tightened automatically, melting and fusing to the body with an iridescent glow before it disappeared completely, leaving no trace on the surface of his skin.

Kerrick whistled, craning his neck as the magic was effortlessly absorbed.

"That should do it," she said, rubbing his skin to make sure nothing remained. "He won't remember finding this place, but you're going to have to pick up shop and set Dionysia somewhere else for a while. I suggest Poland."

The goblin sniffed. "You don't have to tell me twice. It'll be a cold day in hell before I park the club anywhere near Detroit."

He turned to the door, but hesitated. "Hey…I don't suppose you have any more of those strings in that little bag? I'd pay a premium, of course. It'd be handy for the troublemaking trolls, you know, to make them forget they ever came by."

"Nice try. Knowing you, you'd use it to make your wealthier patrons forget they'd paid their bar tab. Or a comely nymph would conveniently forget she had a boyfriend around you."

Kerrick did a good imitation of being affronted. "I'd never do that," he said, crossing his arms.

Serin raised an eyebrow.

"Well, I wouldn't do it to you, anyway," he said.

"You forget my mother made these. It won't work on me, or any one of my line." Her Elemental sisters were safe from the charm's influence as well.

The goblin shrugged. "Can't blame a guy for trying. Although, come to think of it, one of those would be useful if any more human hunters get wind of this place," he added, nudging Romero with the toe of his boot.

"I don't think you have to worry about that," she said, standing to take her leave. "Something tells me a hunter as skilled as Agent Romero is a rare breed. You won't have to worry about him after this. My mother's charms have never failed—not once. He won't remember anything when he wakes up."

12

Daniel got on his hands and knees, feeling the wall for edges that could disguise a doorway. "I'm telling you it was right *here*."

Ray was watching him with a placidly patient expression, but the skin around his eyes was tight. "Sure it is, buddy."

Daniel scrambled to his feet. "There was a hidden doorway here. They must have had a light embedded in the wall because when I passed through, this crazy design glowed like neon. It actually blinded me for a second. When my eyes stopped burning, there was a big nightclub full of people inside." He threw up his hands. "And the music was *loud*. Half the block should have been able to hear it."

His partner winced. "I'm not saying there wasn't a door and a club. What you describe has too much detail to be a dream, but you took a bad blow to the head. You're confused and with good reason. I'm surprised you're on your feet at all."

Daniel shook his head, but then regretted it immediately. He shut his eyes, breathing through his nose until the pounding pain receded.

"Granted I'm a still a little muddled," he admitted, putting his hand behind his back to hide a tremor. "But this isn't some intense hallucination or anything like that. I remember everything that happened up until I got knocked out."

He was starting to sound plaintive, as if he were begging or badgering Ray into believing him.

"I'm not saying it didn't happen. You convinced me in the car on the way down, but the actual club has to be somewhere else. There's no glowing door here, and the rooms on the other side of the wall are just overflow storage for the local book press."

Ray kicked the wall. "There's never been a club in this alley or anywhere on this street. It's all hipster-owned wannabe mom-and-pop shops. This whole area is gentrified up the ass. It's worse than Portland."

Daniel straightened, putting his hands to his aching head. "I know it was here," he said, but even he was starting to doubt himself.

He studied his surroundings, knowing he was right. The alley was exactly like the one from his memory—length and shape. Even the graffiti and the trash were the same. When he glanced down to the street, his adrenaline surged.

"*Wait*. I can prove it." He pointed down the mouth of the alley. "I took fire from an unknown shooter right around the corner. The locals made a full report. Check the address with them if you don't believe me."

Ray shrugged, still confused. "I already did, which is why I brought you back out here instead of taking you to the hospital like I should have."

"I told you, I'm fine," Daniel lied, slowing down to avoid jostling his head any more than he had to.

"Yeah, you look it," Ray drawled. "After this, I'm taking you in to get your head scanned."

Fuck. Was Ray right? Daniel rubbed his wrist. Like his head, it had been bugging him all day, ever since he woke up in the alley. It wasn't painful exactly—just sensitive. And every time he touched it, he could see Eileen in his mind.

"The bartender called her something else," he murmured, little fragments drifting back. Daniel turned to Ray. "He called her Serin."

"Who called who what?"

Daniel screwed his nose up, replaying the exchange between the woman he knew as Eileen and the male bartender. Eileen Knight was actually named Serin. He was sure of it.

"*Se-rin*," he repeated, testing the syllables. It could have been another alias, but somewhere deep in his brain, a switch flipped. Instinct told him he was on the right track. As if on cue, his memories of the night sharpened. He remembered heavy drum and bass music, the weird clompy shoes the blonde barkeep wore, and a few gigantic and smelly customers.

Ray was really confused now. "Are you talking about a gas attack now?"

"No. I'm telling you... I think I know Eileen Knight's real name."

"*Wait*." His partner flushed, his hands fisting. "That bitch was *here*? Why didn't you tell me that earlier?"

"Do me a favor. Don't raise your voice like that." Daniel winced, the pounding in his head resuming. "And yes, she was here. I told you that earlier."

"No, you didn't. I would remember if you'd mentioned her."

Daniel ignored his partner's scowl. He almost certainly had a mild concussion, so Ray could just deal with his less-than-perfect memory.

"Well, I meant to," he grumbled. He turned back to the wall, picturing the club on the other side. "What's more, I was totally right about her fighting ability. I saw her land a mean roundhouse kick that took down this monster three times her size."

That image was burned into his brain. It could have been a snippet from the video of the fight in the alley, only this had been live and in living color.

His stomach clenched suddenly. He couldn't remember what happened to her afterward. Daniel forced himself to take a slow breath. Serin-slash-Eileen was all right. In fact, he'd bet a week's paycheck she was in better shape than him at the moment. And whatever else was true, he now had proof the woman could take care of herself.

Unless one of those guys got the drop on her. She could be lying somewhere hurt, needing help...

"At least we know who hit you now," Ray groused.

"No," Daniel dismissed. "I'm pretty sure it was the bartender. Or it could have been the blonde with the horse shoes, I guess. But Eileen, I mean Serin, was in front of me holding off that trio of assholes."

He scratched his head carefully, skirting the edge of the massive bump. "Now that I think about it, I'm sure those guys were coming for me. I might actually owe her one."

Ray snorted. "Now I know you have brain damage. If that woman was involved, then it wasn't to do you any favors. In fact, we should test your blood for traces of Rohypnol. For all we know she slipped you a mickey and that's why you can't remember anything."

"The bottle broken over my head is the reason my memories are fuzzy," he said, rubbing his wrist before touching the wall again. "I don't know how they managed to disappear a whole club, but they did it. This is some next-level Houdini shit. I just hope Serin made it out unharmed."

His partner shook his head in pity. "I think that's enough for today, lover boy. No more stalling. I'm taking you to the hospital."

Head aching, Daniel let himself be loaded into the rental car. Maybe a trip to the doctor wasn't a bad idea. His wrist was itching like crazy now.

13

Daniel picked his way through a waist-high bracket of shrubs with a silent swear. Ray was busy hunting down a promising confidential informant from his old ATF days so he'd run out here on his own over his partner's protests. He'd assured Ray it wasn't a big deal—the doctor had given him the all clear and this lead was almost definitely a dead-end.

Instead, it appeared he'd stumbled on a major buy. What for, he wasn't sure...

Cars and motorcycles surrounded a derelict building that used to be a country mansion. The sprawling three-story structure belonged to a timber baron. After that industry waned and the city had grown enough to encroach on the extensive property, the land was sold and the house was abandoned by the family. The bank owned it now.

Some of the trees had grown back, but the bulk of the plant life was thick spots of scrubby brush. Many a bum had slept in the home over the years, but occasionally, a criminal enterprise would set up shop on the grounds. Every couple of years, the local authorities would clear them out. According to their records, this place remained empty after the shooting of a low-level drug dealer late the previous year. Ballistics had matched the bullet dug out of the body to one of the guns used to take a shot at him and that bystander he'd never identified in Midtown.

Despite what the television shows would have people believe, unregistered guns changed hands all the time. The lax regulations around firearms made it a bitch to track them. Daniel didn't hold out much hope he'd be able to tie the death of the dealer to the attempt on his own life. Unfortunately, he was fresh out of other leads, so he'd made time to drive to the old crime scene, never expecting to find anything.

He'd been over a mile out when he saw the reflections bouncing off the windshields of all the cars surrounding the building. Hoping the shine of his own vehicle was missed by the occupants, he pulled his car off the road near a particularly dense patch of sun-bleached shrubbery. Then he continued on foot to get a closer look.

The slim chance this was a group of kids getting ready to party at an abandoned house was nixed the moment he spied the first man holding an AR-15. A second man joined him moments later, similarly armed. They scanned their surroundings, rounding the corner in a regular circuit. Inside, multiple men passed behind the windows. It appeared to be a full house.

Fuck. Daniel ducked, texting an alert to Ray and the local police. He snapped a quick pic of the house, taking care to fit the guard and a few other men in the shots before turning to head back to his car to wait for backup.

He hadn't gotten far when he spotted her. Serin was there, on foot, climbing out of a culvert. She was dressed head to toe in black leather, like the club, but unlike the armed guards patrolling the grounds, she had a sheath strapped to her back.

It held a *freaking sword*. There was also a small hand-held trident strapped to her hip.

Overhead, a sudden unexpected rumble of thunder sounded. Daniel scowled at the sky. The previously cloudless day darkened, a huge bank of black clouds racing toward them.

The first fat drop of rain hit him as Serin slid past him on silent feet.

Daniel had seen former Navy seals turned agents move like that. He could almost always hear them when others couldn't. It was a party trick, one he could do blindfolded. Serin was less than ten feet away, and it was as if she weren't there. He strained his ears to hear something of her movement, but there was nothing except the drops pelting the ground.

He half expected some action movie soundtrack to start playing —her approach was that badass. She didn't even appear to notice the sudden cloudburst at all, keeping her attention fixed on the house ahead. She never turned her head in his direction.

Daniel had to press his lips shut hard as a sudden hot flash heated his wrist, the same circle of skin that had itched like mad right after the club incident. It had stopped a few days ago, only to flare up now at the worst possible time.

His first instinct was to go after the crazy sword-wielding woman, but Ray's loud voice in his head held him back. If Serin was here, there was a good chance she was involved with whatever was going on inside the house.

His long years on the job told him that was the case, but his instincts were screaming otherwise. And why the hell was his fucking wrist hot to the touch now? It didn't hurt at all, but it was throbbing as if he were wearing vibrating handcuffs.

Ignoring the sensation, he refocused on Serin as she approached the building. It didn't appear as if she was trying to avoid the patrols, but they didn't see her as they altered their circuit. They hugged the walls of the house, taking advantage of the roof's overhangs to stay drier.

His shirt was sticking to his chest now. Daniel wiped his eyes, struggling against the rain obscuring his vision, but he was transfixed with Serin's every move.

Any second, the guards were going to come back around.

Ray's right. They're going to recognize her and wave her in.

At least that was what he told himself. Doubt tightened his gut, but he forced himself not to move as he tracked his suspect's progress.

Serin bypassed the back door, heading to the side of the house. What happened next was surreal. One second, she was on the ground... and the next, she was hanging from a third-story attic windowsill.

What the ever-loving fuck? Before his mind had finished processing the sight, the window sash lifted and she twisted, slipping inside in a move Jean Claude van Damme would envy. Ninjas had nothing on her.

For a moment, elation coursed through him. Ray had been wrong about her! But Daniel's smug satisfaction melted faster than the rain. The chances she was here to do business was out the window, pun intended. But now he had a bigger problem.

She took out an entire motorcycle gang, he reminded himself. If anyone could take care of themselves, it was her. Except there were at least eight cars here. There could be two dozen men in there for all she knew.

You are not moving. You are waiting for backup.

The woman he'd been tracking was some sort of specialist slash mastermind. No doubt she had a carefully laid plan. If he went in there, he might mess things up for her.

And if you don't stop her, you'll have her dead to rights.

Vigilante or cutthroat competitor, Serin wouldn't be able to avoid jail time if she got rounded up in this bust. Then there was the fact the woman was carrying a sword. There might be literal throats cut if he didn't intervene...

Daniel clenched his jaw, fighting a losing battle. He waited for the guards to duck around the corner before sprinting toward the house.

Taking a page out of Serin's book, he headed for the same side of the house she had. He glanced up at the third story window, but there were no real handholds under it. How the hell had she gotten up there?

He didn't have time to think about it. Instead, he went for the first-floor window, craning his neck to make sure there was no one on the other side.

In comparison, his break-in was less than graceful. His hamstring was screaming, dangerously close to snapping like an old rubber band as he clambered over the sill. Daniel landed with a grunt, surpassing a cough as he dislodged several decades worth of dust.

The walls were bare save for some torn wallpaper. Next to him was a dilapidated couch and a few beat-up armchairs. Discarded plastic cups littered the floor. Milk crates were positioned strategically next to the furniture, makeshift coffee and end tables for the stoners who came here to party.

Fortunately, the room was empty. He picked himself up, debating leaving his sidearm hidden under a stained couch cushion. In these clothes, there was a chance he could bluff the people into thinking he was a part of the group. It depended on how well the parties involved knew each other.

The cop in him knew he couldn't leave his service piece behind, so he pulled it out, keeping it close to his side as he followed the faint noise of conversation. He crept along a dingy hallway, but he couldn't make out the words. The door at the end of the hall was slightly ajar. A body was blocking his view but then it moved, revealing a large rolling suitcase full of money on a pitted table.

It was a fuck-ton of cash. If the suitcase was as full as it appeared, then it was somewhere in the ballpark of five million dollars—far more than would usually be seen in a standard drug deal.

What the hell was going on here? Figuring it out wasn't his priority. Making sure Serin didn't get herself killed was.

Gritting his teeth, he forced his legs to get in gear, backing away from the open doors so the kitchen's occupants wouldn't see him pass.

He continued his search for Serin, creeping from room to room, narrowly missing getting caught more than once.

It was his text alert that did him in—the little buzz it made even on silent sounded, echoing in his head much louder than it was in real life. Swearing, he fished it out of his pocket to turn off the vibrate function, but it was too late.

The actual volume of the buzz had been muted. The gun cocking a few feet away, however, was deafening.

He turned around, scowling at the wet man pointing a massive Magnum at him.

"What?" he snapped, deciding to bluff his way out. "I'm texting my girl."

The moron was dripping water on the floor. Daniel assessed him in a blink—low enough on the totem pole to be relegated to outdoor patrol and stupid enough to carry a cannon that no doubt bucked like a mule instead of something light and utilitarian.

"Who the fuck are you?" the goon snarled.

Daniel put his phone in his pocket with a casualness that belied his racing heart. "I'm Joe, smartass. Who the hell are you?"

The guard blinked, lowering the gun a fraction. "Pretty sure you're not supposed to be here Joe," he said, elongating the name into two syllables.

"My boss told me to check this whole floor out," Daniel said dismissively, taking his phone out again.

Be there in fifteen, the text from Ray said.

The mouth breather was confused. "Then why didn't I see you earlier?"

"So you always meet every employee of the men your boss does business with?" Daniel waved at the windows. "My car got stuck in the mud. This fucking rain, huh?"

His expression clearing, the guard lowered his cannon. He shrugged. "Yeah. It came out of nowhere. Even my boxers are wet."

"I'll take your word on that," Daniel added, trying not to cast worried glances at the door.

With luck, the rest of the criminals would assume muscle-man with the cannon was talking to another guard, but he couldn't bet on it.

He opened his mouth, about to make an excuse about taking a leak, when a crash upstairs rained dust all over them. It was swiftly followed by another before shouting began.

"Serin," he breathed, taking off at a run. The goon followed at his heels.

14

Serin hadn't planned on fighting all the way down to the lower level. This whole floor should have been empty, but two of the men had made their way upstairs to plot a bloody betrayal in the next room.

"I'm telling you, we can do it if we act fast," the first man said, loud enough for her supernatural hearing to catch it through the thin plaster.

"Or we get our heads blown off trying," the second one replied.

"All we have to do is take them by surprise. Do you know how much money is in that briefcase?"

"And do you know how many other guys are downstairs?" The second man broke off, saying something she couldn't make out.

"With this, we won't need to worry about them."

Serin edged around the corner, peeking into the room to see one of the would-be mutineers holding a massive machine gun. The weapon was straight out of a sci-fi movie, like the firearms in *Fifth Element*, Logan's favorite movie.

She swore under her breath when the man held the gun up like a showroom model.

"This baby is all we need," he insisted, waving it around. "One can take out a fucking army."

"And that Puck guy is buying two *dozen*. What makes you think he and his men won't grab them and take *us* out?"

The first man pointed the barrel at the floor, holding the heavy weapon with one hand.

"Because the clips on these are custom made... and they're locked up in *my* trunk." His tone self-congratulatory, he smirked. "Too bad I didn't fork over the real key to Sal. The boss won't know what hit 'em. Neither will the buyer."

He nudged the other guy hard. "Puck deserves to get fucked over, the way he talks down to everybody."

The second man passed a hand over his face. "All right, but we split the cash and the rest of the guns fifty-fifty."

Well, crap. If she didn't intervene now, these two idiots were going to start shooting up the place. They could very well kill Puck before she got a chance to question him.

Serin moved into the center of the doorway, blowing air through her lips to puff her hair out of the way. The men in the room froze with hands-in-the-cookie-jar expression. Their faces darkened first with confusion and then suspicion.

"No, I'm not with any of you. I'm here to kick your ass and take those guns." Irritated, she rolled her eyes when they continued to stare at her like idiots.

Affecting boredom, she yawned, then held out her hand, signaling them to come at her. Being naturally stupid, they obeyed, completely forgetting they were holding what might qualify as a weapon of mass destruction.

The gun was the first thing she broke, snagging it in a blink and twisting the barrel so they couldn't fire it.

Disbelief was barely dawning in their eyes when she followed up with a punch, one she had to pull back on to avoid killing the first. The man went flying through the dilapidated wall of the bedroom before she landed a kick to head of the second man.

The sounds of their skirmish attracted attention. Men flooded in like rats escaping a flood.

Grinning, Serin pulled out her sword. It sang, cutting the air—and some body parts—with a hum that guaranteed death if anyone got too close.

Her muscles warmed rapidly as she fell into the rhythm of battle. Instinct and training took over, acting and reacting to block punches. She used the sword only when someone was about to raise their gun—and even then, it only took a strategic cut to certain fingers to get them to drop the weapons.

She would never admit it to her sisters, and especially not to her family, but Serin was enjoying herself.

The Water Elementals of T'Kaieri were fierce warriors, but they had been trained from birth that using violence was a last resort. They were supposed to use their talent to take out their enemies. Relying on brute force was beneath them.

But it was so much more satisfying, she thought as a goon twice her size crashed at her feet with a thud that rattled the floor. She couldn't help her smile at the sight.

Until Agent Romero shoved through the door, knocking down another man to get inside.

Serin froze in surprise, allowing one of the newly fingerless men to tackle her.

At least, that was his intention. She absorbed the force, dissipating it and standing firm. The man's eyes widened with fear when Serin glared, her gaze ice cold. She batted him away, then scowled at Agent Romero.

Her heart sank. *Wait*. Romero wasn't Puck, was he?

That suspicion lasted until the idiot fished out his badge and tried to arrest everyone.

"Get on your knees with your hands up," he yelled when his first shout was ignored. "You are all under arrest."

When he started reciting Miranda rights, she took pity on him, grabbing him by the collar and dragging him downstairs.

"I don't know what the hell you are doing here," she hissed, "but you need to shut up and stay behind me. I've got an asshole fairy to find."

And once she got her hands on Puck, he was going to regret crossing her and her sisters. There was Loki's shooting as well, not mention that whatever Puck was doing appeared to be giving Agent Romero here the means to track her.

Her list of grudge material against the fae crime lord was getting damn long.

Regrettably, Agent Romero was not keen to take a backseat. He jumped in front of her on the stairs.

"You're the one who needs to get behind me. And where the hell did you get that sword, let alone learn to use it? Do you know how many hands you cut off back there?"

"Only one and it was still technically attached," she corrected in low voice. "The rest are fingers and those can be sewn back on now—medical science has improved by leaps the last few decades."

She huffed, wiping the blade on her sleeve. "I remember when I used to maim an asshole they stayed maimed. Not the case anymore."

Romero stopped short at the bottom of the stairs, baffled frustration clear on his face. "What are you talking about?" he asked, raising his voice.

Biting her tongue, Serin clapped her hand over his mouth. "*Shut it. There are at least half a dozen more men running around down here. Don't broadcast our location unless you want the rest on top of us.*"

"They should be on top of us anyway," he countered, shifting to that stance cops on television used when moving through hostile territory—gun held in front, finger on the trigger. "Your fight upstairs was loud enough to wake the dead."

That showed what he knew. There were at least a dozen bodies buried nearby, but not one zombie.

"I know that," she said from behind gritted teeth, wondering why he could irritate her so easily. She shoved him behind her again, forcing him to stay by moving forward, sword in hand.

"Are you insane? You have a sword. I'm the one with the gun. *Get behind me.*"

"One more word and I'm locking you in the nearest closet," she said, contemplating doing just that.

Serin never reacted this way with anyone. She was not a green beginner, struggling to control her emotions or her craft. Diana and Logan were the firebrands. She and Gia were the calm and centering influences.

Unless she was in Agent Romero's vicinity. Then she flared up like an underground steam vent. Somehow, this human managed to get under her skin. However, she'd be damned if she let him know that.

"They must be outside," she muttered, considering her unwanted tagalong with pursed lips.

Agent Romero put his hands up. "Don't even think about slipping me whatever you gave me at the club. I'm on to your tricks now, Serin." He stopped to scratch his wrist.

Her lips parted and she staggered back, blindly groping for the wall. The memory charm was beating, glowing with unearthly brightness just under the surface.

"How did you do that?" Serin frowned, moving to grab his arm. And where had he heard her real name?

She rubbed his wrist, feeling the thread just under the surface. The spell should have been absorbed within minutes of being put on, faded to nothing. But this had barely been taken up at all. It was just lying there as if his body had rejected it.

His aura had no other ticks, no signs of damage anywhere, not that it should have made a difference. Dalasini's spells worked on *everyone.* They had been used on powerful witches, the fae, even the *angelii.* It was overkill to use one on a human, but they were infallible. Only she and her sisters were immune. And, of course, her mother herself.

You can't leave it there.

Serin swore aloud this time, covering his wrist with both her hands and rubbing. The spelled band rose to the surface, breaking when she applied a little pressure.

She tried to hide the remnants of the string in her hands as she removed it, but Romero wasn't having it.

"What the hell is that?" He snatched at her hands, tugging at the string with his mouth open. "Was that *inside* of me? It was, wasn't it? I felt it come out."

His face twisted, went white, and then a shudder passed through him.

"Err..." This had never happened to her before. Clearly, the agent was some sort of anomaly.

You're forgetting your surroundings, a little voice warned her.

"Sorry, Agent Romero. You are a problem I don't have time to solve." If one of her mother's memory charms hadn't worked on him, there was little chance one of her own spells was going to.

"Well, I can always knock you out," she mused.

People subjected to blows to the head frequently had issues recalling the events just before the injury. Of course, she would have to hit him pretty damn hard to wipe out all memory of her.

His eyes flared with disbelief and irritation. "You can *try*," he said, puffing up.

She was tempted to take him up on his mocking challenge. "Relax, I have no wish to cause you permanent injury."

A mental image of the agent sucking his dinner through a straw flitted across her mind. That was the last thing she needed on her conscience.

The infuriating human snorted. "How comforting. Sweetheart, let me tell you now—I wouldn't go down as easy as those losers upstairs."

Serin grunted, a biting retort on the tip of her tongue. But if her mother's charm didn't work on him, there might be some truth to his boast.

"We don't have time for this. Puck is getting away. You need to stay here." She turned on her heel, heading for the door.

"To hell with that." Romero followed, just a step behind, crowding her. Ignoring him, she threw open the door.

A wave of bullets cut through the rain—and it was aimed right at her and Romero.

***

Time slowed down as the bullets flew at them, but it wasn't long enough for her to mutter a counter-spell. Acting on instinct, she reared back, grabbing Agent Romero and diving sideways for the floor.

He yelled something as they fell, grabbing at his arm. Blood spread out from beneath his fingers as she crawl-dragged them out of the line of fire.

I guess they managed to bust into moron number one's car trunk.

Bullets sprayed the wall, shredding the rickety wooden wall. Splinter-shrapnel rained like knives, slicing through the agents' thin cotton shirt.

Her leathers fared much better, but the shots kept coming, turning the walls into swiss cheese. Serin covered the agent, checking him rapidly for more holes.

"I'm fine," he shouted, trying to tug her behind him even though he was lying flat on the floor.

A really foul-smelling couch provided some cover, but it wouldn't last long. She turned to the agent, smacking his hand when he tried to yank her against him.

His arm was covered in blood.

Serin covered the wound with her palm. She had some healing ability—not as good as her sister Gia, but her talent did give her a bit of control over the water in his body—enough to staunch the flow of blood at least.

Romero didn't notice he wasn't bleeding anymore. He was busy trying to save her life, getting to his feet and pulling her out of the living room. She let him drag her to the hallway, peeking out to gauge where the gunmen were.

The agent exploded. "Do you want to get that pretty head blown off?" he growled, pulling her deeper into the hallway.

"Hey, this is your fault," she snapped back. "If you hadn't been here to distract me, I would have done some recon and glanced out the damn window. We wouldn't have been caught with our pants down!"

"*You* shouldn't be here at all. There was a major arms deal going down."

"Oh, gee, really? I hadn't noticed. What tipped you off? The hole in your arm or the blitzkrieg of bullets?"

He raised his arm. "It was just a scratch. See, it already stopped bleeding."

She clenched her jaw to keep from taking credit. *He really does bring out the worst in me.*

"And why the hell don't you have a scratch on you?" he asked.

"Well, it's not because I'm bulletproof," she said.

Her spellcraft was good enough to redirect some of those bullets, but the sheer volume being thrown at them was enough to overwhelm even the best deflection spell. Protecting Romero was another story—for her talent skillset, shielding a human would have required a laboratory full of spellcasting equipment and ingredients. Maybe Logan or Gia could have redirected the bullets with their talents, but she was restricted that way.

She was still weighing her option when the assailants took the decision out of her hands. Wood banged on soft plaster as the door was kicked out—or at least what was left of it. She caught a brief glimpse of a dark figure silhouetted by the dim afternoon light.

Serin held out her hand, calling the water to her.

Outside, the rainwater she'd called for earlier coalesced, rushing toward the house like it was escaping a broken dam. But the raised foundation depleted the force out of the wave. The best she could do was knock the gunman off his feet.

That was enough.

"Follow me." Serin grabbed Romero's hand, running to the back of the house.

If only they'd been able to get outdoors. Even though it was ramshackle, the house provided enough protection from the elements to interfere with the use of her water talent.

She mentally scanned the pipes in the basement level for water, but the house had been abandoned so long they were dry as a bone.

Serin kept running, tugging the agent behind her. A bullet whizzed past her cheek, going through her hair. She stopped to throw the agent across the hall and out of harm's way, preparing to charge at the gunman who'd flanked them.

She threw up her hands, preparing to disarm him, but the man went flying backward.

Serin started, blinking as the gunman groaned, picking himself up.

She had done that, hadn't she? Moving him without touching him, she meant. *Do it again.* She gestured, but nothing happened.

Only a few Waters could manipulate a body's water. This was why most Elementals drowned their victim, even if they had to manipulate the heavens to ensure their weapon of choice was on hand when they went on a case.

Manipulating a person's water was a different story altogether. It was bound to the body by an individual's chi and protected under the thick layer of energy—the aura that surrounded all living things.

She gave the man another experimental nudge. A much harder one. The man's sneakers squeaked on the wood as he was propelled backward. The expression on his face as he crashed against the wall was comical, up until it was wiped clean by unconsciousness.

She wanted to throw her hands up in victory, but there was no time to celebrate.

"Hey," Romero yelled as he appeared in the doorway of the room she'd thrown him in. "They're coming."

A flurry of footsteps pounded on wood. At least three more men were coming. From the sound of it, each was weighed down with one of those massive guns.

She didn't have time to think. Serin turned, following Romero into the room before she realized it was a bathroom...and it only had one door.

The men were in the hall. Caution had slowed their steps, but she could feel their water as they crept along.

This was bad. She might be able to block most of the bullets, but she knew from experience the protective semi-bubble only covered a small surface. It was only a matter of time before the gunfire decimated the walls, giving the bad guys one-hundred-and-eighty-degree access. Another gunman firing from outside would complete the full circle of death. There was no way Romero would survive.

She only had a split second to process that. A barrel peeked into the doorway.

Serin put her hand on Romero's shoulder, then let go of her corporeal form. She splashed to the floor, rising in a controlled wave.

Water splashed into the cast-iron bathtub. Liquified Serin escaped down the drain, taking the agent with her.

15

Serin found a branch in the drainage system that led to the sea. She burst out of a large corrugated pipe on the beach.

She reformed with ease. The agent...not so much. When she nudged the puddle imbued with his aura, he came to, sitting on his butt, arms and legs flailing. His mouth gaped as if he'd been trying to swim in whitewater rapids while screaming his head off.

Taking one look at her, he started shouting for real.

She winced. "You were actually much quieter on the ride here, you know. I was impressed for a moment. Now, not so much."

"*You...you...*"

"I saved your life," she said, backing away from him. "We were about to be blown to kingdom come. Or, more precisely, *you* were about to be riddled with enough lead to build a bridge. I would have been fine."

Probably...

"Wha—what?" he sputtered, his eyes wild and wide. Then he started swearing, holding up his hands and rubbing his fingers to his palms.

Serin felt her lips twist into a wry grin. "Yeah, it takes a little while for your extremities to feel like yours again the first few times you go non-corporeal... Why don't I give you a minute to collect yourself?"

She walked a little way down the beach, casting a perplexed glance back at the agent as he began to pat himself all over, touching his arms and legs—and between them—in a regular rotation.

She couldn't blame him. Serin couldn't believe it herself.

He shouldn't have been able to travel with her. Yes, she had made the attempt to bring him along, but it had been a Hail-Mary pass—desperate, stupid, and ultimately doomed to failure.

Kind of like the rest of this venture.

Tired of running in circles, Serin had cut to the chase after double checking the list Alec had drafted. Many items had been missing from the archives—enough for them to know the thief had been operating systemically over a long period of time. Some of the stolen goods were merely valuable, like the jewel-encrusted toad. Others were imbued with enough black magic to alter the course of history. But a few of the missing items had little value at all—at least to anyone other than an Elemental.

She hadn't seen the stolen Sai since her first decade of service. They hadn't been made in Asia. These were an ancient pair that had been crafted somewhere in India for Onake Ova, a little-known Earth Elemental who'd disappeared in the seventeenth century. Onake had lost the pair in battle, but it had been a moot point because the woman herself had vanished along with them.

Serin had inadvertently solved the mystery when she'd discovered the pair of Sai in the horde of a deadly Vodyanoi, a type of water demon, at Lake Gurudongmar in Sikkim. She recognized it the moment she'd picked them up. Whether they meant to or not, Elementals left a mark on their weapons, one their successors could feel.

Serin had taken great satisfaction in using the tridents to kill the ancient predator who'd murdered her long-departed sister. She'd taken them back to T'Kaieri where they had been stored in an elm wood case carved for them by the head archivist himself. The etching on the lid commemorated the moment justice had finally been served. It had been one of Serin's first major kills, one her parents still bragged about. But though she had found satisfaction in avenging the death of one of her sisters, Serin hadn't thought about the Sai again until Alec told her one of the pair was missing.

Why would the thief steal it? And how the hell had it ended up in the hands of an arms-slash-drug dealer?

She still wasn't sure, but the fact she had the other one let her cast a common mate-finding spell. She'd tracked it to the farmhouse, but hadn't found who in the gun-runners gang possessed it because of Agent Romero. Getting him safely out of danger was the priority.

In the end, that had been easy...but it sure as hell shouldn't have been.

Only her sisters had ever successfully traveled with her in her medium. She could move in theirs as well, but no one outside of that select circle could do it. Not even Jordan, her mate, despite the fact it was one of the perks of bonding with an Elemental...unless that Elemental was a Water.

Hers was the most difficult element to master, something even Gia, her Earth counterpart, acknowledged. Water was also riskier than the others.

Unlike Earth, Air, and Fire, Serin's element was a living thing, something with an innate will of its own. Giving herself over to it required a complete commitment combined with a plasticity of mind that wasn't as easy to achieve as some might think.

An Elemental had to trust in the Mother—their faith in her had to be absolute. It was She who kept their minds and auras intact as they sped through the world without their bodies. Then once an Elemental let go, they had to resist the siren's call of the water.

In their history, a handful of Water Elementals hadn't been able to cope. They had given themselves over to the great ocean's cold embrace and become one with it—permanently.

Because of this, many of her predecessors had intentionally circumscribed their own talent. All wielded water as a weapon, calling storms and drowning their marks when those souls had blackened past the point of no return, but they themselves eschewed the ability to become one with it unless absolutely necessary. They preferred to travel overland or in the sky to avoid it.

There were other limitations to their abilities as well. Before today, Serin hadn't been able to touch her opponent's water without physical contact.

Though island training actively discouraged the use of force, Serin had learned quite early on to direct her ability when she fought. In a word—her kicks and punches landed with more force than was normal because she was pushing her foe's water away. But touch had always been a prerequisite. Acting at a distance had always been beyond her skill. It was the fabled talent of only the most illustrious of her ancestors, the legendary Elementals who changed the course of the world during their years in service.

And now she could do it, too...and perhaps more. Talent like hers was like an onion. Peel one layer away and there was another just below it.

She had leveled up, as Logan would say. Serin laughed shortly, a trace of bitterness coursing through her. In a few short years, she was slated to give up all her gifts in the name of tradition.

"And I don't want to."

It was the first time she'd admitted it aloud. She hadn't even been able to say so in her head, although her heart had ached in protest every time her mother brought up the subject of retirement.

"That makes no sense. Haven't you been listening to me at all?"

The agent was on his feet, watching her with his hands on his hips. His dark eyes flashed like diamonds. Still a little damp, his t-shirt was molded to his chest. He had a very impressive physique. She could actually count each individual ridge of his six pack.

"I wasn't listening," she admitted, unwillingly admiring the carved planes of his face. For a human, Agent Romero was an attractive man.

His was an ascetic type of male beauty. The Mother had drawn him with spare lines. Cut cheekbones, solid square jaw, and dark fathomless eyes. The only lush bits were his dark eyelashes and the moderate fullness of his lips. The slight pigment in his skin saved him from being too severe.

Why was he different?

His cheeks reddened under her scrutiny. He slashed the air with his hand. "Are you going to tell me what just happened over there?"

"No." Serin turned her back on him.

"*No?* Just *no*?" He stomped in front of her, even though it meant splashing into the surf. His hair was a bit damp, but they were both otherwise dry. She hadn't lost her touch.

Agent Romero grabbed her upper arm. Serin tilted her head to glare at the offensive hold, her face darkening.

Slowly, the long-fingered hand unfurled and he released her, stepping farther back into the water.

"I *need* to know what the hell happened back there. What did you do to me?"

The plaintive note in his rough voice was affecting. She hurt for him, but what could she really tell him?

Not much. But he wasn't going to let this go, not unless he decided to.

"You must be...important. Not many individuals can take that ride and live. I think the Mother wants you to be saved for some reason. That itself is significant. She doesn't stir for much these days. Why that is, I couldn't say, but for your own sanity, it would be best if you forget everything you've seen and experienced since we stumbled across each other."

His baffled expression was a combination of frustration and rapid calculation. "You're a witch, aren't you?"

"No," she said, her tone icing over.

"Then how did we turn all liquid and shit?"

His head drew back, an expression of dawning horror twisting his expression. His hands flew to his hair.

"Wait, was that a sewer drain? *Ugh*. It was, wasn't it?" He shuddered. "I need ten showers. *Now*."

She couldn't stifle a chuckle. "Relax, you're clean."

Even when Serin was forced to travel those less-than-desirable avenues, she could separate any liquid from any solid at the molecular level.

"Then why is your hair dry and mine wet? *Why is mine wet*?" He smelled his fingers.

She knew better than to laugh. "I meant what I said. Stay away. I'm tracking a dangerous individual, one you have no hope of being able to deal with."

He stopped fussing with his hair, moving his hands to his hips. "Are you sure about that?"

His cockiness was almost endearing. "Not even if you had the resources of your entire department behind you. Trust me. This is way above your paygrade, Agent Romero."

His eyes narrowed. "You can't be serious."

"I'm not saying forgetting will be easy. I'd take the memories away if I could. It would be easier for you that way."

His expression grew thunderous, and he lifted his wrist up. "*Hey*! You already tried that, didn't you?"

She shrugged. "Since you're standing here, we can safely assume it didn't take. But believe me when I say—this is not a good thing. I was trying to help you. People who learn about this side of nature generally don't cope well. Mental hospitals are full of those unfortunates the Supernatural world swept up and spit back out again."

"You are fucking unbelievable, lady." He pointed a finger at her. "You can't mess with people's heads and expect to get away with it! Who made you judge and jury over our lives?"

She sighed, suddenly tired. "It was the all-powerful Mother, creator of this world and all its inhabitants."

His mouth shut with a satisfying snap.

"I'm an Elemental, one of four chosen to maintain the balance between good and evil. I do that with my power—my dominion—over water. I've served Her for almost a century."

"Oh." He almost looked like he believed her.

She moved toward him, reaching out to touch his cheek. He clapped his hand over hers.

"I am sorry you were drawn into this business," she said. "Very few humans can survive in our world. Somewhere, something went wrong, and I can't fix it. Mother knows, I've tried. But if you heed my advice, your life should continue just like it was, or at least something resembling normal."

He didn't say anything. Instead, he pressed her fingers harder against his cheek.

They were warmer than she expected, sending an unexpected heat coursing through her. She pulled away abruptly.

"Goodbye, Agent Romero." She turned into the surf, diving into the deeper water like a mermaid going home.

Letting go, she let the cold ocean consume her body. She directed the currents to begin carrying her away when she realized she could still hear the human on the beach.

"You haven't seen the last of me!" he was yelling. "And it's *Daniel*, not agent!"

16

Daniel kept touching the keys on his keyboard every other second as he pretended to write his report on the events at the farmhouse.

He told himself he was just figuring out how to explain the day's events without sounding like a madman. However, the reality was the small tactile sensation reminded him he still had fingers.

This better not develop into a permanent tic. That was the last thing he needed. His coworkers were already giving him grief for calling in the cavalry to the farmhouse and then disappearing.

None of the men had been apprehended. Whatever bodies Serin had felled with that sword or with one of her killer kicks to the head were gone, dragged away by the others no doubt. The only proof they were ever there was the multitude of severed fingers and that one hand. Oh, and the thousands of fresh bullet holes and spent shell casings everywhere.

Daniel had to hire a cab to take him out to the house after Serin had abandoned him on Sand Point Beach. By the time he got there, Ray and the locals had established a perimeter and forensics was on site. But the actual suspects were long gone.

One of the assailant's cars was still there. Gun oil practically saturated the carpet lining the interior, but the big guns had been removed.

Daniel had been able to describe the weapon he'd seen after the fact, despite only catching a glimpse of it. Thanks to its distinctive shape and coloring, they had a good idea what it was—something new to the entire team. The boys in forensics identified it as the Jakat five-eight, nicknamed the Warmonger. The experimental weapon was supposed to be on the drafting board of an overseas gun manufacturer.

The company board denied having any in production, but conceded the shell casings matched. The bastards were claiming intellectual property theft and even thanked their office for bringing the problem to their attention. However, they couldn't say when their super-secret blueprints for the weapon had gone missing. An internal investigation was ongoing.

A junior pair of investigators passed Daniel's desk. They eyeballed him. One nudged the other, murmuring something he couldn't catch.

He clenched his teeth in irritation. Those guys used to worship the ground he walked on. His superstar status in the department was taking a real hit with this mess.

"What do you expect?" Ray slapped a couple of files on Daniel's desk. He'd come up behind him while he was having a pity party.

"First, you stumble on a major arms deal following up on a nothing lead and you do the right thing by calling it in, but then you decide to go inside for some unknown reason—and I'm not buying that you were just trying to ID them, because if you'd stayed put we could have slapped names to faces afterward."

Daniel swiveled in his chair to glare at his partner. "I told you once they spotted me in the yard, my best bet was to bluff my way out of there by pretending to be one of them. Once I got made, I had to wait until they decided to leave to call for backup."

Ray sat in his own chair, scooting closer and lowering his voice.

"And despite the fact you were alone and they went Rambo on you with a gun straight out of Wayne LaPierre's wet dream, you chased them—but not in your own car."

"It was too far." That was his story and he was sticking with it. "If I'd gone all the way back to where I concealed it, I would have lost them."

"So you jumped in the nearest perp's car, which just happened to be empty, and you went after him. Did you hotwire it?"

Daniel shrugged. "I didn't have to. The keys were inside."

"But then you lost the car somewhere *and* all trace of the suspects. Judging from the state of that house, there are some very big assholes out there armed to the teeth with guns capable of storming Omaha beach on their own."

Daniel rubbed his head. "I'm aware of that. Why do you think I decided to pursue them?"

Ray tsked. "I know you meant well, but why didn't you go back to the rental for your kit? You could have put a tracker on their cars. Then they'd be in a cell now, and everyone would be kissing your ass as usual. But you lost them, which I know is bullshit. You are the best tail I've ever seen. Unless the fuckers can fly away, there's no way they managed to elude you."

His partner glanced around, making sure no one was too close. He leaned closer, his forearms braced on his knees. "Now do you want to tell me the real reason you went into that house? And who the hell cut off all those fingers? Was it a Yakuza spring cleaning?"

Fuck. Ray knew him too well. Daniel had been tight-lipped with the rest of their coworkers, pleading ignorance about the fingers. What little he felt safe sharing, he put in his report, but he should have known his partner would never accept his abbreviated tale.

And honestly, Ray deserved better. The man had his back for years, and now Daniel was forced to lie to him.

Well, you can't tell him the truth. Ray would have him locked up for his own good, but Daniel could give him enough to satisfy his curiosity.

He glanced around them. The other agents and their supervisor were all busy. "All right—Serin was there. She's the one who sliced all those fingers off. Did it with a sword. She was trying to stop the arms dealer."

Ray sputtered, spraying spittle on him. "The fuck, man?" he burst out.

Grimacing, Daniel wiped his cheek. He turned to see who might be watching but swearing a blue streak was common in their office. It was a testosterone-rich environment. Even Edie the IT girl would curse like a sailor whenever she had to reformat one of the office computers.

"Lower your voice," he admonished.

Ray reached over, then pinched him as hard as he could.

"*Ow.*" Daniel smacked his hand away before rubbing his arm.

His partner dragged his chair over the last few inches with a jerk forceful enough to bang their chairs together.

"Are you telling me that woman was there? *Again*?" Rubbing his face, he shook his head. "Unbelievable." He dropped his hand, narrowing his eyes. "She's why you went inside."

"I saw her walking up to the house with nothing but a sword. I thought she was insane. I had to help her." Daniel leaned back in his chair, letting his eyes unfocus. "Turns out she didn't need it. She ended up saving my ass, giving up her chance to get at Puck."

Ray leaned back, too, crossing his arms. "I get it. You ended up taking her car when you went after them."

"Something like that," Daniel muttered, his mind going back to that crazy ride in the storm drains.

The hell of it was, he would have enjoyed something that wild and dangerous under normal circumstances. He was a tried and true speed demon and adrenaline junky. Sky-diving, car racing, white-water rafting...he'd done it all.

"What else aren't you telling me?"

He weighed telling Ray the truth about Serin. Would his partner believe him or would he strap him into a straitjacket before he even finished the story?

"Not here, man. Let's go up to the roof."

A few minutes later, they had chased away the smokers who haunted the roof on their breaks. Daniel watched the grey sky.

"It looks like rain," Ray said.

Daniel said nothing.

"So what is it? Was I right about the Yakuza or is the mysterious lady working for someone even worse?"

Daniel racked his brain for the right words. "Not worse. More powerful, or at least that's what she claimed. And from what I saw, she's not lying. There are some serious forces at work here, some heavy-duty shit."

"So she works for Uncle Sam?" Ray asked, jumping to the obvious conclusion. "Is this just some big cross-departmental communication fuckup? Did we not get looped into the right channel?"

Daniel nodded. "It's something along those lines, but us not being looped in wasn't an oversight. We weren't meant to find out. I'm out of my depth here."

Scowling, Ray rubbed his eyes. "So...again, let me get this straight: Eileen—Serin—is part of some black-ops group, one of those super-secret off-the-books operations?"

Just say yes! But this was Ray, the man who'd had his back for the better part of a decade. "It's not the government. It's above that."

"What is higher than 'the man'?"

A woman. That was assuming Serin had been sticking to traditional gender roles when she said Mother.

Daniel took a deep breath. "Ray. I have something to tell you."

"Okay..."

Daniel just stared at him.

"I'm waiting."

"Magic is real."

He hadn't meant to say it, but once he'd started talking, he hadn't been able to help himself. He didn't have any secrets from Ray.

"Huh?" His partner scratched his nose, waiting for more.

"Serin is some kind of witch... Although, she really hates being called that. I saw her do magic. She did it on me. It's how she saved my life. And when I mean magic, I mean *wave your hand and break the laws of reality* type of magic. Not special effects, not classified advanced technology. *Magic* magic."

That was as specific as he wanted to get. Getting turned into a puddle and hurling through the pipes to escape a team of gunmen was too much information for day.

Ray cocked his head. Comprehension flashed across his face. "I should have known."

"What?"

His partner threw him a disgusted glance. "That girl dosed you once. The fact you let her do it again is unforgivable. For Pete's sake, you are a seasoned agent, but you keep letting this girl get around you. God only knows what hallucinogen she slipped you this time."

"That's not it," Daniel insisted.

"Look, I know you're embarrassed. You should be. Getting drugged once was bad enough, but twice is a pattern of failure. If anyone else in the office finds out, you'll be a laughingstock—and that D.C. job will be off the table. "

"Err..." Daniel didn't know what else to say. He'd witnessed something miraculous, but that was the nature of miracles. If a person didn't see it with their own eyes, how would they ever be convinced?

"Don't worry. I'm not going to tell anyone, but you have to get checked out by a doctor. You never know what damage might have been done. There are some crazy-ass drugs out there these days."

Daniel was a little surprised. Ray was a bit cynical, but he went to church whenever he could. Maybe he was just paying lip service to the divine, but he'd expected a tiny bit more openness.

"Maybe you're right... Not about the drugs, but about what I saw. It was a high-pressure situation. My mind could have been playing tricks on me."

Ray rocked on his heels. "If that's the story you want to stick to, fine. But when there are guns, there are usually drugs. I'm going to head back downstairs. There's a lot of traffic-cam footage to go through if we're going to find these guys. And Serin or whatever she calls herself. "

Daniel turned around, alarmed. That wasn't a good idea.

Even if Serin was a criminal, could he, in good conscience, go after her knowing what she could do?

She had been spot-on. The department was totally unprepared to handle magical criminals. What would they do if they managed to catch up with her again? Cuff her and throw away the key? There was no jail in the world that could contain her.

Belatedly, Daniel realized how she'd managed to get off the Reaper's estate. If she could escape from there through the pipes, she could bust out of anywhere. Hell, she could turn into a puddle and blend into the groundwater.

He turned back to the horizon "I regret pursuing this case. It's gotten...complicated."

Ray swore. "Are you suggesting we stop going after these guns?"

"I didn't say that. But we should stay as far away from Serin as possible."

"You mean *you* should stay as far away from her as possible, which is just fine by me. I, on the other hand, intend to bring her in and charge her ass with assault and administering a controlled substance, among other things. The president himself would have to bail her out. *In person.* Because no one messes with my partner, even when he's gone soft in the head over a crazy, sword-wielding, Beyoncé knock-off."

"*Hey.* There's no need to get nasty. Why bring Queen Bey into this?"

Ray rolled his eyes. "Go home or to the doctor. Either one works for me. Don't come back until you get your head straight. I'm gonna go back to my desk—where I'm going to do your job and mine for the rest of the day. And stay away from the boss. He's kind of pissed at you."

Well, who isn't?

Daniel watched Ray go. As much as he resented his partner's honesty, he couldn't fault the man his opinion. If their position was reversed, he'd be giving Ray a serious talking to as well.

But Ray hadn't seen what Daniel had seen. He didn't understand. Daniel wasn't sure he did, either.

The question was...who had he lied to? Had it been when he told his partner he was going to drop it, or when he'd told Serin she hadn't seen the last of him?

A drop of rain hit his cheek. He waited, but no more followed. Despite the dark clouds promising rain all day, only a single drop fell on him.

It was the tiniest of nudges, but it was all he needed.

17

Serin slammed her head into the man's face once and retreated, feinting right to avoid the second assailant's inept thrust. He waved the ancient trident weapon like a switchblade or a prison shank.

The first man screamed, blood spurting from his nose. When he doubled over, he knocked over several flasks and decanters from the counter. He dropped the Sai she'd used to find them on the floor. At the other end of the room, a thin curly-haired mark was crawling to the door, unable to stand on his feet because she'd broken his ankle.

Her blind ambush was going well, all things considering.

She hadn't expected to find the Sai a second time. Anybody with half a brain would rid themselves of it. But the arms dealers she was tracking weren't very bright. They also hadn't been treating the Sai with any special significance as far as she could tell. One of their lowly underlings named Tony had been using it as a backscratcher in between playing with it, pretending he was a cartoon mutant reptile.

"Really?" Serin huffed, putting her hand on her hips when the Sai clattered the ground. "I scryed for hours to find that. It's over a thousand years old."

She tsked, picking up the trident and slamming the tip through the shoulder of the second man as he ran up to her.

This one didn't scream. His mouth dropped open in shock. "But you said it was a thousand years old," he wailed.

"And I honor it by employing it for its intended use." Serin pulled out the point, punching him with her free hand.

He went down, groaning before losing consciousness. She turned her attention to Tony, who was still doubled over, holding his broken nose.

Serin bent at the waist, holding the weapon in his line of sight. "Where did you get this?"

Tony only glared, breath ragged. "You crazy bitch!"

Smiling sweetly, she reached for his hand and bent one of his fingers back.

"Fuck!" he screamed.

"Name calling will only get you more broken bones."

Kicking him over, she straightened and examined the lab. It had two long workbenches. They were covered with vials, Bunsen burners, and welding equipment. There was a smelting setup in one corner. Dozens of boxes of bullets were stacked haphazardly on it. Some very large guns and a few other less utilitarian firearms were lined up neatly on the shelves—they even had a medieval crossbow hanging on the wall.

She withdrew the second Sai from the sheath she wore on her back, admiring the pair together for a moment before holding them up to the three men groaning on the floor.

"They're a pretty picture, aren't they?" With practiced grace, she twisted them in the air, spinning them acrobatically. "Pretty, but not valuable despite what Alec thought. He's a scholar, so he underestimates the public's general lack of interest for true craftsmanship. Maybe they'd be worth something to the right collector, but there aren't enough of those on the ground to make stealing them worthwhile. So why are they here?"

No one replied. Serin narrowed her eyes at the skinny man with the broken ankle. He had head geek written all over him.

She stepped over him, peering down at him with the eyes of a predator. "Are you sure you don't know?"

The man's eyes flared and darted to the other two, but he wisely weighed his options and decided, quite correctly, that she was a bigger threat.

"He thought it might help," he said, gulping. His pronounced Adam's apple bobbed up and down. "We tested it because it was supposed to be special, but while the metal is old, it's not anything rare for that time. So we set it aside and focused on his other instructions."

"Shut up, Hyde!" Tony shouted.

Serin rushed over and kicked him in the testicles, eliciting a shriek from him, but at least he stopped talking. "Whose instructions?"

"The client."

Finally, she was getting somewhere. She knelt in front of Hyde. "I know you're the brains these two are supposed to be protecting. Tell me, do you make all of your outfit's next-gen guns in here?"

Hyde nodded, his thin mustache clumping with sweat. "I was supposed to test the metal. Our client said it might be special. He gave it to the boss a few days ago."

"I said shut up!" Tony wheezed, clutching his crotch.

Serin and Hyde both ignored him. "Tell me about this new client," she coaxed. "Have you met him?"

Hyde's thin shoulders shifted, curving in slightly. "No, I've never spoken to the man. But he's really involved. Always calling with instructions and recipes. He wants very specific mixtures of alloys and coatings."

"Coatings? Do you mean on the bullets?" Coating the guns would have been pointless.

Forgetting about his ankle for a moment, Hyde leaned forward conspiratorially. "It's a little weird. I mean, who cares what they're coated with? It's the form of the bullets and how the metal pierces the body that matters, but he insists we dip every bullet in these vats of premixed solutions. The mixes aren't even poisonous, but the stuff is foul to work with and the ventilation here sucks. But the boss won't shift our operations to a proper lab, not until after we get paid for delivering the product—and it won't matter afterward."

After standing, Serin started checking the benches around them. There were some noxious substances here, ingredients that could be components in a spell if this were any other place.

But these were humans, not witches. Nevertheless, there had been a taint of magic throughout this affair. And they were taking their instructions from someone else. The outfit was adept at customizing or adapting to someone else's needs.

A witch or fae practitioner was tangled up in this. And they were dictating to arms dealers, making sure their instructions were being followed, all while helping the process along with ingredients and tools like the Sai.

"This client has given you a lot of other things to test and incorporate into your weapons, right?" she guessed.

Hyde nodded. "Not as much as I would like, but yeah. He's been doing business with our boss for almost a year now. When the deal started, he shipped us boxes and boxes of stuff—weird herbs, acids, and raw spices from all over the world."

"Were there any pre-mixed solutions?" A few of the scattered vials would have been ideal to hold spells, and they didn't fit the appearance of the other glassware. Corked bottles with beveled edges were too traditional. Modern laboratory vials were smooth and had screw-on caps.

"How did you know?" Hyde asked. "He wanted me to take the mix apart, figure out the components, and then play with the proportions. But I'm not a chemist. Eventually, the client gave up on having me work it out. I figured he outsourced it cause he started calling in with more specific recipes for the coatings."

A rush of disquiet filled her.

This bizarre tie of arms dealer and renegade fae was starting to make a lot of sense. The Supes had largely ignored the human world's issues with firearms, but the explosion in the use of such weapons was impossible to ignore completely.

Logan's mate had been gunned down just a few months ago. He'd survived, but what if the bullet had been coated in wolfsbane or silver nitrite? Silver did work on wolves, but it took some time for the metal in the bullets to leach into the blood. A colloidal silver compound—something that dissolved and was easily absorbed—would be far deadlier.

The possibilities were chilling.

Large swaths of the fae were allergic to iron, but there was a big chunk who wasn't. They did have other vulnerabilities. Every Supernatural species had their own weaknesses.

Vampires were thought to be too fast for guns. That had been the case since they'd been invented, but from what she'd seen at the farmhouse, machine guns were evolving, closing that gap. Even an old vampire would have trouble outrunning that wave of bullets.

The guns this outfit was making decimated the farmhouse. She had barely escaped with Romero. And Loki was taking too long to recover. She hadn't given his sluggish healing much thought, but now she was worried.

What if this mystery client had purchased items from the Elemental hoard as raw material for the manufacture of weapons, ones tailored to work against specific Supes? Or worse—those that worked on more than one kind?

"Well, that's the problem with bosses," she commiserated with Hyde, her mind rapidly following different scenarios. "They find it remarkably easy to ignore their men in the trenches. Believe it or not, I know how you feel."

The Mother's silence weighed heavily on her, but she shook it off. She pointed at a laptop case on the bench. "Is this where you get your information? By email?"

Hyde shook his head. "It's on Tony's phone. He's the only one the boss calls."

"For fuck's sake, shut up!" Tony cried from behind her.

Hyde stiffened. It was her only warning. She spun on her heel. Tony had grabbed a jar of liquid from the bench. She didn't have to read the label on it to know it was acid—she could smell the caustic solution the second it began to fly, straight at her face.

Serin reached out, calling the water all around them.

It was a wild overreaction.

Hyde may have been right to complain about the ventilation, but his boss hadn't skimped on the emergency showers. They were part of all legitimate labs, ready to douse a hapless scientist when they spilled something toxic on themselves or their clothing.

The taps on the sinks also worked.

Water exploded from all sides, a sentient wave that splashed over her at the same time the acid did. Her skin heated, already burning, as the water rushed over her skin. It diluted the corrosive liquid before it could do any permanent damage.

She flung an arm out, sending the water to slap Tony down with enough force to knock him off his feet. His mouth was too full of water to call her another name. He flailed on the ground.

"Um...magic lady?" Hyde asked in a whimper.

Serin scowled at him. "What?

"Sorry to interrupt, but I think Tony keeps his phone in his pocket."

Swearing, she shut off the flow of water abruptly. Her leather boots splashed in the large puddles surrounding Tony. She reached into his pockets, fishing out a dripping black smartphone. Tony was coughing too hard to put up a fuss when she slapped one of her mother's braided charms on his wrist.

She took out two more and turned to Hyde, testing them with her mind to make sure they weren't defective.

You know they're not. What was happening with Romero didn't have such a simple explanation.

"Thank you for your help. I appreciate a degree of chattiness in an arms dealer. In your case, I would strongly suggest a career change.

Unfortunately, you won't be able to remember my advice, so let's hope you're as bright as you seem and come to the conclusion on your own."

His eyes flared as she knelt next to him, then began wrapping the charm around his wrist.

18

Loki knew Serin had forbidden this form, but he couldn't resist taking her skin out for another spin—not after he raided her closet.

Grinning like a fool, he put on one of her old dresses and turned up the music, dancing around carefully to avoid opening his wound again.

Even the air felt different in this apartment. Wiggling his hips, he stroked the gemstone countertop bar that separated the kitchen from the sunken living room. The leather and wood barstools were perfectly matched. Serin must have picked them out. She had such an amazing innate sense of style.

He loved it here. The Elemental safehouses were always choice penthouse suites overlooking a city or cool little houses tucked away in glorious natural spaces. He'd been milking his injury for all it was worth, playing on Serin's sympathies and extreme busyness to stay on here.

Whenever she was around, he would throw himself on the nearest flat surface, usually the expansive leather couch, making sure to be shirtless to better show off the still-healing wound in his side. He walked only when necessary, his pace that of a geriatric sloth.

The minute she was out the door, he dropped the act. True, he still wasn't fully healed, so he had to shake his booty with care, but he wasn't immobile, either.

It was a little odd how long the injury was lingering. As a lower-caste fae, he didn't have the same sensitivity to iron his royal superiors did. He'd always imagined if he were shot, he'd snap right back, but what did he know? Getting a bullet wound hadn't been high on his *let's-try-this-and-see-what-happens* list.

After Serin had went out earlier, he'd realized her well-stocked fridge was out of several of the major food groups—namely sugar and grease.

I have to ask her who fills this fridge. There had been fresh fruit, vegetables, and cheese, but he had no idea how it had gotten there. He'd never seen Serin come home with anything as plebeian as a grocery bag.

On the grounds he needed junk food to heal, he ordered a pizza before going on a quick bodega run. He returned with bags of gummy worms and cheese puffs, which he would need to finish or hide before Serin returned home.

Munching on a fist full of cheesy crunchy goodness, he opened a bottle of excellent wine he found in the cupboard after he'd picked and put on an ethereal teal silk gown that floated and fluttered around him like a swarm of butterflies was holding it up.

Loki grabbed more cheese puffs, then stuffed them in his mouth. *Damn*, he thought as cheese dust rained over the silk. He shook the bodice away from his body with his only clean fingers to dislodge the mess, hoping she wouldn't notice.

She wouldn't, he assured himself. Serin hadn't been wearing this kind of thing lately. She'd adopted a style similar to her other sisters —lots of leather and kick-ass boots with steel toes, some of which he'd found in the closet as well. He didn't dare touch those just in case they belonged to Diana. That one had a short fuse.

Dancing his way to Serin's mirror, he admired his glamour, pouting and preening while glorying in the dramatic contrast of the tropical shade against his dark skin before gently shaking his booty around some more.

With luck, Serin would be out for a few more hours. She'd been gone all day yesterday, following yet another Puck lead.

Loki had to hand it to the bastard. Puck had laid so many false trails, most people had no hope of ever tracking him. But Loki's favorite Elemental was tenacious. Serin never gave up. It was why he loved her...or wanted to be her. Either worked for him.

The doorbell rang. Wineglass in hand, Loki sashayed to the door, throwing it open with a seductive come-hither pose Serin wouldn't be caught dead doing.

"You're not the pizza guy."

The man on the other side widened his eyes, his thick lashes fluttering as he took in Loki's scantily clad Serin suit.

Oh shit... It was the cop trailing her—the one who had saved Loki's life.

"Uh..." Loki hurriedly straightened up, taking a step back before panicking and slamming the door shut.

Romero started knocking. "*Serin.* I—I can't believe you're here. I was searching for someone else. We need to talk. Please open the door."

Whoa. Since when was this human on a first-name basis with an Elemental?

Curiosity took a nibble before quickly consuming him. Loki cautiously opened the door a crack. Romero pushed it wide, stepping inside like he owned the place.

"Rude," Loki chided, pointing at him with the wineglass. He retreated to the sunken living room, hyper-aware of the orange cheese dust on his free hand.

"I'm sorry," Romero said, his brow creased as he watched Loki, still in Serin's likeness, search for a towel. "It's just that I needed to talk to you. You disappeared so...thoroughly the last time, and I didn't know where to find you. I didn't want it to be in the middle of another firefight."

The cop stepped closer in a rush. Loki stumbled back, the wine in his glass sloshing as the man put his hands on either side of Loki's—Serin's—face.

Romero's expression wasn't one of friendly concern or even confusion. In fact, his eyes weren't even on Loki's face. The agent's gaze was fixed on the well-filled neckline of the dress.

"*Excuse you*," Loki chirped, affronted despite the fact the cleavage in question wasn't his.

The agent finally deigned to meet his eyes. Frowning, he let go and stepped back. "What the hell? Who...who are you?"

Loki's mouth dropped open. How could the cop tell? Loki's glamours were foolproof. He doubted even Serin's parents could see through him that fast.

This was big. Loki circled the agent excitedly, studying every muscular limb with avid eyes. "Wow. What are you?"

The man read as human, but there was clearly more to him if he could see past Loki's glamour.

"*Loki.*"

Flushing, he started and turned to the door with a slow pivot

Busted. Serin was standing in the doorway, her eyes like arctic ice.

"I told you to stop *wearing me.*"

"What the fuck?" The agent whipped his head back and forth from him to the real, far-more-angry version standing in the threshold. Romero's nostrils flared as if he were trying to smell which one of them was the real Serin.

Loki put his arms down. His was the more fashionable outfit, but Serin's fully clad leather form was somehow ten times sexier than the gown he was wearing. "How do you look better than me? This is silk..."

Agent Romero moved to Serin's side, his irritated expression remarkably similar to hers. "What is going on? Who is this?"

Loki threw his head back and tittered, his hair doing a pale imitation of the rippling wave the Water Elemental's did when she moved.

"*Loki*. Take me off now," Serin snapped.

He blinked, dropping the suggestive pose with a scowl. "But he's watching," he pouted.

She slashed at the air, an abrupt *get-on-with-it* gesture.

"Fine," he huffed, dropping the glamour with a ripple. He held out his arms like a cheerleader, revealing his favored male-greaser persona. "Ta da!"

Romero watched him with something like horror in his eyes. Loki stifled a giggle, remembering how close he'd come to getting mauled by the man.

He was on the cop immediately, cozying up to him and batting his baby blues. "You can still kiss me if you like," he teased.

The agent pushed away, pointing at him with his mouth open. "You're the guy from the shooting outside the club."

He turned to Serin. "I didn't know where to find you, but I stumbled on footage of this guy on local traffic cams. He was down at the corner store when I pulled up. I decided to follow him, but I didn't expect...whatever *that* was."

Serin's lips were a thin line. Glowering at Loki, she swept past them to set her pack down on the kitchen counter.

"Your room. Go before I change my mind and deal with you now."

Shamefaced, Loki nodded like a bobble-head, but the bag's pungent odor distracted him. He stopped in the middle of the living room. "Whew. What did you bring home?"

She put her hands on her hips. "I stopped at an herbalist in Chinatown to make you a poultice because you've been healing so slowly. But if you're well enough to be wearing my skin and making junk food runs, you can make it your damn self."

Chastised, he came forward to take the bag. Hugging the smelly contents to his chest, he gave her a quick peck before skipping backward. "Thank you, thank you, thank you..."

He turned back at the doorway of the guest room. "Don't worry...

I'll turn the music up loud. Won't hear a thing," he said, winking and mugging at the pair suggestively.

The Elemental rolled her eyes. "That won't be necessary," Serin huffed, but Romero's mouth twitched.

Loki flashed into the body of an old wrinkled man. He cupped a hand over his ear. "What was that?" he warbled in a thin frail voice. "I'm quite deaf you know."

"*Loki.*"

He ignored the warning tone, materializing a cane out of thin air to wave at the pair. "Sorry, sugar doll. I can't hear youuu…"

19

Serin was in a foul mood. Not only had she accidentally wrecked the phone and possibly her only lead to Puck, but now the safe house was breached by Agent Romero, who'd apparently been cozying up to Loki in his drag form.

Romero was shaking his head. He thumbed in the direction of Loki's closed door. "So the guy from the shoot-out is one of you?" he asked.

Serin's lips tightened, debating. What was worse? Too little knowledge or too much?

He's traveled in your medium.

Romero had already seen too much. Once opened, some doors couldn't be closed. A man with his tenacity wasn't about to give up without answers, and the last thing she needed was to have him running around, dogging her steps, trying to get those answers on his own.

She let out a long-suffering sigh. "No. He's a Loki."

The line between his brows deepened. "I thought his name was Loki."

"It is. It's also his species. All Lokis are named Loki."

"That makes no sense." He frowned. "How do you tell them apart? Especially when they can do all that shapeshifting?"

She sniffed and picked up her backpack, unloading the herbs and dinner supplies she'd picked up on the kitchen counter. The phone she'd confiscated was at the bottom of the pack, wrapped in napkins the herbalist had kindly provided.

"He's not a shifter. He's fae. What he does is a glamour—an illusion."

Romero continued to frown, now at the pears and blueberries she was unpacking.

"What is that?" he asked.

She narrowed her eyes. "It's fruit."

"But not like, magic fruit?"

"No. It's regular fruit." She was tempted to laugh but bit her tongue, remembering Diana's run-in with the Apple of Discord. Not all fruit was just fruit.

"What do you do with it?" he asked, studying the food like he expected it to start levitating or glowing at any second.

She did laugh this time, continuing to unpack the fish filets she'd picked up for dinner. "I eat it. I do *eat*."

Romero drew back. "*Oh.*"

He sat on the stool across from her. Whatever hesitation he'd felt seemed to melt away. His body relaxed, lounging, making himself too comfortable.

"Is there enough for two?" he asked, a suggestive note creeping into his voice.

"Yes." His face lit up at the word.

"For me and Loki," she finished.

The little glow faded, but Romero was irrepressible. He lifted one shoulder. "Don't worry about him. He ordered pizza."

She rolled her eyes. "I don't know how he expects to get better eating like an unsupervised child."

"You sound like his mother." He blinked, a thought occurring to him. "You're not... right?"

"*No.*" Again, she laughed, unable to stop herself.

He shrugged. "Sorry, I'm trying to piece this stuff together. You said you were old."

Serin raised an eyebrow in warning. He coughed. "Well...older."

Romero opened his mouth to say something else when the doorbell rang. Loki, back to his normal youthful self, sailed across the room with his hand over his eyes. "Don't mind me. It's just my pizza."

Serin waited until he finished paying the deliveryman. "Loki, what did I tell you about ordering takeout?"

"Uh... Don't have anything delivered to the super-secret safe house or it won't be super-secret anymore?" he said, grinning sheepishly. "In my defense, I didn't think you'd be home tonight."

He held out the pizza box, opening it and offering a slice with a winsome smile.

Romero stood, reaching over to take a slice. "There, now you don't have to cook for me." He scarfed down the greasy triangle while Loki made himself scarce again.

The slice was gone before she'd finished washing her vegetables. Her uninvited guest came around the counter to wash his hands at the sink.

"You haven't told me why you're here, Agent Romero," she said, focusing on her own meal preparations.

She nearly jumped out of her skin when his arms came around on either side of her, trapping her against the counter.

"I told you—the name's Daniel," he said in a low voice before he bent his head and kissed the skin next to her ear.

Serin spun around, intending to give him a piece of her mind, but she lost the thread the moment his lips touched her.

Time slowed down. A wave of sensations crashed through her, pinning her in place. The feeling was familiar and new at the same time—a rightness that was difficult to describe but easy to recognize.

Ah, hell. Romero was her mate.

She should have been surprised. No Water Elemental had been mated to a human in...ever. In all of their recorded history, their mates were selected for their supernatural gifts. It was their duty to pass on their talents and abilities to any offspring they might have. Her parents had selected Jordan because he had been a skilled practitioner. If her parents had known the truth...

Serin had to remind her body that it had a skeleton. That the disembodied boneless feeling was a trick. Apparently, Romero had skills of his own. He was a damn good kisser.

And he can travel in your medium. It hadn't been a fluke, nor was the cop an outlier.

Daniel. His name was Daniel.

Serin pushed him away, giving herself a little shake to jar her senses back in place. "You know I could punch a hole *through* you for that, right?"

The agent's face was flushed. He appeared thoughtful, as if he were thinking about his answer. "Will I turn to water because you're touching me?"

She snorted. *Maybe.* The Mother afforded true mates a fair amount of protection from their partner's gift, but Serin was clueless about this new development. Swearing softly, she pushed him away and turned her back on him to resume cutting vegetables.

This is not right. Serin had been bonded to Jordan for years—he'd only been gone a few months. But Romero was here now.

What the hell had gone wrong with the Mother's plan?

Serin was suddenly too full. A storm of emotion was roiling inside her, but she refused to acknowledge it. Her dry eyes stung as the knife pierced the eggplant she'd bought, methodically cutting it into thin slices.

Romero had no idea what was wrong with her. He was watching her with concern, a slightly panicky expression on his face. He was probably worried she was going to start weeping or worse...

That wasn't going to happen. Serin had spent a lot of time training herself not to show any emotion. She couldn't cry, even if she wanted to.

"What did you get wet?"

Pulled from her thoughts, she murmured a confused, "What?"

He reached into her open bag, pulling out the thick bundle of damp napkins.

"A phone. It's not mine," she admitted. "I took it off a suspect."

He unwrapped the napkins, revealing the sodden cell phone. "I see. Was it in this state when you found it?"

Hesitating, she bit her lip before glancing away. "Yes." A fib.

"Really?" He held up the phone. A few stray drops fell from it.

Meeting his gaze again, she shrugged. "Technically, the entirety of the suspect was that wet at the time."

His lips quirked. "I guess that's one of the drawbacks to having water superpowers."

She snatched the phone out of his hands, set it on the other side of the cutting board, and then returned to slicing—the fish this time. "I don't have superpowers. I am talented or gifted. There's a distinction."

"That's splitting hairs, isn't it? Just different words to describe the same thing."

She focused on her meal preparation. The last thing she needed was to cut off a finger. "No offense, Agent, but you don't know what you're talking about."

Crossing his arms, he leaned on the counter. "Then why don't you enlighten me?"

"I don't have time to teach you about my world. In case you haven't noticed, I'm on the trail of a thief and a killer. Maybe more than one...." She paused to gauge his reaction. "Does your partner know you're here?"

His mouth turned down. "Ray wouldn't understand. He's a good partner, but he's a by-the-book kind of guy."

"I'm sure he's a peach, but that's not the point." After setting the knife down, she wiped her hands on a dish towel.

"Is this the part where you warn me off—tell me I'll never understand your world, let alone fit into it?"

Crossly, she shook her head. "It's not just you I'm concerned about. You're a man with ties. I'm sure you have a family, friends. Humans in your position can't stand where you are—with a foot in the door to the Supernatural world. It either sucks you in and consumes you...or it spits you back out. But neither happen without collateral damage."

"Well, maybe I'm lucky. I don't have a family. Since work doesn't leave me time to socialize, I don't have friends, either.

He was a stubborn one. "But you have your partner and other colleagues."

Romero's eyes became hard. "Let me get this straight. You're not threatening them, right?"

"Of course not." Her weariness came out on an exhale. "But people without gifts tend to get hurt when Supernaturals are involved. Some die."

"Ouch. Way to pull your punches."

Serin threw up her hands. "I'm not exaggerating for effect. You're out of your depth, Agent Romero."

"Or you are."

She put her hands on her hips, taken aback. "What does that mean?"

He cocked his head at her. "How many times have you tracked a suspect? Or fought with one who was ungifted enough to need a cell phone? I'm guessing it's not a frequent occurrence for you, else you'd know not to soak them until after you've frisked them."

Serin glared at him.

"Just saying." Romero's expression was smug. He gestured to the phone. "You know I have access to an entire lab of non-gifted techies. They can do wonders with a broken phone."

"Don't worry about it." Serin brushed past him, reaching for the oven controls to turn on the broiler. "I'm sure there's a spell to fix it."

There might even be one in their library. Every safehouse had a stash of weapons and reference books. The latter were constantly being updated as they met and experienced new challenges. She was sure Gia had written down how to recover a waterlogged device somewhere. And if there wasn't a way, then she would craft one. It would be an easy task with a bit of study.

"I'm sure there is...or you could put it in a bag of rice."

Serin turned to find Romero holding up a little plastic sack. She raised a brow. "Is that an evidence bag?"

"I always carry some. It's a tool of the trade," he said, digging around the cabinets until he found a bag of rice and poured some into the baggie.

After he sealed it, he presented it to her with a flourish. "*Et voila*."

"A spell would be faster."

He wagged the bag at her. "You're welcome."

She snatched the bag, then shoved it into her pack again. "Thank you, now stop helping."

Romero leaned in, crowding her again. She told herself she should stop him, but she let him put his hands on her hips, pulling her close to him.

"I think we both know that's not going to happen."

"Yes, I do." She reached out, putting her palm against his cheek. He started to lean down for another kiss and Serin focused, channeling her talent through her hand.

Again, it shouldn't have been possible for her talent to act on him, but if Romero was her mate, the normal rules wouldn't apply.

The agent froze, the color of his skin paling and growing translucent. The counter and room behind him shimmered through his water form.

"Sorry about this," she said softly, sending the cascade of water splashing into the sink. "But I can't have you interfering anymore."

Romero may have been water, but his voice was still loud in her ears. He went down the drain, swearing up a storm the entire way. Serin waited until his voice faded in her head.

She turned to Loki, who was watching wide-eyed from his doorway, a slice of half-eaten pizza in his hand.

He whistled. "Damn, girl. That was harsh."

Her stomach hurt, but she couldn't waver. Letting Daniel in would be a huge mistake. "Agent Romero doesn't belong in this business. He needs to learn to stay out of the way, and you need to learn to be more careful. He found this place because of you. Now we need to move safe houses."

Loki tiptoed up to the counter, brushing off the reprimand. "But isn't Romero your special-some-pony?"

"My *what*?"

Loki grinned. "You're not a *My Little Pony* fan, I guess... Where did you send him?"

She turned back to the cutting board, but she wasn't hungry anymore. "The beach. He knows how to find his way back to town from there."

She turned off the oven, tossing the entire lot of food in the trash bin. They didn't have time to eat. They had to pack.

Theoretically, it should take Romero a few hours to get back here, but he was a resourceful man. She reached for her bag, groped inside, and then swore.

The agent *was* very resourceful—and apparently skilled at sleight of hand.

"That ass took the phone!"

20

The cute female tech handed over the phone, but continued to linger at Romero's desk.

"It's an older model, but it has most the capabilities of a smartphone," she said.

"Yeah, I see that," he murmured, scanning the report she'd written.

He glanced up when she didn't move. "Anything of note?"

She blushed, reaching out to touch his sea glass paperweight. "We recovered most of the data. There's a complete contact list, so plenty of leads to follow, but no texts of anything incriminating. They could be using a code, of course, but it's not an obvious one if they are."

"Great, thanks," he said, skimming the contact list for any red flags.

"There were some audio files," she added. "But they're probably nothing. It sounds like they recorded someone's recipes. We only got fragments of those, but they're not likely pertinent to your case."

He twisted his lips. "That's it? Recipes but no porn?"

Laughing, she shook her head. "Um...do you want to discuss it further over coffee?"

"No, thanks. I've got some here." He held up his half-filled mug, his eyes fixed on the report.

"All right." She started to turn away but hesitated. "Let me know if you need anything else."

"Mm-hmm."

The transcript of the audio files was a bit weird. It sounded more like someone was preparing some sort of holistic medicine than cooking, but since it was just a fragment, he couldn't tell what it was for.

He raised his head, surprised to see the tech still standing there. "Was there something else?"

"No, no." Her face was tomato red now. Ducking her head, she turned and hurried away.

Daniel leaned back in his chair, already dismissing the encounter, until Ray reached over and smacked him over the head with his copy of the report.

"*Hey*. What was that for?"

His partner snorted derisively. "Isn't that *the* Sandy, the same tech you've been making eyes at for over a year?"

Daniel hit him back. "What does that even mean? Making eyes. Sounds like I'm a serial killer. Worse, like a kid in high school." He took a sip. "And I haven't done anything like that."

"How quickly you've forgotten. You actually went for coffee with that girl twice before you started hunting the woman in the white bikini."

Daniel shrugged. "Sandy is a colleague. I have coffee with lots of our coworkers. Are you going to give me shit for having a cup with Jeffords, too?"

Ray rolled his eyes, waving in the direction of the middle-aged and overweight agent. "Not unless you were trying to get him into bed like you were with Sandy."

"I was not," Daniel protested.

A corner of Ray's mouth pulled down.

"All right," Daniel admitted. "I kind of was. Maybe. But she wasn't interested. I moved on. No big deal."

Ray leaned closer. "Except it kind of is because it's not what happened. Sandy is totally into you. She was angling for another coffee date. But you forgot all about her the minute you got the Knight case. Admit it."

"So I put my love life on the back burner. It's a big case. Work happens. Besides, if I get that promotion—and it's a big *if* these days—D.C. is where I'll be transferred. Not a good time to start a relationship."

Ray threw up his hands. "Since when do you do relationships? What happened to Mr. Hit-It-And-Quit-It?"

Daniel scowled. "I was never prolific enough for that name."

Ray pointed at him. "See, asshole!" he crowed in triumph. "You just spoke in the past tense, and it's because of the Knight woman."

"Enough." Daniel rubbed his forehead. "We've been over this already."

Ray turned his chair, facing it back to his screen. "You already admitted it's where you got this phone," he said over his shoulder in a low voice.

"And unless one of these phone numbers turns up a name, lifting it was pointless."

Daniel frowned at the handset before turning to his keyboard. He pulled up the login window, accessing the internal database. On impulse, he sent the audio fragments to his office-issued cell phone.

Serin had stopped at a Chinese apothecary to get a bunch of herbs to help her weird shapeshifting friend. Something told him she'd recognize the ingredients in the transcript. They seemed innocuous to him, but that meant nothing. *It's probably some kind of magical roofie or worse.*

He wondered how he was going to get Serin the list. Going to the high-rise apartment in Sherwood Forest was pointless. He knew because he'd already tried. But Serin and Loki had split the minute she threw him out of the apartment.

Daniel picked up the baggie, fingering the flat screen. How the hell had he managed to hold onto it during that second wild ride through the drainage pipes? It was baffling, but the phone had been in his back pocket, right where he'd left it.

Magic was weird.

DANIEL GLANCED AT HIS WATCH. IT WAS ALMOST MIDNIGHT. HE'D BEEN waiting for three hours.

She's not going to show.

He'd racked his brain for a way to track Serin. He watched hours of traffic cam footage, trying to track the pair following their exit from the apartment. It had been a complete waste of time. They hadn't been caught on any of the neighborhood's cameras. He hadn't bothered to check the footage farther out.

He'd hoped to get lucky with the cams again, but after Loki's illicit convenience store runs, Serin must have him on a short leash.

It had taken Daniel the better part of the night to realize he didn't have to hunt her down. He had the phone. Serin would find him. So he had gone to the nearest pub to wait.

Despite the cold, he sat outside at one of their sidewalk tables, nursing a beer with only the die-hard smokers for company from the sparse Friday night crowd.

A sour-faced waitress approached, asking if he needed anything for the second time. He lifted the bottle. "Still working on this one, thanks."

Her mouth tightened. "If you change your mind about another round, I should warn you—we close in two hours," she said sarcastically, sweeping away to check on other patrons.

He tracked her progress to the door. When he turned back, the chair opposite was occupied.

"You're late," he said.

Serin stared at him coldly. "I had no idea we had a rendezvous scheduled, Agent Romero."

"C'mon, Serin, I thought we were on a first-name basis," he said, nodding at the waitress when she dropped off his beer. "And who says rendezvous anymore?"

The woman looked good enough to eat. She was wearing rust-colored leather pants and a sleeveless top. Even though she was still, there was a preternatural grace to her form.

Anyone else dressed like that would appear fake, like an extra in a bad sci-fi movie. But Serin was the real deal. His mind flashed to her as the lead in a Matrix-like movie. He bet she could do any of those gravity-defying moves without wires.

Somehow, knowing how badass and deadly she was only made her hotter.

Fuck, I've got issues.

A thought checked him in his tracks. He scowled. "You are Serin, right?" Because if it was Loki again, he was going to have to wash the inside of his own skull with lemon juice.

"No, I'm over here!" Daniel twisted to see a Serin double in a flowing purple top and sparkly silver skirt strutting toward him.

Heads turned as she dragged an empty chair and pulled it up to the table.

"*Loki,*" Serin scolded. "You were allowed to come with me on one condition—that you not do that anymore!"

Loki shook out his arms, making the gauzy see-through sleeves flutter as he sat down. "But someone has to wear these fabulous clothes again. I miss your old style so much. You simply can't let these babies hang in the closet unused—-it would be a crime against fashion."

Serin scrubbed a hand over her face. "Take me off," she said from behind gritted teeth.

Loki blew his—*her?*— hair from his eyes. His head whipped back and forth with an exaggerated put-upon air, like a teenager told to clean his room. Once he was certain no one was watching him, he changed. A mind-bending ripple of reality later, there was only one Serin. Loki was a twenty-something male again, wearing pressed jeans and t-shirt the same shiny purple as the blouse he'd been wearing.

"Thank Christ," Daniel muttered. Two Serins screwed with his hormones.

Loki beamed at him, fluttering his lush lashes.

"Well, hello again, Agent Romero," he said coyly. "Did you miss me?"

Daniel blinked, realizing the fairy's interest was genuine. Well, of course he was bisexual. Loki could be both a man and a woman. Why would he limit his prospects?

Daniel took another sip of beer. "I missed you like crazy," he told him, straight-faced.

The shapeshifter laughed, turning sparkling eyes on the Water Elemental. "Can we keep him, please?"

Serin rolled her eyes. "I need a drink."

The waitress materialized in front of them as if by magic.

"Would you like something?" she asked Serin, her eyes warming as she checked out the gorgeous woman. She didn't give him or Loki a second glance. Daniel didn't blame her.

"What's your best rum?" Serin asked.

"We've got a bottle of Appleton Estate gathering dust. It's too pricey for this crowd." The waitress flicked her lashes disdainfully at Daniel.

A fifty-dollar bill appeared in Serin's hand. The waitress took it and slipped it into her bra, her eyes inviting more than alcohol. She moved away to place the order, putting an extra sway to her hips.

"That's okay. I didn't want anything," Loki said to no one in particular.

"Good, cause I don't think we exist when she's around," Daniel said, nodding at Serin.

Serin didn't reply, simply nodded regally when a very generously poured glass of rum appeared in her hand a few moments later. Satisfied with that crumb of attention, the waitress wandered off with a smile.

All hail the queen.

Daniel leaned back in his chair. "Damn, that was quick. Maybe I should try pouring myself into skin-tight leather pants next time."

A hint of a smile played on Serin's lips. "Something tells me you wouldn't get the same reception even if you did."

He shrugged. "I'm going to leave a really big tip just to disappoint her." Daniel reached into his bag, grabbed the tech's report, and then dropped it in front of Serin.

She sipped the rum, glancing down at the folder.

He tapped the papers. "It's everything we pulled off the phone—contact list, text transcripts, and weird homeopathic recipes."

That got her attention. She straightened, flipping through the papers until she reached the list of ingredients. Her expression didn't shift one iota, but he could sense the change in her.

"What is it?" Loki asked as Serin closed the file.

"The recipe is not complete."

Loki took if from her hands, rifling through pages until he got to the transcript portion. He whistled. "Not good."

Daniel shifted, aggravated at being left out. "What are those ingredients used for?"

Serin turned away, taking another sip of the amber liquid. Her eyes fixed on a point to the right of him. "Like I said, the recipe is not complete, but it confirms something I suspected."

He took the report back. "Our techs decided it's unrelated to the weapons manufacturer."

Loki leaned forward as if he were about to burst, but he subsided on a signal from Serin.

Her mouth tightened. "They're wrong."

The ominous tone sent a chill through Daniel. "What can it possibly make? I mean, there's some rare herbs in there, but most of it is a standard bunch of plants and oils—it's all-natural shit."

Her smirk was derisive. "Just because something is natural doesn't mean it's safe. Everything is poison in the right amount, although I suspect this wouldn't kill you. That wouldn't matter, of course. It's the bullet itself that would cause the damage in your case."

Daniel stilled. "Are you saying the guys we're chasing are doctoring their bullets with this concoction? Are they targeting... um...magic people?" he asked, waving to Loki as an example.

"It would appear so." Serin turned to the now-subdued fae. "It's why you're still not fully healed, despite being shot weeks ago."

Loki's face had paled considerably, his formerly twinkling eyes dimmed. He put his hand over his middle, covering the place where he'd been hit.

"I guess I know why you and I were shot just steps away from Dionysia," he observed.

"Yes. Maybe it was random, but my guess is it wasn't. Puck was taking the opportunity to test his formula."

She turned to Daniel. "Dionysia isn't a place for high fae. It's a hangout for the lower classes. Most of the lower fae aren't susceptible to iron, so they'd have to use something else to take them out. Shooting you and Loki was a test. They wanted to know if their poison worked."

Loki grimaced. "I guess I'm lucky they haven't gotten it right yet."

Serin fingered the crystal glass's rim. "And Dionysia is lucky you came along just then. Puck may have intended to shoot up the entire club. But when you didn't drop dead right away, he knew he had to go back to the drawing board."

Daniel's brow creased. "And they have to use *bullets* and deliver them via machine gun to get their poison in? Isn't that overkill?"

Loki shrugged. "Some Supes have surprisingly tough hides. Others are fast, *really* fast."

"Ugh," Daniel grunted. "Not sure I want to know the gritty details about everything that goes bump in the night."

Don't say vampires exist. Don't say vampires exist.

He cleared his throat, trying to refocus. "Let's make sure we are all on the same page. This outfit we've been tracking is customizing weapons that can kill anything—my kind, your kind. Basically everyone."

"It's a working hypothesis."

Fuck. This was worse than he thought. "Okay, then. What now?"

Reaching over, she snatched the report out of his hand. "Now we part ways. Thank you for recovering the data from the phone. I want that back by the way. Where is it?"

"Uh...I didn't bring it."

Her face darkened. "Where is it?"

"Still with our techs. I had to catalog it as evidence to get the workup done. Why do you want it?" He nodded to the report. "That's everything that was on there."

"Maybe, maybe not."

He raised a brow. "Don't tell me there's a magic spell to reconstruct data from damaged SIM cards?"

She cocked her head, drumming her fingers impatiently on the table.

"*Oh.* I guess I should have brought the damn thing."

"Gee, ya think?" Loki's shoulders wiggled with attitude. For a second, his face morphed into Serin's as if he couldn't help himself.

"Enough, Loki," she warned, turning back to him. "I have a friend who is very skilled with electronics, even damaged ones."

"Do you mean Gia? It's Gia, isn't it?" Loki asked, nudging her repeatedly.

Daniel was lost. "Who's that?"

Loki was almost vibrating with fangirl excitement. He leaned closer. "It's the Earth Elemental. She's got skills with electronics cause they're made of metal and plastic, which is made of petroleum."

"Huh. Interesting," Daniel muttered, focusing on Serin. "I want to help."

"Good." She reached into her pocket, took out a small card, and handed it to him. "Send the phone to that address."

"I meant help in person. Also, this is blank."

"Is it?"

When he flicked his gaze down he started slightly. Blank only moments before, now the card had a local P.O. Box printed in neat cursive.

"Aw, now you're just showing off," he said, glancing back up. Both chairs were empty.

Damn it. He leapt to his feet, turning in a circle.

There was no way Serin pulled another Houdini on him, not in front of an audience and not with Loki in tow.

Despite the cold night, the smokers were still out, clutching their butts in mittened hands.

He caught a glimpse of Loki disappearing around the corner. Daniel ran after them, nearly knocking over the waitress on his way past.

Fuck, the bill!

"I'll be right back," he called behind him.

"Yeah right, asshole," she screamed after him, waving her tray menacingly.

Double fuck. He was going to have to hit an ATM so he could leave a tip big enough to make up for this.

Daniel rounded the corner, relieved to see the pair hadn't disappeared after all. For some reason, Serin's hands were up, high above her head.

"What the—" he began. A few more steps in and he saw him.

"*Ray?*"

His partner was standing a few feet away in the middle of the alley. He was holding a gun. It was pointed at Serin.

<h1 style="text-align:center">21</h1>

Serin shoved Loki behind her, wondering if the man holding the gun was part of the arms manufacturing ring. The barrel of the gun twitched slightly as Romero ran up behind them.

"I knew you were acting squirrelly, Daniel," the man said, waving the pistol in an angry arc at the papers in her hand. "I figured you were meeting her, but I never imagined you would give her classified information."

Daniel came to rest at her side, close enough for their arms to touch. "So you followed me? What the hell, Ray?"

Oh... It was Agent Doyle. Belatedly, she recognized the small paunch and receding hairline. The two men faced off, staring each other down. Testosterone tainted the air. Serin kept her hands up, hoping to appear nonthreatening.

"Would you two like to be alone to hash this out?" she asked.

Doyle pointed the barrel at her aggressively. "Hey, you shut up! I've had it with this cloak-and-dagger shit. We're taking you in."

Raising an eyebrow, she flicked her eyes to Romero. "*We?*"

Romero shook his head. "Ray, we can't do that."

"Why the hell not?" Doyle's eyes were wild. "You're the one who said she wasn't government. Which means she's the *bad guy*."

Serin winced. She could feel Ray's frustration. Romero and Doyle had been partners for years. It was nowhere near as long as she had been serving with her sisters, but she understood where he was coming from.

There was a solidarity and fellowship that came with jobs like theirs. Doyle was understandably freaking out because he thought the person he trusted most in the world had been compromised. And truthfully, Romero's loyalty *was* divided. She had put him between a rock and a hard place.

It wasn't as if you didn't warn him.

"This all started when *she* showed up," Ray shouted, the veins in his neck popping out in stark relief. "I knew you were keeping secrets, but I never thought you would do this. Are you working for her now? Are you selling information to the other side?"

The atmosphere around them darkened, the air charging with negative energy. It was resonating within Doyle's indignation and betrayal. Loki grabbed the back of her jacket, glancing at the sky apprehensively, but the humans were too engrossed in their argument to notice.

"Ray, you just have to trust me." Romero was pleading now. "This isn't what you think. This is way over our heads."

"If it's not what I think, then why does that woman have the report?" the other agent said, making *woman* sound like a swear word.

"Serin needed the information off that cell phone. She's the one who found it in the first place."

Doyle threw up his hands. "So now we're doing her dirty work? Why?"

The gun swung back in her direction, shaking with Ray's growing agitation. The man was starting to crack. She didn't want him to lose control.

"I'm very sorry, Agent Doyle," she said, altering her accent. The

British clip softened, knocking it down a few social classes. "But your partner is right. This is above your pay grade."

Slowly, gesturing that she had something to show him, she reached into her back pocket for one of the handy badges she and her sisters carried around for occasions like this.

When she held it out to him, he squinted at it. "I'm supposed to believe you're Interpol?"

"This is a real badge just like this is a real investigation."

"The hell it is," he said, raising the barrel of the gun again, his finger on the trigger. "There are rules about conducting investigations on American soil—paperwork needs to be filed. There would be a trail."

Serin's smile was derisive. "And what makes you think you're important enough to be read in on this?"

Doyle stiffened, but he didn't lower the gun.

"C'mon, Ray," Romero said. "The only reason I got read in was because I wouldn't let it go. I wanted to tell you, but I was ordered not to by Serin's superiors. They leaned on me kind of hard, but after everything was explained, I understood. Sensitive information can't be spread all over the place or people die."

"Is that why you came up with that crazy story? Fuck, Daniel, I'm *your partner*. What did they tell you to make you leave your partner in the dark?"

Romero's face darkened, his eyes going slitted. "They said there was a mole."

Serin leaned back on the balls of her feet. She had to hand it to Romero. He was one of the finest liars she'd ever seen—and she'd rubbed elbows with enough politicians to know some accomplished dissemblers.

"What the fuck?" Doyle exploded. "Do you think it's me?"

"Of course I don't think it's you," Romero said, his hands up. "But the powers-that-be were very clear. This was *need-to-know*, and you didn't need to know. They were afraid the mole might get tipped off if word leaked. But trust me when I say Serin is trying to stop those next-gen guns from getting on the market. I'm just pitching in since she doesn't have her Interpol resources on hand."

Doyle scowled. "So now it's all about the guns. It has nothing to do with the fact you're in love with her." He sneered, gesturing to her with the firearm.

Romero's mouth tightened. He glanced at Serin to gauge her reaction, his expression...was that worry? No, it was something closer to embarrassment.

No one said anything. Romero stood there, watching her.

Oh. This was awkward. What was she supposed to do now?

Loki piped up, gesturing at the mouth of the alley. "The bar is still open in case anyone needs a drink."

Romero rubbed his face. "I sure as hell need another one. I actually have to go back there to pay the bill I kind of ran out on." Shrugging, his face turned sheepish. "It was an accident."

Ray's stance relaxed, his face sagging. "You know, I think I could use a drink."

He started to put down the gun. The blast caught her unawares.

Serin clapped a hand to her ear before realizing her midsection was stinging. Dropping her head, she stared dumbly at the blood pouring down her front. The bullet had caught her high in the stomach.

Fire and ice exploded across her stomach. Her ears were ringing, but she could just make out Loki screaming and Romero yelling. Agent Doyle gaped, his feet fixed to the ground. He looked as shocked as she felt.

Her hands trembled slightly as she touched her fingers to the front of her shirt. The sight of the dark red blood transfixed her.

"Something's wrong," she whispered.

Large hands grabbed her roughly. Romero was saying something, but she was having trouble making it out. "Something's wrong," she repeated.

"Yes, something is fucking wrong. Ray shot you. What the *fucking fuck*, Ray?" Serin had never heard him sound so menacing.

Ray Doyle was white as a sheet. "I'm so sorry. It just went off."

She fixed her gaze on the wound, muttering the strongest healing spell in her arsenal. "This was one of their bullets...a newer one." She pressed her hands to her middle, fighting the lightheaded swimming sensation.

It wasn't her first gunshot wound. In her decades of service, she'd been shot, beaten, and stabbed. Such incidents grew less frequent as she gained experience, but they still happened occasionally. Getting injured on the job was a numbers game. It didn't matter. She was somewhat skilled at healing herself. It was an aspect of her talent. The human body was mostly water.

But this wound wasn't responding.

Romero was still holding on to her, but Serin pulled away, staggering backward and then forward, trying to walk through him.

But the water didn't come. She couldn't shift into her medium. With that not working, her chance at stopping the poison was gone. It coursed through her veins, leaving fire in its wake. Every passing second made it worse. The poison was burning her up from the inside out. The pain grew exponentially with every breath.

It should have been easy to isolate the toxin and expel it from her system. Whatever this poison was, it had instantly dispersed and bonded with her cells, making it impossible for her to get rid of without pushing out a large amount of her own blood. And maybe an organ or two...

She gritted her teeth, trying to will the burning pain away. It felt like she was being sliced up by thousands of razor blades while trying to staunch the flow of blood with lemon-infused towels.

"Where did you get that gun?" Romero sounded as if he were in a tunnel.

Serin staggered, falling to her knees. She reached down, using the last bit of her strength to break through the asphalt, thrusting her hand into the barren soil underneath.

Gia. Gia. I need you.

"I asked you where you got the *goddamn* gun?" Romero yelled louder, his hands pressed to her middle just over hers.

Agent Doyle said something. His voice was strained and desperate, but Serin could no longer make out of the words over the sound of her own fading heartbeat. She wanted to laugh. but she stifled it to conserve her strength.

It was ironic. Serin had survived pitched battles with vampires, black witches, and out-of-control shifters, but right now, she was in the worst peril of her life because of a cop with an itchy trigger finger.

Well, given the color of her skin and where she was in the world, that almost made sense.

She was having trouble focusing now, but she made one last desperate plea. *Atabey, Mother mine, can you hear me? I need help.*

Unlike her younger sisters Diana and Logan, Serin felt the guiding hand of their Mother, or at least she had at the beginning of her career. It was never anything as distinct as a voice in her head, not the way Gia felt their Mother. For Serin, it was subtle warmth when it should have been cold, an answer when she'd been lost.

It's been so long, please... But the Mother didn't break her silence.

Serin closed her eyes, but Romero pried them open. He was still shouting. Her vision was darkening at the corners.

Then she got her answer.

It wasn't from the Mother. Her body, always a little colder than normal, stayed cold. This was local, a rumble in the earth. There was a hazy vision of a body in motion, and Doyle went down, crashing to the ground in front of her.

Gia.

"Yes. I'm here."

22

Daniel wheezed, hitting his face and spitting out sand that wasn't there. He spat again, touching his mouth. Nothing. He had just traveled under the earth—and there was nothing in his eyes or mouth. The ground simply ejected him spotless and baffled hundreds, perhaps thousands, of miles from his last location.

On his right, Loki was whacking his ear and head, shaking out the imaginary sand. "Stop, stop," Daniel said, grabbing the fae's hand before he hit himself again.

"Where are we?" Loki asked, twisting his head left and right.

"I have no freaking clue," Daniel said, staring at the vision in front of him. It was a beach, but not the same one Serin had dumped him at twice now. That one was as far from this place as night was from day.

This place was a vision that only existed in sci-fi movies or photoshopped pictures. The moon hung in the night sky like a giant pearl, illuminating a long stretch of sugar-white sand. And the water was glowing—literally.

Daniel knew it was phosphorescent algae that made the interface of water and sand light up like a carpet of bright blue stars. but that was too simple an explanation. It was as if the hand of God had taken a piece of the night sky and carelessly tossed it here.

"Oh my God, this is so cool!" Loki sprang up and ran a few steps, leaving a trail of sparkling footsteps in his wake as he disturbed the algae in the sand. "Where are we?"

Daniel lifted his hand, rubbing his face. "We just had this conversation. I also don't know who that scary-ass woman was who brought us here."

The vision of a small Hispanic woman tossing his two-hundred-pound partner like a sack of potatoes was burned into his brain. *Dear Lord, dangerous things come in small packages in the magic world.*

"Oh my God, I think that was Gia. *The* Gia. She's Earth."

"Earth as in Earth like Serin is Water?" Daniel asked. He vaguely remembered Loki mentioning her earlier, but magic travel had a way of scrambling the brain.

"Yes, there are four of them in total. Fire, Diana, is a ballbuster; you don't want to meet her. Then there's Air. Her name is Logan. She's the youngest and she's cool, but not as awesome as Serin. Earth is the most senior. I don't know that much about her other than she's really old."

Daniel blinked. "So this Gia person is like Serin's boss?"

He couldn't picture anyone telling that woman what to do.

"I don't think it works like that. It's more like a cross between being an independent contractor and a Charlie's Angel with superpowers. Some come, some go—they decide when. They can work together, but typically act alone unless something big is going down."

"But this Gia person has more magic? Can she heal Serin?"

Loki hesitated. "I thought Serin could heal herself, but she wasn't, was she?"

"No," Daniel said. Still disbelieving, he murmured, "Damn it, Ray, what were you thinking?"

Daniel got to his feet, searching for signs of civilization. The beach was surrounded by a high cliff edge that stretched as far as the eye could see. Except for the moon and algae, there were no lights to indicate the presence of people.

"*Fuck.* Why do they all have to do this?" he said. "There must be a town or village or *something* here. They wouldn't leave us stranded on a deserted island...would they?"

Loki gasped like a teenager who'd just found out Taylor Swift was coming to town. He smacked him on the arm. "Shit, shit, shit! I know where we are."

The fae spun around, holding his arms out. "This is T'Kaieri."

"And?"

Loki stopped, crestfallen. "*Seriously*?"

"That name means nothing to me." Daniel started walking, searching for a break in the cliff line.

The fae hurried after him, catching up and trudging along beside him. "I was expecting a bigger reaction."

The sand was pristine and sugar-fine, but it was hell to walk on. "And that would be why?"

"Because this is the legendary home of the Elementals. Well, the Water ones, anyway. It's basically Atlantis, or as close as you can get without breaking into the realm of fiction."

"They can call this place God's Golden Butthole for all I care—as long as they know how to heal Water Elementals. I'm good. Now, where can we find everyone?"

Shrugging, Loki scrutinized the cliff line. "I honestly didn't think it was this big. I don't know how they keep it off the charts. Surely planes can spot this place from the air?"

Daniel cursed, his steps turning to longer strides. As the minutes stretched, he grew angrier and angrier.

"Didn't we pass this damn shell already?" he asked, lifting a cartoon-level perfect conch off the sand.

"Why are you asking me?" Loki was still playing with the glowing footprints, drawing what Daniel assumed were fairy swear words with the toe of his shoe. The shapeshifter lifted his hand, pointing. "Look up there. Is that a torch?"

Daniel spun around, spotting a bobbing yellow light. The flickering flame grew closer and closer, weakly illuminating a thin path through the cliffs. He would have missed if someone hadn't been coming down it.

"Don't they have flashlights around here?" What was up with this place?

They jogged toward the light, meeting the torch-bearer at the base of the cliff. The stranger was an attractive woman of indeterminate age. Her gauzy green dress fluttered in the ocean breeze.

She inclined her head. "Hello. My name is Noomi. The elders sent me from the village."

"Are we really on T'Kaieri?" Loki asked, standing on his tiptoes. He craned his neck to peer behind her.

"Uh...yes. I'm here to tell you that Serin is with the healers."

"Oh, thank fuck." Daniel wiped his forehead. "I don't know why Gia dumped us all the way out here. Can you take us to her?"

Noomi winced, her free hand fiddling with her robe. "I'm sorry, but no one can set foot on the island without invitation. That is why you were left here until one could be extended."

Daniel nodded, arms out toward her in a *get-on-with-it* motion. "Great, let's go."

Noomi's face crumpled as if she'd swallowed something foul. "I'm sorry. I understand Gia herself brought you here with the expectation you would be invited. But..."

"But what? What the hell is the problem?" Daniel could feel the blood rushing to his face, impatience and worry making him snappish.

"Well, Gia told us you were here and then she rushed to consult the healers with Serin's parents, Caimen and Dalasini," Noomi said, stumbling over the words. "The remaining elders held an emergency council meeting to discuss your presence. They voted whether or not to extend an invitation...and the final vote was *no*."

She said the last as if someone were pulling out her teeth.

"Why the fuck not?" Daniel was an inch away from exploding.

"Calm down," Loki said, putting a restraining hand on his arm. "It's not her fault. She's just the messenger."

He was right. The poor woman cringed, shrinking away.

"Shit," Daniel said, ashamed. "I'm sorry. I know it wasn't your decision, but I have to see Serin."

It was his fault she'd been shot. If he'd found another way to deal with Ray beforehand, his partner wouldn't have come to the meet armed and she wouldn't be in danger now.

"You have my sincerest apologies," Noomi said regretfully. "I know Gia wouldn't have brought you here if she didn't think you had a right to be, but things are very tense in the village. There's been a lot of upheavals as of late."

Her head hung as she cast her gaze at the ground. "I'm afraid I bear some responsibility for that. That is why the elders sent me down here to tell you of their decision."

Loki's face fell. "How are we supposed to get home from here?"

Her shoulders rose an inch. "I believe there was some talk of conjuring a boat."

Daniel swore long and loud. "I'm not leaving this goddamn rock without seeing Serin. Once I know she's out of danger then fine, I'll fucking swim home if I have to. But not until I'm convinced she's going to be all right."

He pushed passed her, heading up the path. Noomi turned, chasing after him.

"I'm so sorry, but you won't be able to go past the cliffs. T'Kaieri is protected, blessed by the Mother herself. The wards won't let anyone pass, not without the incantation that allows you to enter," she said breathlessly.

Daniel ignored her, continuing his stomping path. Loki and Noomi hurried after him.

"Please stop," Noomi called. "I don't know what will happen if you try to cross the wards!"

She lowered her voice to a hushed whisper, asking Loki in a slightly scandalized tone, "He's a human, isn't he?"

"Definitely. Well, mostly," the fairy said, huffing after him. "Enough for the wards to register him as one. But damn, he moves fast for one, doesn't he?"

Daniel ignored them and crested the ridge, sucking in a breath at the sight below him. The village of T'Kaieri wasn't nestled in a valley. It rose to a peak behind the barrier of the cliffs that formed a half-circle around it. At the very top was something that resembled a castle or a cathedral, and all along the edges were the most spectacular homes.

The buildings were difficult to describe. It reminded him of Santorini or some other exotic Greek island, except instead of being uniformly white and square, the houses came in many shapes and colors. It was like someone had scattered flower petals on a hill.

Noomi and Loki finally caught up to him, the woman bracing her hands on her knees and breathing hard. The fae man squealed like a little girl, clapping his hands over his mouth. "It's so beautiful I want to cry."

"You can cry all you want later." Daniel turned to Noomi. "Which one is Serin in?"

Noomi straightened up, pointing to the castle-like structure at the top. "She was taken directly to the temple, where our connection to the Mother is the strongest. There are rooms devoted to the healing arts in there, where our most-skilled physicians conduct their work. Most of the village is there, praying for her recovery."

"All right then," he muttered, starting down the path that would incline again to take him to the peak.

"Stop!" Noomi cried right before he passed under a stone arch.

Once on the other side, he turned, scowling at the pair. "I told you I'm not leaving. Are you coming or not?"

Noomi stood stock-still a few yards away on the other side of the arch. Her hands covered her eyes. Loki gave her a hard nudge, and she slowly put her hands down.

She gaped at Daniel. "How are you standing there?"

"I really don't know what you mean," he snapped, tired of the games.

Noomi crossed the arch. "The wards were supposed to keep you out."

She glanced at the stone structure, her hand on her chin. "I didn't realize they weren't working... Oh no! Perhaps they were deactivated. It would make sense. The last visitor to cross was...well, it was Jordan. That was back when Uncle John first brought him here, but he had an invitation so he wasn't stopped." Once again, she stared at her feet instead of him when she talked. "Sorry to babble, but this is a rather alarming turn of events in a string of alarming events."

Loki moved toward her, his hand out, probably to pat her reassuringly. He only made it a few feet before he reached the arch and rebounded off what seemed to be nothing, landing on his ass.

"*Ow*," he groaned, picking himself up.

Daniel did a double take. "What the hell did you do?"

Noomi's mouth went slack. "I don't understand."

Tentatively reaching out, she touched the stone arch. "Wait, I can feel the spell. It's vibrating the stones, which means it's functioning."

Frowning, Daniel place his entire palm on the rock. "I don't feel anything."

"The vibration would be imperceptible to one of your kind." She turned to Loki. "I'm so sorry. Are you hurt?"

"Only my pride." Loki's expression was that of a child who'd lost his puppy. "It's okay. Go on without me."

Daniel stalked to the gate. "I am sick of these made-up magical rules getting in my way." He reached through the arch and grabbed Loki by the shirt, starting to yank him through the unseen barrier.

Loki squealed again, cringing as he moved closer to the arch, but nothing happened. He flew through the air like nothing was there, causing Daniel to have to right them both since he'd been expecting resistance.

Once Loki was on his feet, they all stopped and stared at the archway.

"Huh," Daniel grunted. "Well, obviously it's on the fritz. Let's get the fuck out of here." He turned his back to the others, immediately starting to jog down the path. The others ran after him.

"Should we tell him it's not broken?" Loki asked the woman in a quiet voice, but Daniel heard him anyway. He chose to pretend he hadn't, not in the mood for guessing games.

"But it has to be." Noomi was panting as she raced to keep up. "Otherwise, I can't understand what happened."

Loki started laughing. "I think I can enlighten you…"

23

The atmosphere in the temple was hushed and somber. Each long bench was filled with people in colorful dresses and robes, their heads bent in prayer.

Daniel tried to ignore them, but he could feel their eyes boring into the back of his head as he paced in front of the healing chamber. The constant susurration of the prayers was making him twitchy.

Loki was across the vaulted chamber, taking everything in with worshipful eyes. Noomi, his self-appointed guide, was with him, whispering and pointing as she answered his endless stream of questions.

There was an altar at one side, but no painting or statue of any god sat on or behind it. Instead, there was a huge tree. He didn't know what species it was, but it appeared ancient. Each limb dripped with delicate white flowers. Their scent filled the room. Ivy clung from every column. In the center of the room, between the benches, there was a raised well with swirling water that glowed brightly.

It's just the algae again, he told himself, but something told him that wasn't the case. It was more like the water was illuminated by life itself. Could water be alive?

Everything here is alive.

He tipped his head back, staring at the vaulted ceiling. It had an operculum, open to the sky. The moon and starlight came straight through, reflecting off the white stone interior in such a way that it lit every bit of the oval-shaped chamber.

He leaned against one of the ivy-covered pillars. It was weirdly cushiony.

"What if it rains?" he murmured, almost to himself, shaking his head at the huge hole in the ceiling.

"Then we get wet."

Daniel spun on his heel. The man who answered was roughly his height, with dark skin and long dreadlocks fastened at the neck with a strip of red leather. His robes were lavender, but on him the color appeared masculine.

He didn't have any wrinkles or grey hair, but Daniel instinctively knew this man was older than Serin. There was something very dignified about him, a quiet wisdom in his eyes that was apparent, despite the soberness of his expression.

Maybe this guy was one of those elders Noomi had mentioned.

"Hey, can you get me in there?" Daniel asked, indicating the healing chamber. "I really need to check on Serin. I won't interrupt any spells or anything like that. I just need to see her."

The man cocked his head, staring at him as if he were trying to understand him—not his words, but more like what he was, as if he'd never seen a man before.

"I know you're not used to seeing humans around here, but I'm hoping you can overlook whatever it is you think about my kind and put a good word in with the healers back there. I really need to see Serin." Daniel tried to make his voice respectful, but his anxiety and impatience bled through.

The stranger tapped a finger to his chin. "Gia brought you."

"Yes, yes she did." That had to count for something, right? If Gia was the senior Elemental, then her decisions should have some weight with the council.

"And you can travel *with* Serin?" the man asked, his expression growing a touch skeptical.

"You mean getting tossed down drains as water?" Daniel straightened with a wry shrug. "Yeah. Serin can basically pull a Dorothy to my Wicked Witch—melt my ass to get rid of me whenever she wants."

"That is...*interesting*."

"Why?" Daniel asked, still wondering why the guy was eyeing him as if he expected him to sprout a second nose.

"Because Jordan couldn't."

There was that name again. Why did everyone in this world keep comparing him to this Jordan person?

The man did an about face, heading to the center of the chamber but gesturing for Daniel to follow. He joined the man next to the well, aware everyone was watching them.

"Please reach into the Well of Souls and touch the water," the dreadlocked man instructed.

Daniel leaned forward, staring at the radiant liquid. "You want me to touch the *what*?"

"The words are a rough translation. It does not contain literal souls."

"Uh-huh." Daniel's nose twitched as he glanced askance at the gleaming water. It looked radioactive.

This is hardly the weirdest thing that has happened to you lately. You traveled as dirt, for God's sake.

There was an air of expectation in the room. If he had to hazard a guess, he'd bet most everyone was holding their breath.

It's a test. If he passed, they'd let him see Serin.

"Okay," he said, jaw tight as he raised the cuff of his shirt. He dipped his hand down.

The damn water *dodged* his fingers.

Daniel swore. "Get over here, you little...."

The water dodged again, swirling and dancing away like he was a magnet that could repel it. Frustrated, he was about to pull away when a ball of it jumped into his hand like a little puppy.

"Damn, look at that." Daniel laughed in amazement, awkwardly holding the perfect sphere of rippling water. He nodded at the man. "This is cool. Does it do this for everyone?"

"No. Only Water talents...and their mates."

Daniel blinked, not sure he'd heard right. "What was that?"

The water responded to his voice, twisting into a rope and running around his cupped hands like a speedy snake.

"Woah, woah, stop that," he said, shaking his hands until the water obligingly jumped back in to the well.

"Did I pass?" Daniel asked, raising his head.

The man wasn't there. Daniel twisted around until he spotted the elder at the door of the healing chamber. He was holding it open for him.

"Finally," Daniel muttered, his whole body flooding with relief.

He ran, stopping at the door to the healing chamber. "I don't know how to thank you. I don't even know your name."

The man nodded, but his face was conflicted, as if he were still torn about something. "My name is Caimen. I'm Serin's father."

***

Daniel forgot all about the fact he'd just met Serin's father when he stepped into the healing chamber.

It resembled a Roman bath with a single narrow oval pool in the center filled with more of that glowing water. Serin was floating in the center, being held up by Gia and three other women. The bullet wound in her gut was very visible. It was as if there were a neon arrow pointing to it. A small amount of blood floated over it.

The Earth Elemental stared down her nose at him. "What took you so long?" she snapped.

He hurried over to the edge of the pool. "Well, maybe if you had brought me straight here instead of dumping me at the beach, I could have gotten here sooner."

One of the women holding Serin glowered at him. "No one enters T'Kaieri without an invitation." She turned to Gia. "Who is this?"

The disdain and indignation in her tone was apparent to all, but Gia interrupted before he could introduce himself in an equally snippy fashion.

"He belongs to Serin, and he's late." Her dark gaze appraised him. "Get in here."

Everyone stared at Gia as if she'd gone crazy.

"*Oh.*" Daniel shut up, his belligerence blasted to nothing. He toed off his shoes and hopped in the pool fully dressed, wading to Gia and Serin.

"So this is what you all do around here instead of surgery," he said in a low aside.

Gia ignored his comment. "Stand on my other side, then put your hands here," she instructed in a no-nonsense voice.

Daniel imitated her movements, aware the other people in the room were having a full-blown whisper-fight.

"He bypassed the wards without even a twitch, then pulled the Loki through the Channel gate even after he'd had already been ejected by the arch," Caimen told the turbaned woman from the edge of the pool.

The expression of comic horror on the woman's face was one Daniel would never forget.

"But he's a...a... Is he a warded witch?" she asked, talking about him as if he wasn't there.

"There is no ward that can pass the Channel gate intact," Gia said, staring at each of the fae in turn. Her clipped tone brooked no argument.

"Sorry, I didn't have time to wait for an engraved invitation," Daniel said. "And no, I'm not a witch. I'm one-hundred-percent human."

"More like ninety-four percent," Gia corrected, not taking her eyes off Serin.

Ah. Well, that news would have to wait to be processed another time. "Am I supposed to be doing something?" he asked, his hands supporting Serin's neck and shoulder.

"Yes. Focus," Gia ground out, her jaw tight.

"That is not a specific enough instruction."

What the hell was he supposed to focus on?

Daniel's stomach roiled as he watched Serin's chest. In the water, it was difficult to tell if she was even breathing.

Gia smacked his arm in an unmistakable sign that meant *shut the hell up.* He resisted the urge to rub the smarting appendage—the woman hit like a linebacker—and finally decided to try concentrating on sending healing vibes through his hands into Serin's body. It felt a bit silly, but he would try anything at this point.

Gia nodded approvingly and held her hand out, palm down, just over the bullet hole.

A hush fell over the room. The moment stretched. Every beat of Daniel's heart sounded absurdly loud in the sudden quiet. Even the lapping of the water was muted.

He bit his tongue to keep from asking what they were waiting for. *One...two...three...*

At four, a flash of something swept over him. The closest he could describe it was an ocean wave made from electricity. It barreled through him as the copper-colored bullet appeared at the entrance to the wound. It floated out of Serin's body and straight into Gia's waiting hand.

Blood filled his mouth. Daniel had bitten through his tongue at the awesome sight.

The Earth Elemental glared at the bullet, turning it over in her palm before a young man outside the pool held out a bowl carved from stone.

"We'll analyze it for traces of the poison."

"It's there," Gia said. "It's infused into the metal."

Fuck, please don't let this poison be the infallible super killer. Let it be a dud like the one that made Loki sick.

"Is there an antidote?" he asked, his eyes tracing the spidery dark line emanating from the wound.

"No."

"That better be no as in *not yet*," he said.

"Even if the healers get lucky, the poison has been in her system a relatively long time." Gia shook her head. "I can feel it—there's a significant amount of damage."

This last was directed at the turbaned woman. The woman's face hardened, her lips firming. There was something about the gesture that was familiar.

This was Serin's mother. There wasn't a strong resemblance, but his gut said he was right. Noomi had mentioned her name...

Dalasini inhaled deeply. "Let us pray to the Mother. Ask her to spare our daughter, Her servant, Serin."

As one, all heads in the room bowed.

Damn. Prayers were all well and good, but the pragmatist in him wasn't ready to trust in a higher power, no matter how much glowing water they had around here. "Um, that's great, but why don't we ask Serin to turn herself into liquid so she can just flush the poison now that the bullet is out?" he asked.

"N-no! Are you mad?" Serin's mother sputtered.

Gia held up her hand. "Dalasini, he doesn't understand your concern."

The Earth Elemental turned to Daniel. "Water is inherently wild and difficult to control. It requires the fiercest will to manipulate it... and an even greater singlemindedness to maintain your own integrity within it. Serin has to be conscious to remain Serin in there. She's too far gone from the poison to make the attempt."

Not liking her answer any more than he liked the whole situation, he reached out for Serin's hand. "Are you sure? Can't we go with her and...I don't know...hold onto her like she holds on to me when I turn liquidy?"

Dalasini made a disgusted noise. "Gia, can you please tell this person to stop speaking? Clearly, he has no idea of what's at stake."

Affronted, Daniel straightened, spine going rigid as he glowered at Serin's mother. "Hey, lady, I know exactly what's at stake—"

Daniel didn't get to finish telling her what that was. One moment, he was there in the pool with the others. In the next, he was formless, floating in the glowing pool.

GIA'S VOICE CAME OUT OF NOWHERE, A FARAWAY ECHO.

"Uh, Daniel, it seems that on some level, Serin must have heard you. Your bodies have merged with the water in the pool."

Feeling as if he were floundering, Daniel tried to contain his panic in this nowhere state of nothingness he'd found himself in. *Fuck. What does that mean? What do I do? Where are you?*

The Earth Elemental's voice surrounded him, grounding him enough to stop his panicking. *"Still standing in the pool. Serin only took you with her. This is on you now. The rest of us are getting out. I'm going to flush the poison out of the pool. You have to hold on to her."*

He wanted to laugh, but a mental image of him drowning was too strong—despite the impossibility of water drowning itself. *I have no fucking idea how to do that.* Serin had always held on to him, never the other way around.

Gia's tone grew impatient. *"You're her mate. Figure it out!"*

The word *mate* flashed through him, but he pushed it to the back of his mind to examine later. *All right. Fuck, fuck, fuck.*

Daniel cast his mind out, attempting to find the bit of essence that was Serin. At first, there was nothing. It was like treading water in the middle of the ocean while wondering where the hell the nearest island was.

"Stop panicking," Gia ordered from somewhere above him.

He scoffed. *Easy for you to say; you've got feet and a mouth right now.*

"Figure. It. Out." It sounded like she pushed the words out through gritted teeth.

Damn that Earth Elemental could be a hardass. Daniel made a move to suck in a breath, but immediately realized how stupid that was. This was a simple case of mind over matter. He just had to picture himself swimming.

Stroke, stroke, stroke. He counted one after another, willing the mental image to be a reality. It took way longer than he would have imagined, but he eventually did a circuit of the tiny pool, collecting Serin's essence and holding it to his heart.

Once he had her, Daniel wondered how he could have missed her. Yes, it was like trying to hug a warm current in an otherwise-cold stream, but it was a Serin-current—and that somehow made it easy.

I did it! He couldn't believe he was cradling a formless Serin to his equally formless body. What was even more inconceivable was how normal it felt in its absolute abnormality.

"Good," Gia replied. *"Now hold on to her. I'm flushing the pool."*

The liquid in the pool began to move, but he held steady in the center, a rock in a very short raging river.

"That should do it." Gia sounded relieved, which clearly told him she'd been more worried than she'd let on. *"Serin, can you hear me?"*

There was no answer. She tried again, but there was only silence.

Okay. Now what? he asked.

"Well...I was hoping the reconstitution would be immediate. Since it's not, I guess you can give it a try."

Once again losing his calm, he sputtered, *Wait! What?*

"Don't shout like that."

Sorry, he winced, somehow feeling his shoulders draw up even with no tangible evidence.

"Just think about both of your bodies. Picture them. Visualize your arms and legs. See them becoming solid enough to walk out of the pool," she ordered.

Okay. His agreement was weak, even to his own non-ears.

Daniel focused on Serin first, because picturing her glorious curves was far easier than visualizing his own body. But nothing happened. He tried himself next. Excruciatingly long, frustrating minutes passed.

It's not working. I don't know what to do, he said, hearing the defeat in his own voice.

Gia sighed, the sound loud even through the water. *"Well, without training, it was a long shot."*

He wanted to throw up his hands—but he didn't have any. *You could have shared that sooner.*

"I didn't want to discourage you," she said, no trace of apology in her tone.

Daniel hugged the Serin-essence tighter to him. *So now what?*

"Now we wait for Serin to recover enough to reform the two of you."

Daniel paused, stomach dipping. *Okay... So what if she doesn't recover? Does that mean we stay like this forever?*

Gia didn't answer. She didn't have to.

24

Loki pushed the fish around in his plate.

"Are you not hungry?" Noomi asked, sitting across from him at the small table.

When it had become apparent that none of the other islanders had spared him a second thought after Daniel disappeared into the healing room, the archivist had opened her home to him, inviting him to share her evening meal.

Her house was the coolest thing he'd ever seen outside of the Seelie Court.

Noomi lived in a seashell. The building was nautilus shaped, a concentric spiraling ring divided into different chambers by walls that didn't fully close. The opening in each was slightly offset to give the deeper parts more privacy while still being completely open.

Square windows let in the ocean breeze, and the walls were a pearlescent pink and silver that reflected the light with a soft iridescence. The main entrance opened in a sitting room and salon, which was followed by an office and then the kitchen. He assumed the innermost part of the curve was the bedroom, but he'd not been invited to see that part...yet.

"I quite like the sushi," he said, admiring the colorful array of fish.

He'd never tasted seafood so fresh or flavorful. The fruit and light leaven bread that accompanied it were equally mouthwatering. The only thing that was missing was a good bottle of wine, so he materialized one. But he pushed it aside without opening it.

"Would you like a corkscrew?"

He cocked his head at her. "Do you have one?"

She shook her head, the neat little braids on her head swinging. "No, but I'm sure I could improvise something."

"That's okay. I just realized I don't feel like drinking. It doesn't seem right while Serin and Daniel are still in danger."

Noomi leaned back in her chair, her face softening in sympathy. "You're in love with her."

Loki felt the confusion cross his features. "Why do you say that?"

The woman smiled. "Because all the unattached males on the island are in love with her. Hell, I'm a little in love with her. Serin is remarkable—strong, smart, and unfailingly kind to those who deserve or need it."

"And a holy terror to those that don't," Loki finished. "And no. I do have a mad crush on her, but I don't love her. Not the way Daniel does, though he'll never admit it. But even though I'm not in love with her, Serin may be my only real friend. We Lokis tend to burn bridges. It's not intentional. It just happens..."

Noomi nodded sagely. "You don't have to worry. She's going to be fine."

She sounded so certain. "How can you know that?" he asked.

"I know her," she said, popping a morsel of something into her mouth and chewing. She swallowed. "I believe she's one of the strongest Waters in history. There are some who come and go—little more than ships in the night. But there are a couple of rare ones. They don't just do their duty, they rise above it, elevating their service to something legendary. I think she is one of those. It's been a privilege to watch her work."

"Have you seen others before?"

Noomi appeared to be very young, mid-twenties at the most, but no one on this island looked their age. She could have been older than him for all he knew.

"No, but I've read and researched all our records on Water talents as part of my work at the Archive." She set down her fork. "This poison is dangerous and very potent, but of all the Elementals, Serin is the one best suited to fighting off its effects."

"Because of what Daniel did? Pushing her to turn into Water?"

Noomi nodded. "It's very dangerous for her to shift while unconscious. But hopefully with him as a focal point, it's only a matter of time before she is able to reconstitute their forms."

"Yes, but..."

She put a hand on his. "You blame yourself, but you are not responsible."

He blinked. "How did you know?"

"You're radiating guilt."

He leaned closer, fascinated. "Are you some sort of empath?"

She shook her head, her eyes lightening to a honey brown. "No, but it is obvious."

"*Oh.*" He scratched his head. As a master of disguise, it should have bothered him that she could read him so effortlessly, but Noomi was a native T'Kaierian. Everybody in this place had magic infused into their blood. This place was like Mecca to Supernaturals.

"Well, that aside, it is totally and completely my fault," he said, sighing.

Noomi was silent, but her eyes widened. She reached over for the bottle of wine, then waved her hand over it. The cork popped out, shooting across the room as if it had been a bottle of champagne and not a fine Koshu.

She poured him a very full serving. "How do you figure that?"

He downed the glass gratefully. After swallowing, he put it down to hold his fingers a little apart. "I came this close to finding the weapons dealer for Serin. Then I got shot, and I had to let Serin take the lead."

"I thought she found the weapon maker," she said after an awkward pause.

"Oh, she did find the lackey who actually made the gun, but not his boss, the one in contact with Puck, the client."

Noomi's angelic face hardened. "Puck is a thief and a murderer." Her sweet voice was filled with venom.

"Among other things," he muttered.

Her delicate nostrils flared. "When he is found, he should be stripped down and beaten in the streets."

Loki blinked, surprised. "I wouldn't have guessed you'd feel so strongly about it."

Still glowering, Noomi dumped out her water glass, then poured herself a glass of wine. "I told you I was the archivist, but I neglected to mention I am the head archivist. All the thefts happened on my watch."

Tears glistened at the corners of her eyes. "I was entrusted with the safety and care of all those artifacts, and I failed. The only reason I haven't been removed from my post is because Gia and the others argued on my behalf. But the truth is that everything that has happened since is all *my* fault. I should have noticed when things first began to go missing. I should have sounded the alarm. Instead, I buried myself in my studies, letting the junior archivists conduct our endless inventory. That is why we didn't discover the thefts for so long...because of my hubris."

Loki absorbed that in silence for a moment before screwing his face up. "No, forget that. It's not my fault, and it's not your fault. Furthermore, I'm tired of being treated like a child forced to sit at the kid's table while the grown-ups make the plans and fight the battles."

He pointed his fork at the tearful archivist. "I had a bead on the gunmaker's boss, the one that brokered the deal with Puck. This guy has some of your artifacts."

Her eyes widened. "Which ones? And why?"

"Puck apparently thought some could be used to enhance the deadliness of those guns."

Noomi shuddered, taking a bracing sip of wine. "I want those artifacts back."

He nodded, pouring himself another glass. The sweet liquid was gone before he could blink, so he poured another. "I think you should get them back."

"*Me*?" It was said in such an incredulous tone, Loki almost laughed.

"Yes!" He waved a hand to encompass over her. "You're plainly a badass witch. Just look at what you did with that cork."

Her expression dampened. "That was nothing. I only study the badass magic spells to write treatises on them. I'm basically a glorified librarian."

Loki realized the bottle was empty so he materialized another one —pre-opened this time. "That's perfect. Librarians are awesome. They know almost everything. If they don't know something, then they know where to find it."

Uncertainty crossed Noomi features, warring with the pink flush of pleasure his words had caused. "Well, I may know defensive spells, but I've never cast them."

He cocked his head at her. "Really?"

She turned left and right as if to see if they were still alone before leaning in conspiratorially. "All right, to be honest, I have tried one or two of them..."

He didn't buy that for a second. "Just one or two?"

She cleared her throat. "Well, perhaps it was more than one or two."

Grinning, he gave her a give-it-up gesture. "Was it more than one or two *dozen*?"

Noomi fiddled with her chopsticks before taking another drink. "Maybe."

Loki grabbed the bottle, sloppily topping up her glass. "So this is perfect. Together, you and I can hunt down the boss and get your artifacts back."

Her alarm was palpable. "I never said I mastered all of those spells. I can only perform a few."

"Combined with my glamour skills, a few is more than enough," he cried, waving his glass around a little too enthusiastically.

Enough wine spilled that he decided they needed another bottle. Several more glasses were consumed, mainly by him, but a few by her—enough she didn't dismiss all of his arguments out of hand.

"I'm telling you we can do this!"

Most of his words were slurred, but Noomi apparently had an excellent ear.

"I don't know," she said. "Alec needs me to finish cataloging all the missing items."

Loki waved that away. "With his freakish vampire speed, he can do that by himself. In fact, he's probably already done. But if you come with me and we get some of those artifacts back, no one can give you anymore shit about losing them."

Noomi's face crumpled, her lip pulling down.

"Not that *you* lost them," he said, backtracking fast enough to get whiplash. "You did your job. It wasn't your fault. This was an inside job. Besides, the guy who did it, Jordan, already paid the price."

She picked up her glass, then drained it with a morose expression. "The Elementals have been so supportive of me since the theft was discovered, but the elders dislike having a vampire here on the island and they *hate* that he is the one fixing my mess."

"Again, it's not your mess—it's Jordan's—but since you insist on taking responsibility, let's do this! We can fix it, or at least some of it."

Noomi gnawed on her bottom lip for a moment before asking, "Why are you so intent on helping? The archive thefts don't have anything to do with you."

"I don't know...I guess I'm tired of being a bit player." Loki popped a big piece of sushi into his mouth. It was so good he shoveled in a few more. "Plus, these guns are bad news all around. They're trying to figure out how to kill lower fae, too. Those are my people."

He leaned back in his seat. "Non-Seelie fae get stepped on all the time—the lower castes are the ones the Court would just as soon spit on than actual acknowledge them as members of the same species. Those are the guys who are going to feel this the most, not the members of the Court. Those assholes are protected by layers and layers of magic, not to mention the soldiers and warriors of the Great Hunt. But the rest of us are cannon-fodder waiting to happen "

Noomi reached for his hand and squeezed it. "I understand. Our history is filled with many stories of the Seelie Court. It is both a wondrous and bloodthirsty place."

Exactly. He was so glad she understood. "I have to do something before the shit hits the fan. It'll still hit the fan anyway, but at least...at least I'll have tried to stop it."

"I didn't think a Loki would have such a strong sense of responsibility," Noomi marveled. She was starting to slur a teeny bit, too.

He pointed at her, realizing her prettiness was making him dizzy. "I don't. This isn't about that. It's bigger than me. It's bigger than you. It's bigger than this damn island."

Noomi scowled. "This island will be here when all other life on earth is rotting in the ground."

She was definitely drunk now, no teeny bit about it.

"Okay, that's a little dark," he said, starting to refill. It was taking too long so he gave up and started swigging straight from the bottle. "But it's cool. You're right. This place is the alpha and omega, and we are going to defend it and get your artifacts back."

Noomi slapped her hand down on the table, lifting her glass up in her other hand in a toast. "You know what? You are right. You and I are going to be a great team. And we're not going to be caught unawares this time. I'm going back to the archives, and I'm going to get a few spell books. We're going to do this!"

"Abso-fucking-lutely we are."

Loki stood up too fast. The room spun, and he promptly fell on his ass.

There was a beat of silence.

"And we're leaving just as soon as we sober up!" he cried.

Cheering, an unsteady Noomi helped him to his feet.

25

Serin could taste the salt in the air, the perfume of the islands many flowers carried on the breeze. There was only one place with this scent. She was home...and against all her expectations, she was still alive.

True, it still felt like her insides had been scraped up with a cheese grater. But the pain wasn't as intense as before. She opened her eyes to transparent white curtains blowing gently in the breeze.

Serin relaxed her hands, smoothing her palms over the sky-blue coverlet of her childhood bed. Relief that she could feel the sensation of the fabric beneath her fingers coursed through her.

"Do you feel better?"

Gia appeared next to her. Her sister's calm expression was a comfort. Serin was out of danger.

She licked her dry lips before rasping out, "I hope you didn't kill Doyle."

Gia poured her a glass of water from the bedside table. "No, but it was a near thing. His partner wasn't happy about the condition I left him in. Fortunately, Romero didn't start complaining until after the healers had seen you and decided you were on the mend."

Serin sat up, leaning against the headboard. "How did they do it? I was dying. I could feel it. I was certain I was beyond their skill."

Serin had been beyond hope. She'd accepted it, but she hadn't been happy about it. *And wasn't that different...*

"They didn't cure you."

Baffled, Serin gestured at herself. "But I feel fine."

Gia nodded. "You are improving. I can feel it. You began to improve as soon as you arrived at the island, but the real turn came when Romero pushed you into your medium. I was able to flush the toxin away then. After you reformed, it was just a matter of time. We just had to let your body repair itself."

Serin absorbed that in silence. Her sister didn't appear as concerned as she should have been.

"It was a single bullet from a handgun. The men at the farmhouse had machine guns capable of leveling that building. If I had been shot with one of those, I don't think I'd be speaking to you now."

Gia's chin firmed. "What about our deflection spells?"

Serin shook her head. "I had one in place at the farmhouse, but it would have protected only me. I had to get Romero out of there...but my charm was active when Doyle shot me. The ingredients to the toxin weren't the only thing coating those bullets. They must have a counter-spell on them, something to neutralize basic deflection spells."

"I was hoping you would say you hadn't had time to cast one," Gia said. "It was a friendly fire after all."

"Doyle wasn't that friendly at first, but he was standing down." She took Gia's hand. "My sister, this is bad."

"Agreed. Someone with a lot of knowledge about us is involved."

"Gia, I know what you're thinking, but Jordan isn't the one behind this. He's gone."

Gia winced. "That doesn't mean he didn't have a hand in this situation."

"I don't see it. Yes, he was a skilled practitioner, but this doesn't mesh with his interests. You know the only spells he cared about were benign. It was all beatification and astral projection and what-ever else sounded like fun to him. His interests weren't dark."

"Maybe not then. But you have a point. He was skilled, but not this skilled. Not in my opinion. It takes a singular mind to combine toxins and spells with human artillery. We need more information."

"Romero had a file with him. Perhaps there is something else of use in it or on the phone his colleagues still have."

"He gave me the report. There was enough there to make out the basics of the toxin, but it was incomplete. Perhaps I can do more with the device than the tech geeks, as Romero refers to them."

Wait. What her sister had said about Daniel belatedly registered in her sluggish mind. "Is... By the Mother, is Romero here on T'Kaieri?"

"Yes."

Holy shit. "You brought him *here*?"

Gia sat on the bed, her ascetic face unreadable, but Serin could see the glint in her eyes. "He is your mate. It was his right. Not that he gave me much of a choice. He was holding you so tightly I had to take you both."

Serin laughed aloud, immediately regretting it as her damaged body shook. They both knew Gia could have knocked Romero flat on his ass with a flick of her little pinky finger. There had been no reason for her to bring him, too. Except for the fact he was Serin's mate...

All the air left her lungs. "Do Dalasini and Caimen know about him?"

One corner of Gia's mouth turned up. "Serin, he wouldn't leave you. He's been staying here at your parents' house."

Oh, by the Mother. "And they know what he is?" Her mind didn't seem to want to accept it.

"That he's human or that he's your mate?" Gia snickered.

Serin weakly smacked Gia on the arm. Logan's snarkiness was rubbing off on their older sister. "Either...both."

"Well, as for being human, they knew right away, of course. I believe Caimen knows all, but Dalasini hasn't seen past the obvious to process the rest. I had to listen to the council lecture me for hours for bringing him here. They finally agreed your recovery was the priority. As for the other thing...I believe Daniel Romero made his claim on you clear, whether he realizes it or not."

"*And*?" How were her parents taking it?

Her new mate—the real one—was human. Her parents came from a long line of practitioners. There had been Elementals in their lineage since the dawn of time. One of the reasons for that was to ensure all the children on the island were as gifted as possible. They did that by finding the most talented male practitioners they could. Matches were made. Power was concentrated. The line lived on.

The island elders didn't call it a selective breeding program. They used gentle euphemisms like 'tradition' and 'matchmaking,' though pretty words didn't change what it was.

Serin's arranged marriage had been inevitable, but her parents had pushed it on her decades too early. She had resented them for it...maybe even hated them a little because of it. Her job had been everything to her. Jordan had been a constant reminder that it would soon end.

Poor Jordan. She'd done her best by him. But that hadn't been enough.

Her bonded had been handsome, talented, and romantic. Jordan was always planning extravagant weekend getaways and dinners. He was constantly buying or making her gifts. And he'd traveled all over the globe, trailing her on her cases, waiting for her at the end of every mission.

Jordan had been everything she could have ever asked for. Who wouldn't love such a man?

Her unhappiness hadn't been his fault. He'd been a devoted partner. In that respect, her parents had done everything they could for her. They had chosen a man who loved her. God knew love wasn't a requirement in these types of arrangements. But being bonded to a man whose love she couldn't return had torn little pieces of her soul.

Serin had thought something was wrong with her. She'd felt like a failure. Over time, she'd convinced herself she was the defective one. And Romero had been out there all that time...

She hadn't been waiting for him. And now that they'd met...

"I don't get to keep Daniel. It's too soon."

Gia's immediately turned down. "I admit the timing is a little suspect for a few reasons. One being you are still in mourning for Jordan."

Serin leaned back on the pillows. "A *little* suspect? First Diana, then Logan. Now Romero turns up. We both know it's not normal."

She met her sister's eyes, reading the deep disquiet there. "Something is happening with Her."

Gia took a bracing breath. "We've known that for a while. The Mother is falling asleep. It's happened before. Things will be uncertain, and there will be more upheaval. Hate and destruction will have a stronger grip on the world. But She will awaken again. We just have to be patient."

"Her slumber shouldn't change anything about us or how we work. She's slept for long periods before, but none of our predecessors met their mates in clusters then."

"There's no reason to panic," Gia said. "If anything, we should be rejoicing. It warms my heart that all of my sisters will know the joy of a true mate. I still treasure the memories of my own."

Tears stung Serin's eyes. "Meeting our mates typically signals the end of our careers. She wouldn't do that right before a period of slumber. That's too much upheaval and strife. Something else is going on."

Gia sighed, turning to study the sea beyond the window. "I know...but whatever it is may not necessarily be bad. Our Mother cares for us."

Swiveling back, Gia took her hand. "We both know things are going to get much worse than this. We'll be beset on all sides—the humans, the Supes, and the ones in between like your Agent Romero. It could be as simple as the Mother wanting to make us happy, or to reward us for our service given the difficult road ahead."

"I hope so. But it doesn't mean Romero and I will be able to make this work. Even if I wasn't in mourning, he doesn't fit in our world. He's a law enforcement officer. He would classify what we do as vigilantism."

Gia's smile was gentle. "I wouldn't discount the agent so quickly. I've spoken to him, answered some of his questions. He has an agile and flexible mind. I could feel the core of his integrity. He's strong, capable, loyal... Men of his caliber aren't thick on the ground in *any* species. We've both been around long enough to know that."

Serin's answering smile was brittle. "I don't understand how you do it. With all that we see and do, how do you hold onto that optimism?"

"I don't always. It depends on what I'm looking at. And right now, all I'm seeing is you. I have good reason to believe our future is in capable hands."

"But I'm at the end of my tenure," Serin whispered. "My century is almost up."

The Earth Elemental rose to her feet. "It's over when you say it's over," she said firmly.

"Gia, you know it doesn't work like that here."

Her sister's hand swept out. "Here is only a place. We are the ones She chose. Fate is ours to make."

Except for thousands of centuries of tradition standing in my way. "Right."

"I'm going to go see if your agent needs rescuing."

"He's staying with my parents. Of course he needs rescuing."

DANIEL PACED AROUND THE LIVING ROOM, HOPPING OVER THE STREAM running through the middle of the living room. This place was fucking amazing. The delicate rounded walls and tropical light were unreal, like something out of a magazine. But despite the warm sun, there was a distinct chill in the air. It was as if the heart of this place was ice.

He stopped in front of yet another seascape, checking out Dalasini from the corner of his eye. Like her daughter, she was stunning, ethereal and elegant. But unlike Serin, the older woman was a bit frigid. Caimen was less brittle than his wife, but he also had the same air of rigid control.

These people must have been a barrel of laughs to grow up with. It explained why Serin rarely smiled.

She smiles at you. Sometimes.

"Did you paint all of these?" he asked, wishing Caimen were still here, but Serin's father had been called away on council business.

Dalasini nodded curtly, saying nothing. *As usual.*

"You're very talented."

"I'm glad you like them," she said tightly.

"I didn't say I liked them."

Dalasini's tone dropped to arctic levels. "I see."

"Nothing personal." He waved at the paintings. "It's just that are a lot of them. All the sea. So many pictures of the sea…"

And not a single family portrait. No pictures of her or her husband. None of Serin. Not even a baby picture.

When he turned back, Dalasini was staring daggers at him. That was all right, though. There would be no pretenses between them. He'd gotten the picture the moment they'd met. A human wasn't good enough for her daughter.

It's like 'Who's Coming to Dinner,' magic edition.

"These are not pictures of the sea," Dalasini corrected. "Water talent has run in our bloodline for countless generations. All the pictures in this room are of Serin in her other form."

Daniel spun on his heel to study the paintings again before focusing back on the woman. "They are?"

His potential mother-in-law—*magic-in-law?*—widened her eyes as if it should have been obvious. "My daughter *is* Water. Of all the candidates, *she* was chosen, anointed by the Mother herself. These pictures are merely snapshots of Serin's other aspect. But this is not something I expect a mere human to understand."

Stifling a laugh, he resumed pacing the room. "Oh, I think I understand a little. Gia was kind enough to explain some of how this works. But forgive me for saying I don't really think you captured Serin's essence," he added, waving a hand toward the monotonous pictures.

"As I said, I wouldn't expect you to understand." She pointed to the nearest seascape. "This is my daughter's true face."

Daniel rocked back on his heels. "It looks like the ocean because it is the ocean. It's not a picture of your daughter."

Serin had a nose and ears and much cooler hair.

"Yes, it is," Dalasini said from behind gritted teeth.

"Does *she* know that?"

The woman appeared momentarily taken aback. "Obviously."

A little snort escaped. She wasn't sure anymore. He could tell. "Something tells me you shouldn't put money on that," he said, continuing his circuit.

Another step and he plowed into Gia, who'd popped up out of nowhere. Daniel rebounded, catching himself before he fell over.

"Damn, woman. It's like running into a boulder."

"That's the idea," the Earth Elemental said with that deceptively benign expression. "Serin is awake now."

"Good," he said, sighing in relief.

He started for Serin's room when Gia caught his arm. "I think Dalasini should see her first."

"Oh, yeah, of course." Daniel nodded agreeably even though he wanted to protest, watching the woman sweep out the room.

How could a mother be so... What was the word he was searching for? *Clueless? Disconnected?*

Gia was amused. "You don't have to be concerned. Dalasini is a caring mother."

He glanced at the endlessly empty seascapes. "Yeah," he said, drawing out the single word into two. "Of course she is..."

26

"You're recovering faster now. The healers say it was the Mother, intervening on your behalf."

Despite the traces of satisfaction in her tone, Serin could tell Dalasini was rattled.

It's Daniel. Serin would have bet anything. Romero certainly had a way about him.

Serin studied her mother out of the corner of her eye. "I hope our houseguest isn't giving you too much trouble."

Dalasini's mouth tightened. "That...man...seems to think he has a claim on you. It's ridiculous. I don't understand what possessed Gia to bring him here."

"He does have a claim. I love him. Unfortunately...for his sake."

It was the truth, one she couldn't hide from her mother and father. Daniel, on the other hand, would stay in the dark until she was damn good and ready to say otherwise.

Her mother gasped. "How can you say that? Jordan was your mate. You're still in mourning for him."

Serin turned to the window, her eyes fixed on the sea. "I do mourn him. He was everything I could have asked for, and certainly more than most of my predecessors had. But he wasn't the one the Mother intended for me. She had someone far different in mind."

Dalasini shook her head. "I don't believe that. You are wrong. The Mother is silent. You don't know what She intended."

"My other sisters knew when they'd met their mates. It may have taken Diana a bit longer to recognize Alec for what he was, but she came around just as I have." But again, knowing what Daniel was meant nothing. Fated mates didn't equal happily ever after, not in their world.

"That simply isn't possible." Dalasini was shaken, but adamant.

"I'm afraid it is."

"But Jordan—"

Serin held up her hand. "Jordan was...an obligation. A burden. Now that he's gone, I'm free." She hated to put it so bluntly, but she had to make her mother understand.

Tears welled in her mother's eyes. "But...but I thought you were happy. It's the only thing we wanted."

Serin shook her head. "That isn't why."

"What?"

"I said that wasn't why you wanted to bond me to Jordan. Not really." She studied her mother's face, saw the similarities to herself there.

Serin chose her next words with care. "I used to believe you were determined to make sure I had a child, so that our bloodline would continue and we would again be chosen to serve Her. It used to hurt me. You see, I believed you had no faith in me to survive— that you thought I would be one of those Elementals who died early in service. You and Father both. I thought you were nervous I wouldn't reproduce. I often asked myself why you didn't have another child."

She cocked her head, reading the truth in her mother's shuttered expression. "I'm close, but there's more, isn't there?"

Dalasini's jaw clenched. Tears glowed like diamonds in her eyes. She pointed at the door, in the direction of the living room. "That *human* had the gall to imply that I don't know you—that I don't truly love you. But I never dreamed you would believe the same thing."

"Of course you love me." Serin released a breath. "I didn't mean that you didn't. But why did you show it *this* way—why insist on bonding me off before the century mark of my service was even over? I never understood what your hurry was."

Dalasini's hands shook as she brushed a stray hair back from her face. When she spoke, her words were halting and strained. "I was honored when you were chosen. But I was terrified, too, and not just because of the danger you would face." Discreetly, her mother wiped under her eye.

Serin was too tired for evasion. "What aren't you telling me?"

There was a long silence. "Marina," Dalasini whispered. "I never told you about Marina."

Serin's brow wrinkled in confusion. "Who is Marina?"

"She was my sister. And she was chosen, too." The tears were coursing unchecked down Dalasini's cheeks now.

"And she died before I was born?" Serin had been told her mother was an only child. Marina wasn't recorded in the archives.

Unless the records are hidden. But if that was true, Gia must have known. Why hadn't she told her?

"Marina served before you were born and only very briefly." Her mother's expression was remote, desolate. "She was older than I— stronger, brighter. Truly gifted among a community full of blessed people. We knew she would be chosen long before she was of age. It was inevitable. Marina was everything I wanted to be. I worshipped her and resented her a little, too, the way younger siblings do sometimes."

Serin reached for her mother's hand, feeling the pain coming from the other woman.

"She didn't die in battle." Their fallen were honored. Everyone knew their names. An Elemental who died in battle was revered.

"No. She...lasted a little over a year."

"I don't understand." Marina hadn't gotten sick and died. That didn't happen to an Elemental in service.

"She...returned to the sea," her mother said in a choked whisper.

Oh. Of course.

There was a saying on the island. The people of T'Kaieri were of the sea. When someone returned to the sea, it meant they had died. But to say that about a Water Elemental was meant in a literal way.

"My sister heard the siren's call of the ocean," Dalasini continued. "She tried to ignore it, but she couldn't. It ended up consuming her. When you were chosen, I wanted to stop it. But I couldn't. After all, it was a great honor. Plus, you chose to serve of your own free will. But I worried each day that you would give yourself up to the ocean and never return. When we suggested you bond with Jordan, it was to give you an anchor, something to hold onto. I wanted to make sure you had a reason to return to the world every day."

Her mother covered her face with her hands.

Serin sighed, but she couldn't soften this. Her mother had to know the truth. "You do realize it had the opposite effect, right?"

Dalasini sobbed. "I didn't until now."

Serin pulled her mother's hands away from her face, keeping hold of one and rubbing the back of it soothingly, but she still didn't understand, not all of it. "I served more than eighty years without incident. Why pressure me to bond with Jordan after all that time?"

"The elders never speak of the Water Elementals who gave up, but our history is long. My sister went early in her service, but the call of the sea gets louder over time. Often those Waters who choose the sea do it *after* their century of service."

"*Ah.*" Serin hadn't realized. It was strongly suggested that all the island's candidates read their predecessors histories, but most of the records stopped when their service ended. If there was more, it wasn't custom for the archivists to add it to their reading list.

"Do you understand now?"

Serin took a deep breath, dislodging a bit of weight she'd been carrying on her shoulders for years. She squeezed Dalasini's hand. "I do."

"But do you forgive me? For pressuring you to bond?"

Serin wasn't certain, but she nodded anyway. "I've always known you had my best interests at heart. Never doubt that."

Her mother rose, still shaky. "Good. I...uh...I will speak to your father about Daniel. He will learn to accept him."

A corner of Serin's lips turned up. "Will you?"

Dalasini's mouth opened and closed. "He's what I always wanted for you."

Her mother didn't mean a human mate. She thought Serin had found her anchor.

Dalasini left after promising to make Serin's favorite meal for dinner that night.

Once the door closed behind her, Serin turned back to the window. "Did you catch all that?"

Romero stepped into view. He'd been standing out there leaning against the wall for some time. "You were holding back. What is it you didn't you tell her?"

Serin leaned forward, staring at his handsome human face. How odd that the Mother would decide this was the man for her. "The call of the sea, the one that whispers in your ear, beckoning you to come..."

"Yeah, that one. I want to know more about it."

He was so fierce Serin assumed he'd heard the call, too, but that didn't surprise her somehow. Nothing about Romero would shock her at this point.

"It doesn't get louder as time goes on," she said after a pause. "It's there from day one, as loud and as clear as you are speaking now."

His dark face paled. "Holy shit."

She shrugged. "Do you know that Irish expression?"

"There are lots of Irish expressions." Daniel's voice was flat. "Which one do you mean?"

Serin put her knees up, wrapping her arms around them. "A body can get used to anything—even hanging."

———

Romero stopped, spinning around at the top of the bluffs in wonder. The jagged rock line above the ocean gave him a spectacular view of the beach and ocean on one side and the island temple on the other. In the center was the mountain, a dormant volcano.

Was that music? It almost sounded like the wind was playing faintly on a set of pipes. *That's so weird. I am Julie fucking Andrews spinning like a fool on a mountaintop.*

It was amazing but strange. Everything about this place was strange in a wondrous and jaw-dropping kind of way. There were plants everywhere, along with lichen and moss, and more mushrooms than he'd ever seen outside of a grocery store.

The air was rich with the scent of flowers, the breeze cooling. Serin had told him everything that grew on the island was edible or medicinal. Even the gorgeous blooms were one or the other. Nothing was ornamental. The water that ran down from Mount Siba was the most delicious thing he'd ever drunk. The island boasted numerous springs and hidden pools, even a lagoon on the east side. The ocean around them was so clear sharks and seals could be spotted miles away from shore. He'd even seen a few whales.

The entire island had an air of unreality. It was as if he'd wandered onto a holodeck. He'd been exploring for a few hours, ever since the healers had shooed him out of Serin's room that morning.

"This place is fucking incredible," he said aloud after a moment. There wasn't a soul in sight, but he knew he wasn't alone.

"You're getting very good at that."

He pivoted to see Gia standing a few feet away. "You can't have hiked all the way up this path without me hearing you," he said, checking around his feet in case he was about to step into a hole.

"No." Gia was amused. "I didn't come up the path. But you can relax; I closed it."

"Yeah, I'm just surprised at how quietly you can do that."

He hadn't caught her coming out of the ground when she'd come to Serin in that alley because he'd been fixed on Serin and the bullet hole in her stomach. The rest had happened like a movie being played on fast forward. He'd turned to see Gia's arm grabbing Ray. His partner had flown through the air and then there had been that unvoiced ultimatum.

"I'm not leaving her," he yelled at Gia, clutching Serin's limp body to him. Loki had come up behind him, grasping his shoulders in silent support.

Gia had stared at him, her eyes narrowed, and then she'd simply given him a short nod. Before he'd known it, the ground was closing over his head. If it made a sound, he'd missed it, but again, he'd been cradling a bleeding Serin in his arms. Gia had been holding on to them all.

And I thought traveling via drain pipe had been freaky. It didn't compare to racing through the soil like a tremor in the earth's crust. He didn't ever want to do that again. It was too much like being buried alive.

"I need the phone Serin confiscated from the arms dealer," Gia said.

He should have guessed she hadn't come up here to chat. "Oh, uh, sorry. I don't have it on me. Serin said your magic might be able to get more from the damaged memory card."

Gia cocked her head. "You sound skeptical, Agent Romero."

"No," he assured her. "Not anymore. Not after what I've seen. I can have it sent somewhere to be picked up, but I think I'm out of range here."

He pulled out his work phone to show it to her. It had no bars.

"There are no cell towers on T'Kaieri," Gia replied, reaching for the phone. She took it out of his hand before waving her fingers over it. "But that doesn't mean you can't reach your people."

Golden sunlight lit the underside of her palm. She touched the cover of the phone, transferring a bit of sparkle. Then she held it out to him.

He hesitated, wondering if the lithium battery could handle magic without exploding.

"It's quite safe. I have a way with electronics."

He nodded. "I believe Loki mentioned that. I'll tell the office I'm having a specialist examine it. I should also text my partner, make an excuse for what happened."

"And to explain where you went," she added dryly.

"Yeah," Daniel muttered, racking his brain for a suitable lie for his superiors. Disappearing on a Friday night had given him a little leeway, but that was swiftly running out. He took the phone, noting with surprise it was cool to the touch. He was about to call the lab tech when Gia put a hand over his.

"Tell them a courier will pick it up. Logan can have it here in a couple of hours."

Nodding, he dialed. An automated message came up. Grimacing, he left a voicemail.

"They're just screening," he explained as he hung up. "If you can pull out more of the recipe, can you help Serin heal faster?"

"Unlikely. She's doing as well as any of us can expect at this point. No, I'm searching for something else."

"Shit." Shaking his head at his stupidity, he pulled out the phone again. "I forgot something. The recipe wasn't from a text or an email. There was a recording."

He dug through the files app. "Our people couldn't decipher anything of significance in the background, but maybe there's something your magic ears can pick up."

Gia wrinkled her nose. "I'm not a werewolf, but I'll do my best."

Daniel pressed play. The man's voice began, droning slightly, listing herbs and chemicals like someone dictating a shopping list. It cut off before it was complete. Daniel was about to play the next one when Gia snatched the phone away. One look at her face made him hurriedly step back.

The fires of hell lit her eyes. *No, not hell.* It was lava and molten rocks, like the brutal burning light at the core of the world.

"What is it?" Daniel was a seasoned investigator. He knew when someone had realized a person they trusted had screwed them over. He'd seen that expression dozens of times. "You know the voice, don't you? Who is it?"

The fire banked higher. "It belongs to a dead man. The words, however, are someone else's." She slapped the phone back in his hand. "Don't play that for anyone but Serin. I have to go."

Suddenly, the ground opened like quicksand beneath her. Daniel scrambled back as the hole gaped wide. He landed on his ass. Worried the ground would solidify around his legs before he could get them out, he skittered back from the pit like a crab.

Gia was gone before he could get back on his feet.

27

S erin picked her way through the archive sub-basement. There was no reason to be here, but her curiosity had gotten the best of her.

Noomi, the head archivist, was unavailable, but her assistant Ksenia cracked the moment Serin asked for Marina's records. The thin volume was on its own pedestal. Even though the elders and her family never mentioned her by name, the archivists could always be counted on to find a place of honor for one of their own.

She flipped through the book, reading the brief notes on her aunt's different missions. Her short tenure had been spectacular. *So much promise...*But this life wasn't for everyone.

Serin bit her lip, tears stinging her eyes for a woman she never met but should have known. She forced her attention back to the page, intent on reading every account before meeting Daniel and her parents for dinner.

That was an event she was more than happy to put off.

"Serin."

Romero was coming down the aisle, deftly hopping over the books the archivists had left stacked on the floor. His hair was wind-blown, and he was wearing a pair of jeans that would make a nun take a second look.

Her heart leapt at the sight of him.

Stop that, she scolded herself. No matter what Gia said, this Romero situation was not cut and dried. Maybe if she had met him ten years from now when she was scheduled to give up her position...

A snapshot of his face when she'd been shot flitted through her mind as he stopped in front of her. He cared. She didn't want him to, but there it was, an unasked-for gift. This was going to end badly once he saw her for what she truly was—a killer.

The Mother had a lot to answer for.

"I drowned the Reaper. You know that, right?"

Daniel stopped short. "I, um, yeah. I guess I knew that."

She cleared her throat. "I didn't mean to blurt it aloud like that. But I just wanted to be clear about what I do. We are not the same."

His expression blanked. "I never said we were the same."

Her hands went up. The air grew heavier despite the many anti-humidity spells in place to protect the books and scrolls. "You have implied that our jobs are similar. Nothing could be further from the truth. On my cases, the suspect has already been judged."

"By a jury?"

"By the Mother and the universe."

He cleared his throat. "Let me guess. This is the part where you tell me you're the executioner. After which you inform me that I won't be able to handle it because I represent law and order as a DEA agent?"

"In a nutshell...yes"

"Believe it or not, I pieced together the details of what you do a long time ago. And I actually have a lot to say about it and us, but I'm afraid we don't have time."

He pulled out his phone, putting his hand on her shoulder to offer some form of comfort. Judging from Gia's reaction, this was going to be a shock. Opening the phone to the right file, he pressed play.

Serin was quiet, her creased forehead her only outward sign of emotion.

"I was expecting a bigger reaction."

Serin wrapped her arms around herself, staring into the middle distance with remote eyes. He nudged her, and she blinked.

"It's nothing earth-shattering," she murmured.

"Really? Because Gia literally shattered the earth when she heard it, then disappeared right before telling me to play it only for you."

Serin nodded absently.

"It's your ex, isn't it? The one who died." He'd heard bits and pieces, but he hadn't wanted to press Serin for the whole story. He assumed she'd tell him in her own time.

Well, time had just run out.

She picked up the book she'd been reading, fingering the embossed leather cover, but he couldn't make out the words because it was written in an unfamiliar language.

"Jordan betrayed us," she said after a long pause. "We assume he was being blackmailed. He stole from this archive and left, then he took his own life."

"*Fuck*," Daniel muttered. That was some heavy shit. He'd known the man was dead, but he'd assumed he'd been killed in some sort of long-ago Supernatural battle or something. "When did this all happen?"

"We buried him a few weeks before I met you the second time."

His stomach dropped a few inches. When he'd started hunting her, the man had still been alive. "That recently?"

Swallowing, she nodded. "I'm not sure why Gia was so worked up. We know that Jordan was guilty now. He apologized in his suicide note."

Christ. This was getting worse and worse. Daniel flipped the recording on again. "It sounds as if he's reading a shopping list. Is there anything in the background your magic ears can pick up?"

Serin touched her ears self-consciously. "I don't hear anything of significance."

Frowning, he took the phone back. It didn't sound like Jordan had been under duress. If anything, the well-modulated voice sounded bored, as if he were performing a chore.

Daniel flipped back to the electronic copy of Sandy's report. He zoomed on the text listing the second recording, the one that had been complete but garbled. The time stamp the message was received was noted before the message, but there was another at the end.

"That's it." He held up the phone. After squinting at the screen, she shrugged. "Look at the timestamps on the audio file."

"What about it?"

"*Them*, what about them." He pointed to the one at the bottom. "The creation date of the recording is here, too, which means it was sent as an audio file they downloaded.

"Yes, and?"

"The creation date was three days *after* our second meeting. Jordan recorded this *after* you buried him."

DANIEL HEAVED ANOTHER SHOVEL OF DIRT OUT OF THE SQUARE HOLE.

"Can you explain why I'm digging up the grave when you're the one with magic powers?"

Serin was pacing like a caged animal at the graveside, squeezing her fist reflexively. "Mainly because you grabbed the only shovel and started digging."

She put something in her pocket before reaching out. "Give it here and I'll finish."

Regarding her thoughtfully, he used the shovel handle as a prop. "Why don't you just flood the hole and bring it to the surface?"

"Because we don't want to alert everyone on the island. This is the home of most of the world's Water talents. My mother is only one of them. Half the elders and their families would be able to sense the movement of that much water moving outside the island's normal rhythm."

She continued to hold out her hand. Reluctantly, he handed the shovel over. With no hesitation, she hopped into the hole and took over.

He climbed out, marveling at her speed and strength. "So why is there only one shovel in the village?"

"We don't farm, not as you know it. The island's food crops don't require that much intervention. We scatter seeds, and they simply grow unaided."

Daniel thought about the neat clusters of maize and tomato plants he'd passed earlier. It didn't bear the hallmarks of mechanical plantation. Nothing square, no neat rows. Nevertheless, there had appeared to be some organization—spirals, circles, and ovals, irregular shapes that made the most of the open space and varied terrain. It was crazy to think they could just drop seeds and those patterns would appear.

He'd never been religious. The grandmother who raised him had been Catholic, but he'd only done lip service by begrudgingly attending service on Sundays. Once she passed away, he'd stopped going. Later, he'd seen too much ugliness in his chosen career to believe in the God the priests had lectured about from their pulpits. But if he had seen this island back then, he would have fallen to his knees in worship.

No wonder the elders spent half of every day at the temple.

"Daniel."

Giving himself a little shake, he turned back to find Serin staring at him, holding out the shovel expectantly. He whistled. In his short minute of introspection, she'd uncovered a rectangular stone slab.

"Is he in a bloody sarcophagus?"

"His uncle chose a plain wooden box, but he requested the stone be overlaid to protect it from the seismic activity of the island. The land shifts more than you would think."

She leaned down and pried the slab up on one end, lifting it up and out as if it were a painted Styrofoam movie prop.

He peered down at the coffin. The lid was roughly carved of one piece of thick wood. Kneeling, Serin touched the lid.

"Who made the coffin?"

"The island's carpenters. This is made of Ash. It's one of the trees with magical properties. It can absorb or repel spells depending on the preparation. This has been charmed to repel them."

He hopped down to join her. "I'll do this. You get up."

Serin didn't move, a mutinous expression on her beautiful face. Daniel would be damned if he let her open the box, though. After a brief standoff, she relented and climbed out of the hole, standing at the edge.

Daniel leaned down and tried the lid, but it held fast. He reached for the shovel lying at the edge of the grave, then wedged the cutting edge just under the lid. It took a minute, but he managed to pry it open, breaking the seal with a hiss.

He tossed the shovel aside and yanked on the lid, revealing a perfectly preserved body. "I thought it was going to be empty."

The man lying in state was wearing an intricately embroidered robe. He was perfect—his face, his hair, the hands neatly folded on his chest. He reminded Daniel of a Hollywood bit player, the talentless hacks so pretty they could skate by on looks alone.

"Why doesn't he seem dead?" Even if he'd been embalmed, there should have been a noticeable amount of decay by now.

This man, who resembled a male model with his thick dark hair and chiseled features, appeared as if he'd just laid down for a nap. Even his cheeks, which were much lighter in color than Daniel's own dusky skin, had a natural pink flush.

He turned to Serin, uncertain what to do next. She stared down at the body.

"It can't have been empty," she explained, her eyes fixed to the man's face. "My parents were here when John brought the body from

Jordan's family home. The elders said prayers over his corpse in the temple."

"Is that why he looks so...alive?"

"No. Our prayers are for a speedy journey to the afterlife. Since we don't traditionally bury bodies, we left the remaining burial rituals to John, his uncle and only family member."

Daniel absorbed that for a moment, a little chill trickling down his spine as he remembered his least favorite stories from church.

"When I was little, the priests taught us about the saints—there is a whole list of them whose bodies supposedly didn't decay. He called them the Incorruptibles," he said, unable to tear his eyes away from the unnaturally pristine corpse.

Serin huffed out what almost sounded like a laugh. "Jordan isn't a saint by any definition."

O-kay. "Where is his home?"

"I believe it's in upstate New York."

Daniel glanced up. "You believe?"

"I never visited. He wanted to show it to me just after we bonded, but I had a very big case fall into my lap. After I was done, I asked to go, but he had changed his mind. He decided he would rather join me on my next case. That's when he began to travel with me."

Daniel murmured something unintelligible, wondering if he should apologize for digging up her ex-husband. What the hell was the protocol here?

Serin gracefully slid down next to him. She balanced her feet on the edge of the coffin, kneeling close to the face.

"Um, Serin..." He blinked, grabbing his shirtfront.

Now that she was next to him, he could feel her emotions like a wave of cold. It wasn't his imagination. She was literally cold, the air around her crystalizing like a winter's night.

I should never have started this. He was an asshole. Yes, digging her ex up had been her idea, but Daniel should have stopped her. He would have if he'd known this was going to happen. Daniel put his hand on her shoulder, intending to nudge her.

It was a mistake. The biting cold swept up his arm. Flinching, he snatched his hand back, ready to argue with her. They had to close the box. Sure the corpse looked weird, but it might be because the guy's uncle had cast some weird preservation spell.

Suddenly, Serin leaned forward and put both her hands on the corpse's face. A hazy ripple of fog passed over it. When she let go, the fog dissolved, revealing a face that was completely different from the one they'd first uncovered.

Daniel staggered, nearly falling over on the body. "Fucking hell. It's not him."

Serin glanced at him over her shoulder. Her eyes could have frozen hell. "No, it's not."

"Uh...do you recognize this guy?"

She shook her head, raising her fingers and rubbing them together. "It's a spell, one of the most sophisticated I've ever seen—something that combines stasis and a glamour."

"A glamour like Loki does?" Daniel asked. He peered around, half-expecting to see the fae trickster coming down the hill.

"Fae glamours are unique to their species. They fade when the body dies. And this person is definitely dead. The question is, did Jordan kill him and leave the body for John to find or did John deceive us, too?"

Having a mystery to solve made Daniel feel better. "I don't know, but we can figure it out. Let's start by finding out who this guy is."

Daniel held up the phone, then snapped a few flash pictures of the man's face, but after the first one, a strange shadow crept over it. Sensing something off, he slowly lifted his eyes to see what was obscuring the moonlight when Serin grabbed his arm.

"Get up!"

Together, they scrambled out of the grave as tendrils of black broke through the body like a hundred tentacles reaching out for them.

28

The counter-spell wasn't working. Serin grabbed one of the tendrils trying to climb her leg like a snake. Her skin sizzled as if it were coated in acid. Reflexively, she let go, but the damn thing dragged her back into the grave, wrapping around her so tightly it cut off her circulation.

With a wrench, she peeled it off, starting another spell at the same time. It had no effect. Instead, more tentacles wrapped around her legs and waist, holding her fast in the hole.

Serin let go, shifting to her water form to jump out of the hellish pit. She reformed at the edge, shouting, "Get Diana! She's with Alec in the archive."

She pushed Daniel as the tendrils lashed out of the hole, trying to grab him as well. Despite the burn, she grasped the wiggling tentacles. Daniel hesitated, leaning down as if to grab it.

"No! You can't touch it. It'll kill you. Go *now*."

With one last tortured glance back, he turned and ran in the direction of the archives.

Serin shifted again, fighting the tendrils back into the grave while muttering counter-spell after counter-spell. Nothing worked. The best she could do was contain them and hope the island's inherent magic would help.

Smoke began to rise from the grave as the writhing mass grew exponentially, burning through the wooden box with a roar. It sounded like an animal or the monster of a science fiction horror movie that had escaped the confines of the screen. Whenever it touched the soil, its acid burned, eating the life inside.

The curse was laying waste to the earth itself, killing millions of microorganisms and nutrients with every squirm and smack.

Serin turned her eyes inward, looking past the writhing mass underneath it. She gasped, fear and dread overriding her control. Sweat broke out over her skin as she traced the path of the tendrils down—its path marked by the death of the bacterial and fungal flora that made the soil of the island so plentiful and rich.

The mass was burrowing deeper, the toxic feelers growing as they lashed out. They had buried Jordan at the heart of the island. From here, it could radiate out, spreading to every end of the sacred landmass.

Breaking the glamour spell had triggered it. Jordan hadn't killed himself. It had been a trap the whole time.

"Serin!" Diana was running down the hill with Alec at her heels. Daniel was some distance behind them, followed by other islanders she couldn't identify.

Serin reformed, snatching up the shovel and swinging it at a flapping tentacle. "The body was cursed. We have to burn it."

She lifted her hand, muttering the spell that would allow her to borrow some of her sister's ability.

As a senior Elemental, Serin could borrow the other Elementals' talents to varying degrees. Fire and Air were relatively easy. To some degree, she could shift the Earth as well, although her control over the latter wasn't as precise.

The ability to wield Fire was only strengthened in Diana's presence. Serin ignited her right hand.

The oily, acidic tendril reared back as if it could sense the flames.

She threw it down, hitting the tentacle. The pop and sizzle were faint. The smell of burning oil and tar confirmed she hit it, but there was no measurable damage.

A much-larger blast of fire joined hers. Diana was there, directing her flames at the monstrous tentacles.

The smoke was different now. It stung Serin's eyes. She called a little of Logan's power, drawing on her sister's mastery of the winds to blow the poisonous fumes out to sea.

The blackened mass in the pit was smaller now, but its size was deceptive.

"*No, damn it.* The curse is burrowing deeper," she called to Diana.

She could feel the moisture wicking away as the soil under her feet died.

The spell had a life of its own. It behaved like a primitive animal, shying away from the dangerous fire and racing under the surface like fungal hypha on steroids.

Diana cast her magic deeper, trying to burn it from under the ground, but this was T'Kaieri. She couldn't make her fire talent work under the soil surface. There wasn't enough oxygen there to feed the flames.

Her sister broke off, her face white as a sheet. "I can't follow it."

"I know," Serin breathed in a low voice.

"Can you redirect the lava from under the volcano?"

Serin spun around to see Alec helping Daniel to his feet. Their efforts were destabilizing the ground around them.

"I don't think so, not without breaking up the island."

She and Diana stared at each other. Images of Pompeii as it fell flitted behind Serin's eyes. *This is not the myth of Atlantis brought to life.* That was not how it was going to end.

Serin shook her head violently. "This is on me. I'll use my power to collect it, drag it out into the open." She hesitated.

Diana grabbed her hand. "What is it?"

Serin took a shaky break. "It's going so fast. The longest tendrils are only a few miles from the beach. I don't know what will happen if they reach the island's borders."

Something told her the spell wouldn't end there. Ice formed in her gut as her mind rapidly calculated possibilities.

"I need the ocean." She turned to the men and the rapidly gathering crowd. "I have to flood this part of the island. Go find the infirm and your young. Take them to the high ground at the bluffs. I will do my best to keep the water away from your homes, but I may not be able to. Go now!"

Alec pulled at Daniel, dragging him away. Behind them, the crowd dispersed with shouts.

Her ears were filled with snatches of prayers. The islanders were begging the Mother for mercy. But help wouldn't come from their goddess. That was why Serin was here.

She extended her arms out in supplication, pictured the beach, and called the rolling waves.

All was silent save for a faint crashing sound. Moments later, the water burst into view on her right, running down into the valley, a furious flash food. The mass and volume forced its way, carving a deep path for itself. But this was more like a raw wound. T'Kaieri would bear the scar for centuries or more. *If* it survived.

Diana became distinctly more nervous as the water rushed down around them. To the untrained eye, it was an undisciplined and uncontrolled flood. Serin relaxed as it splashed down, leaving her in a circle of dry land.

Her head was already pounding. This was nothing like diverting a river or manipulating a pool of water. Even calling down a storm was easier than this. "I'm going to dig it out. Be ready to call your hottest fire."

She let go, joining the torrent of water lapping at her feet. For a moment, it was glorious. She could feel the ocean's joy as they joined as one. It bubbled and frothed in celebration, the way it always did when she let it consume her.

This was the feeling Marina felt when she let go to become one with the sea. The echoes of Serin's long-departed sisters could be heard in the roar.

Warmth touched her as the water splashed around Diana's feet. It sizzled, which told her that her sister was heating up, getting ready.

Serin stopped hesitating. She let the ocean water flood into the open grave, following it down like a speeding train.

Her body seeped into the soil, letting her follow the path of death and destruction. Her heart ached at the damage done to life of the island.

The beast of a spell reacted to her presence. It shed something like a skin, releasing a foul sludge as if it were melting, polluting the water. She could feel its noxious will, a primitive intelligence, trying to wrestle control. It wanted to take over the water—to use it to spread the poison farther and faster.

But she was here, in the flow. Serin threw herself at it, sending her water out in jets, chasing the tendrils throughout the soil. She surrounded the tentacles one by one, but her magic couldn't force them back.

Drowning them wouldn't work. She had to force them back another way. A movie image flitted through her mind—of Ursula the Sea Witch getting impaled by a ship's mast. She'd watched the movie once at Logan's insistence. Both had marveled at how poorly Disney had captured the ocean and its inhabitants. But it gave her an idea.

The whirlpool.

Serin stretched out with her mind, focusing on the end of each tendril. She swirled the water, directing the flow in a circle over and over again until she'd formed thousands and thousands of vortexes, all spinning madly.

The tendrils were caught in the multiple maelstroms, their poison concentrated in the center. Desperate now, she threw out lash after lash of water, sending it after every toxic thread.

Controlling this much water at this level taxed her control. Serin's mind was stretching thin, her very essence at threat. She wasn't meant to act at on a region this large. With each rivulet of water she was forced to cast out, the concentration of will and magic that held her together weakened.

This was how her aunt had gone. Marina had done it willingly. Serin was being torn apart by the spell's speed.

All around her, the island was dying. She could feel the evil burning through the ground and then a void, a little vacuum where life should have existed.

The soil was this island's lifeblood. It was the T'Kaierian's connection to the Mother, and it was being severed.

Serin. The voice called her, its distinctive timbre alien to her in this form. It wasn't the Mother. It was Daniel. He was yelling at her, tone demanding. *Serin, come back.*

Oh. Of course. He could feel her unraveling. She refocused on his voice, the sound like a light at the end of the tunnel. Another joined it. Diana was yelling at her now, too.

Her mother's voice joined the chorus. Then her father's. Cousins, friends, and neighbors came together. Their voices rose as one, cresting until it was all Serin could hear, a wall of sound and song that encouraged and fortified.

The little cracks in her will stopped widening as the prayers wrapped around her. Bolstered, she redoubled her efforts, drawing the whirlpools in, churning out a hole of mud and water. It felt like hours but must have been minutes until she was able to drag the writhing mass out, forcibly yanking it out of the ground with the last of her strength.

Somehow, she managed to find her body within her dying energy. She reformed her hands, driving the mass of water into a sphere. The bottom rested on the surface of the ground right next to the grave.

Serin and Diana were surrounded by a large group of islanders. Some of the elders, her parents, and many others. Their youngest and infirm were out of sight, but the able-bodied of their population had disobeyed her. Everyone with talent was there. Their hands were raised as if joined in prayer, but they weren't chanting to the Mother. They were casting a spell of fortitude.

It was aimed at her...and it was their wills holding her together.

Diana put her hands on Serin's shoulder, silently imparting some of her strength. Serin coughed, remembering to breathe again. "You have to burn it!"

A bewildered expression crossed her sister's face. "How? I can't burn water."

"In the center," Serin ground out, her head threatening to split open despite the islanders' efforts to help. "I have to separate the molecules. Water won't burn, but hydrogen will."

"What?" Diana's mouth dropped open. "Can you do that?"

No. "I can try."

Diana's milky-white skin turned even paler. "But...but won't that be like an H-bomb?"

"No, that's fusion," Serin corrected. "Think more like the Hindenberg. But you have to be very careful. You must control the blast from beginning to end or you'll destroy the island."

"*Fuck,*" Diana swore before stepping to the right. Alec flashed to her side. He took hold of her waist, leaving his mate's hands free so she could work.

Daniel came up on Serin's left. He pressed against her side, his arm wrapping across her back as if he could physically hold her together.

Serin didn't speak to him. She had to conserve every particle of energy, but his presence was welcomed. The edges of her hands started to glow as she began to separate the individual molecules to create a cushion of flammable hydrogen around the curse mass.

There was no spell for this. Serin was flying by the seat of her pants, calling on the last of her resources for the taxing precision work.

A blast of air swept over them, roaring in her ears, but she paid it no mind, shutting out everything but the bubble of death and destruction in front of her. Slowly, the cushion of air and hydrogen thickened.

"*Now,* Diana," Serin ordered. It was all on the Fire Elemental now.

Serin wanted to help, but she didn't have the strength. It was taking everything she had to hold the huge sphere of water together.

Diana swore under her breath. "Alec, get out of here."

"Take Daniel with you," Serin ordered. "Get the crowd back."

"I'm not going anywhere," Alec said.

His words mixed with Daniel's fervent, "*Hell no*."

"Romero, get my parents farther away or I will never speak to you again," she yelled, her eyes burning.

Daniel swore, but he turned on his heel and started running toward the crowd. Serin felt him go, but the warm pressure of his hands remained.

"Diana, *get moving*," Serin urged.

Her sister's hands went up. At first, nothing happened. There was only a shifting of the molecules. Diana was touching the cushion, shifting the molecules around but not igniting them. Her fear was palpable. Serin didn't blame her for her hesitation, but she was on the verge of collapse.

"We need more, Di. It's not igniting."

"Fuck, fuck, fuck."

For a second, the wind abruptly ceased as if the world were holding its breath. Then a single spark ignited, setting off a chain reaction inside the bubble.

A massive explosion followed—forcing the bubble of water outward. Wind swirled around them as Serin cried out, her muscles locking and tearing as she willed the sphere to hold together.

A deafening screech filled the air as the sentient spell began to burn. Serin could barely see it as the flames consumed the evil thing. She wanted to let go, but she held the bubble, continually separating water molecules to feed more hydrogen into the fire so it wouldn't snuff out for lack of oxygen and fuel.

Her brain was aching. She couldn't tell where she ended and the bubble began. All sense of time eroded. All she felt was the strain of her effort until she didn't anymore.

Spent beyond all measure, Serin fell into darkness.

29

The ground was hard, but Serin didn't care. She could sense it still held some life, and that was all that mattered.

She cracked her eyelids apart a fraction. Daniel's concerned face hovered over her. Logan was bending over her, too.

"When did you get here?" It was meant to be a normal question voiced in a normal tone, but it came out in a thin raspy whisper. Her lips cracked in the process, bleeding into her mouth.

"I got here just before you and Di blew that shit to kingdom come," Logan said, her animated face glowing.

Connell, Logan's mate, appeared next to her. He was pale as a sheet. Serin guessed he had just realized how close the island had come to becoming a giant fireball.

"We were close by in Florida," Logan said. "I could feel you and Diana—the power you were pulling on—so we booked it over here. I'm sure Gia is on her way here, too."

Serin tried to nod, but her body didn't cooperate. Her head lolled, and she gasped as pain coursed through her body. Even her cells burned in protest.

Daniel scooted closer, lifting her a little so his knees could support her.

"*Diana?*" she asked, worried she hadn't seen her.

Her sister was being helped to her feet by her mate. Diana gave her a weak thumbs-up. Serin let her head fall back into Daniel's lap, the relief crushing the breath out of her.

A bottle of water appeared in Logan's hand. Instead of putting it to her lips, she poured it over Serin.

"What are you doing?" Connell asked, horrified.

"She's Water. This way works just as well as drinking. It should make her feel better."

"*Should?*" Daniel asked, his eyes rapidly scanning the sister he hadn't met, as well as sizing up her extremely large mate.

Daniel's hand landed on Serin's chest as if to protect her. He lifted it a moment later, startled. Her shirt and front were bone dry. Her parched body had thirstily absorbed the water.

Her father's voice crackled through the air as if he was on a loud speaker. Other familiar voices rose. Serin ignored the byplay, letting her mind drift over the island to scan the damage.

Daniel picked her up. "Logan is right. You need water to heal."

Her body rose in the air, supported by his arms. The surf grew louder. He was carrying her away, not to the temple, but to the beach.

"So much damage," she whispered. She could feel the dead lengths of soil as they passed over them.

They radiated like spokes out from the grave, reaching across the island. They stopped just short of the beaches and the bluffs. Some of the most fertile land had been laid waste. Their crops would suffer.

Unless the Mother intervened, it would take the island years to heal.

But it didn't reach the ocean. Diana had done it; she'd kept it from spreading farther.

"You did it," Daniel said harshly, apparently knowing where her thoughts were. "You pulled that monster out of the ground, then you put it where it could be killed. Yes, your sister helped, but she would have never gotten the chance to burn it up without you."

Serin smiled weakly. "Are you worried I'm not going to get credit?"

"No." He laughed, his gait changing as he began to walk on the sand beach. "Everyone saw what happened. There's no question you are the most amazingly badass woman who ever walked the earth. Not that credit matters when you're saving the world."

There was a splashing sound as Daniel carried her into the water. She expected him to set her on her feet, but he kept right on going until he was chest deep.

Serin closed her eyes as the warm ocean caressed her body. Despite Daniel's arms holding her, she was floating, absorbing the life-giving liquid, replenishing herself down to the cellular level.

It was like being filled with moonlight. A quiet joy suffused her, deep and calm. The water shifted. Daniel let go of her body, allowing the sea to support her. He took her hand, holding it fast as he stretched out beside her. The ocean cradled their bodies, suspending them in the vibrantly glowing surf.

More than anything, she wanted to forget about the others waiting in the valley, about her responsibilities, so she could keep floating here with Daniel under the stars. The desire to stretch out the stolen moment was more than tempting. Logic said she would have many others like this. This was only the start with Daniel, but Serin had lived long enough to know the truth.

She would never get this moment again.

Serin stared at the moon. "The man in the coffin..." she began.

"What about him?"

"His death must have been the catalyst for the curse. Breaking the glamour on the body was the trigger. Jordan must have killed him, then deliberately left the body to be found."

"Like a supernatural booby trap?"

"Yes. He must have planned for me to find it and trigger it where it lay."

There was a splash as Daniel stood, anger vibrating the air before he controlled it. "He was trying to kill you?"

Serin swished the water with her hand. "Most likely. But he failed because I wasn't the one who found the body...and after I avoided it, by letting the others take charge of the burial arrangements."

Daniel put his hand out, pulling her to him. He held onto her for a long moment. Neither spoke.

"I thought I'd failed him," she said, her voice devoid of all emotion.

She didn't have to see Daniel to know he was scowling. "Why would you feel guilty for what he did? He's the one who stole from us. Given everything that went missing, he was at it for months, lying and sneaking around."

Serin kept her gaze fixed on the moon, noting his use the word *us* with a little squeeze of her heart. "Yes, but he did it out of revenge."

"Against who? The son of a bitch was *married* to you."

She laughed. "You say that like it's a privilege. But for Jordan, it must have been hell after a while."

"Why?" Daniel sounded furious.

She curled her body forward, standing in the waves. "Because he eventually must have realized I was never going to love him back."

30

Ray Doyle was wearing a hole in the sidewalk next to the bar. He checked his watch again. It wasn't yet four, and his partner was always at least five minutes late for everything. That was unfortunate—Ray was only two or three away from heart failure.

Daniel had been gone for weeks. Ray had stumbled into the office the day after their confrontation in the alley to find their boss had received a request to temporarily reassign his partner. Romero was going undercover, and he wouldn't be able to communicate for the length of his assignment.

Doyle knew that was bullshit. This whole situation was bullshit.

Ray pulled out a cigarette case, lit one, and took a deep drag. A woman at one of the tall tables near the entrance of the bar frowned at him as smoke drifted over her. He glared right back, checking his pocket for the evidence bag.

This morning, he'd received a text from his partner's number asking him to come to the bar where he'd been meeting with that Serin woman. It was just a hop, skip, and a jump away from the alley where Ray's life had turned into a nightmare. He hadn't even been able to talk to anyone about it out of fear they'd come for him with a straitjacket. His girlfriend was pissed at him because he'd been such an asshole since that day.

Ray rolled his shoulders, checking his watch again. The text had probably been fake. Anyone could have spoofed the phone number. Pranksters did it all the time in his line of work.

Daniel was dead in an unmarked grave, and Ray had let it happen.

He spun on his heel, his eyes flaring when he spotted his partner, alive and well, at one of small tables a few feet away.

Daniel was the picture of health. Even his skin was darker, making him appear as if he'd been lying on a beach instead of a ditch. Disgusted, Ray spat out the cigarette, hurling it into the gutter. He stalked to the table, giving his partner a blistering once-over.

Something was different. Ray had spent years working side by side with the man. Daniel was a dour, hard-as-nails motherfucker. When it came to his work, he was ruthless. Now the asshole was practically glowing with happiness even though the shit wasn't smiling.

Ray checked behind him to make sure no one was eavesdropping.

"What the hell, Daniel?" he hissed, turning back to thump on the table. "Where have you been? And don't tell me it's some undercover assignment because after what happened over there, I know better," he said, jabbing a finger at the corner leading to the alleyway.

Daniel nodded somberly. He was playing with a length of string. "What do you remember?" he asked.

"I remember shooting your girlfriend," Ray mumbled, staring at his hands. "I still don't know how it happened. I was just holding the gun. I could've sworn my finger wasn't even on the trigger anymore."

He raised startled eyes, searching Daniel's face. "Then a female ninja tossed me over her shoulder, and the fucking ground opened and swallowed you up. My head was killing me, but I know that wasn't a hallucination. You were holding Serin, and there was someone else there—a guy. That's in addition to the bitch who tossed me. Who the hell are these people?"

Ray broke off, wringing his hands. He hadn't gotten a good look at the second woman, but he knew she hit harder than was humanly possible for someone that size.

He dug through his jacket pocket for his pack, then lit another cigarette with shaky hands. "I've been going crazy thinking you were dead or worse for weeks, and all I get after all that shit is a *text*?"

Ray couldn't remember his last good night's sleep. He'd lost over twelve pounds. Yes, he still needed to drop at least a half dozen more, but that wasn't the fucking point.

"I keep replaying that night in my head over and over," he continued when Romero didn't say anything. "Either it's some next-level government MK-Ultra shit or I'm losing it."

Daniel sighed, but his eyes were calm and resigned. Reaching out, he took Ray's hand with both of his.

"You've been a great partner, the best a guy could ask for. I lucked out when we were assigned together. The only reason I could do my job as well as I did was because I knew you always had my back."

Ray studied his arm, wondering where he'd gotten the woven string bracelet. It looked like something his niece had made. *Yeah, that's where it came from.* Little Emma made it for him.

He blinked and raised startled eyes, wondering why Daniel Romero was holding his hand. Ray smiled politely and leaned back, forcing his former partner to let go.

"Oh, um...hey. What's up? Long time, no see. How is D.C. treating you?"

Romero hesitated, withdrawing his hands. "It's good," he said. "Really good."

"Great, great." Ray waved the waitress over, ordering them a few beers.

It was the least he could do for old time's sake. The two of them had never been close, but they had been partners for years. It wouldn't kill him to have a beer with the guy whenever he was in town.

After a few minutes, Daniel asked for the phone.

"What?" Ray asked blankly.

"It's in your pocket. You brought it from the office. The techs were running something down on it for me."

Ray glanced down at in the bulge in his pocket. Removing the object, he frowned at the cell phone with the cracked screen in the evidence baggie.

"I didn't put this in here..."

"I asked for it, remember? You were probably so busy this morning that you threw it in your pocket and forgot about it."

Ray wrinkled his nose, but handed it over. "Does it relate to your top-secret case?"

"It's a long shot, but the powers-that-be think it's worth checking out."

Ray shrugged, and they sipped their beers, both lapsing into silence.

"Is the new job exciting at least?" Ray hoped the move had been worth it. There wasn't enough money on this earth to convince him to live in the capital. Office politics were bad enough, but they must be ten times worse in a place like D.C. Then factor in the cost of living... forget it. He'd rather have a slower-paced office and a bigger apartment, but then he'd never been as ambitious as Romero.

"There's something I didn't mention about the new job," Daniel said.

"What is it?" Ray asked, scratching his stomach and belching quietly.

Romero fiddled with his glass. "It involved a change of agency."

"What?" He sipped his beer, raising an eyebrow in question.

"I'm CIA now."

Ray laughed. "You asshole! I can't believe you defected."

His ex-partner shrugged. "I just wanted you to know in case you don't hear from me that often what with the overseas assignments and everything..."

"Oh, yeah. Of course," he said, wondering why Romero was making a big deal about it. An email once or twice a year would suffice. "I get it, man—you'll be busy playing James Bond, chatting up dusky femme fatales. I am so jealous," he lied.

He glanced at his watch again, wondering when he could politely excuse himself.

"You don't have to stay," Daniel said, nodding toward the road. "I've got to head back to the airport in a few minutes anyway."

"Do you want a ride?" Ray asked, feeling generous.

"I'm set, thank you," Daniel said, polishing off his beer a little too fast. He coughed, then smiled stiffly. "Say hi to Bette for me."

Had Ray's ex-partner met his girlfriend? He couldn't remember introducing them. "I'll do that," he said, standing up and dropping a few bills on the table.

Ray walked off with a whistle, deciding to surprise Bette by picking up Chinese on the way home. He was starving.

———

DANIEL WATCHED HIS PARTNER GO, BUT THE WEIGHT IN HIS GUT DIDN'T budge.

"It was for the best," Serin said, reaching for the phone from the seat Ray had just occupied.

He leaned back in his chair. "Yeah, that worked...exactly the way it was supposed to," he said slowly, as if the words were weighted down by sandbags.

Serin's ocean-blue eyes darkened in sympathy. "My mother's very talented with memory charms. Her spells have never failed...with one notable exception."

He nodded, waving over the waitress. The girl approached with narrowed eyes, trying to place him. Daniel ordered another beer, paying in advance and throwing another twenty on top with a murmur of apology for not paying the last time he was here. Finally recognizing him, she pocketed the twenty and stalked off with a swish of her ponytail.

"I don't suppose we can use one on the waitress." He should have asked for a bottled beer and not a draft. "She looks ready to spit in our drinks."

"I'm sorry."

He smiled at Serin, well aware she wasn't referring to the wait-staff, injected reassurance into his voice. "I'm fine."

Raising a dark eyebrow, she waited.

He sighed. "All right. If you'd asked me a few weeks ago if I'd ever keep something from my partner, I'd have said there was no way. Now, I've rearranged his brain and implanted new memories."

"It was your idea," Serin reminded him gently.

"I know, I know. But this is harder than I thought it would be. "

He hadn't erased himself from Ray's head entirely. Dalasini had explained that would be difficult because their partnership was too established and known to so many others.

Instead, he'd diminished one of the major relationships in his life to a footnote. Whenever Ray thought of him now, Daniel would be unremarkable, just someone Ray used to work with who rarely crossed his mind.

"I'm sorry if you're having second thoughts, but it's too late to change your mind. It can't be undone. Not on Ray. He's not like you. He's not flexible."

Daniel took a big swig of his drink before nodding. Dalasini had explained that, too. "It's for the best. It's like I told you before—Doyle can't handle the supernatural."

"No." There was something in her voice, a little edge, as if she were wondering how capable he was of handling it.

"I'm not having second thoughts about staying on here," he assured her. "If I have to choose you or my old life, I will choose you and everything that comes with you every single time. I think I made that clear."

Serin's shoulders dropped, but the lines around her eyes didn't relax. "You did."

Rising, she pocketed the phone and held out her hand. "Let's get moving. There's work to do."

31

Alec bent over the tiny script. He wanted to shout with joy. Instead, he allowed himself a single *'fascinating'* as he made another note.

The swish of robes made him turn around. "Oh, good," he said as Ksenia, one of the junior archivists, approached with a parchment in hand.

"Is that the updated inventory list for the amethyst room?" he asked

Each of the vast cavern-like chambers of the archive was organized along a distinctive color spectrum, a rainbow of gemstones. When one room in the warren was filled, another magically appeared, its walls pre-embedded with the gemstone that would give it its name.

Checking the contents of each room would have been an impossible task without the existing archival records. Nevertheless, checking those lists against the actual inventory was a daunting task for any group, so he'd broken the junior archivists and some of the retirees up into teams. They'd been working day and night in shifts while he supervised and spot-checked their work. Not that he was slacking off and making them do all the work. He was busy making sure the more dangerous artifacts weren't replaced with fakes or forgeries.

"I'm afraid it is still in progress," she said, fingering the parchment nervously. "This is about Noomi."

Alec perked up. "Is she back?"

Work had slowed considerably since the senior archivist had left. When he learned she'd taken it upon herself to escort the Loki back to the mainland, he realized she was going to be away for a while. Things had a habit of getting off course around a Loki. But this Loki was Serin's friend, so he wasn't worried about Noomi. Not yet, anyway...

"No, she hasn't returned, but the elders wanted an update on our progress." Ksenia cleared her throat gently. "They decreed that no sensitive volumes could be checked out by the island's inhabitants, so they sent some of us out to collect them from people's homes."

"Damn and blast. No wonder everything has been taking so bloody long." The junior archivists were running all over the island, collecting overdue books. "What does this have to do with Noomi?"

Ksenia gripped the paper in her hand tighter. "Well...the volumes Noomi checked out just before her departure are all of a very sensitive nature."

With a frown, Alec plucked the parchment from her hand and scanned the list. "Waddell's *Advanced Spellcraft*, Coriander's *Practical Magic*, the *Shadow Codex...*"

The list went on and on. Damn, he hadn't realized the archive had a copy of the *Branium Vivitae*.

Though it mainly contained defensive spells, a talented practitioner could do a lot of damage with that text.

"Hmm, I can see how they would have a problem with these going missing," he observed.

Ksenia's eyes flared in alarm. "They're not missing. Noomi is only borrowing them. She will return them when she gets back."

"Of course she will," he said bracingly.

That didn't seem to calm her. Ksenia stared at him as if waiting for him to do something else.

"Tell you what," he said, rolling up the parchment. "Why don't you and I keep this list to ourselves for now?"

Her breath escaped in a whoosh. "Oh...I don't think that's wise. The elders told me to report anything of note to them right away."

Alec could hear the incipient panic in the young woman's voice at the thought of keeping anything from the elders. He stifled a sigh. Those tightwads were mere figureheads. It was clear the power of T'Kaieri rested with the family lines the Elemental Water talent bounced between. However, the elders had a habit of running roughshod over the young people, the junior archivists in particular.

"Then you should," he assured her. "Right after you finish the inventory of the amethyst room. Maybe after the tourmaline room is done, too."

Awareness dawned, and she coughed. "Yes, I see. The inventory has to take priority."

"I'm glad you agree. Noomi will surely return before we're done. Then this small concern will be a moot point."

Ksenia nodded, her breathing deepening. "Yes...I should get back to it," she said before bowing deeply and hurrying away.

Alec watched her go before turning back to the list with a whistle. "I hope you know what you're doing, Noomi."

<h1 style="text-align:center">32</h1>

"Are you ready?" Loki asked as he crouched.

"No!" Noomi flattened herself against the massive wooden crate, doing her best to stay below the line of sight of the men gathered across the warehouse. "How did I ever let you talk me into this?" she whisper-wailed.

Loki peeked around the corner at the cluster of armed men. "I believe it involved lots and lots of wine."

He took the spell vials she'd prepared out of her hands. "Don't worry. This is going to work. We just have to wait for the guy in the suit to step out. He's clearly the boss. Once he's out of sight, I'm going to glamour myself into him so we can get the drop on the remaining guards. Once they're out, we can corner the boss and make him tell us where the amulet is."

The amulet was how they'd found Armand, the head arms dealer. Noomi had taken a page out of Serin's book. There has been an amulet on the list of missing items. Alec hadn't known the innocuous silver pendant had an overlocking bronze oval. The two pieces were never stored together because when they had been in the past, they had an unfortunate tendency to attract hordes of squirrels.

It hadn't occurred to her that the bronze overlay could be used to scry for the other piece until Loki mentioned it was what Serin had done for the Sai.

"He's going," Loki hissed. Noomi took a deep breath before risking a peek around the corner of the crate.

The long-haired man in aviator glasses was walking away. He was flanked by a dangerous-looking brute as they headed down a side hallway.

"He's taking his bodyguard with him," she whispered. Their plan to isolate the boss was compromised.

"We can still do this," Loki insisted. "I'm just going to need you to hit the big guard on the back of the head with one of these knockout spells after I take out these three."

Reaching into the bag strapped to her side, he removed two spell vials. He pressed one into each of her hands. "You have to make sure you hit them hard enough to break the glass," he warned.

She gulped aloud, but took the vials. "This is a stupid idea. We should send for Serin or at least text Daniel."

"*No*," Loki whined. "They have their hands full tracking Puck. The least we can do is mop us this little mess for them."

She studied the remaining three men. They were all big males, the kind with naturally grim faces that made people cross the street to avoid them.

"You call this bunch a *little* mess?"

"Sure..." He waved dismissively. "We've got that crackerjack protection spell you found. Even if my glamour doesn't trick them, they won't be able to shoot us."

"The spell is not going to make us bulletproof." Noomi didn't have the talent to create those spells. They were too difficult to sustain for any useful amount of time. "The potion I brewed is just going to confuse the men."

She'd spent the better part of a week getting the spell ingredients together and mixed properly, in between trying to talk Loki out of this reckless course of action.

The bitter brew tweaked an observers' perception. It made anyone who saw them register their bodies two feet to their right or left instead of their actual location. With luck, if any of the men managed to shoot, their aim would be off, or at least that was the idea... They hadn't had time to fully test it.

There were so many things that could go wrong. But Loki was determined to do this, and she couldn't let him go it alone.

That doesn't mean you can't try to make him see reason one last time. "Are you sure you don't want to wait for Serin to get here?" Noomi had the messaging incantation memorized.

Loki wasn't even listening to her. The ripple of bending light passed over him, sending the wave of glamour over his body. "One...two..."

He was gone before three. Disguised as Armand, he strutted down the middle of the warehouse through the narrow lane made by the boxes stacked in neat rows on either side. Waving at the men impatiently, he cleared his throat.

"Get over here," he ordered in a surprisingly decent imitation of the arms dealer's voice.

One of the men frowned, but the other two shrugged and began to approach him obediently.

Noomi's held her breath as they came closer to her hiding spot. Clutching the two spell vials, she waited, sweat trickling down her back.

Her heart began to race as the men closed the distance. *You don't have to do anything.* This part of Loki's plan was bound to work. The trio got closer and closer. Loki waited until they were almost six feet away.

The fae man pulled his arm back, launching two of the spell vials as hard as he could. One vial broke as intended, and the man went down, falling to the floor unconscious.

The second vial hit the shorter guard in the middle. His belly fat acted as a cushion. The glass bounced off, landing on the floor and cracking open.

"Shite..." Loki reached down, trying to scoop up the liquid with his hand.

"Boss, what are you doing?" the slowest of the three asked as his partner scowled at the fallen man, still not putting two and two together.

"Hold this," Loki-slash-Armand said, slapping the liquid onto the retreating man's cheek. He dropped like a stone.

There was only one man left standing. Noomi squeaked aloud, her terror escaping at a higher pitch than her normal voice. She hurried around the safety of her corner, stumbling a bit as the goon stood gaping at the man he believed to be his boss.

Loki reached into his pocket for another vial. That was when the mouth-breathing bruiser finally came up with four. He slapped at Loki, his meaty paw knocking him to the ground.

Whimpering, Noomi ran forward, throwing one of the vials in her hand out in a wild arc. Her aim was terrible. Instead of striking the man in the chest, it hit him in the ankle and wedged there, unbroken.

She and Loki locked eyes, trading panic back and forth like an invisible hot potato.

Loki crouched as if he were going to leap on the man. Gulping, Noomi rushed forward, slamming her foot down on the vial. It broke open on the goon's thick leather boot just next to the lacings.

"Ow! You bitch." He flung his arm out, knocking her against the crates with a backhanded slap.

"Don't you fucking touch her," Loki yelled, launching himself at the guy. Both fell to the floor, the guard twisting so Loki ended up on the bottom, Armand's wiry compact form completely engulfed by the other guy's massive bulk.

Noomi darted forward again, prepared to break a second vial over the man's head, but she soon realized he wasn't moving.

"Oh, he's out." She had knocked him out after all. "The potion must have soaked through his shoe."

"Great," Loki grunted, straining. "Can you get him off me?"

"Sorry!" She reached down and tugged a thick arm, but it was like trying to lift a tree trunk.

Loki heaved, trying to squirm out from under the weight. "You would have picked the tallest one."

Noomi tsked, changing tactics. Instead of pulling, she started pushing until the top half of the man rolled off Loki's chest.

Taking a deep breath, he held up a finger. "When we tell Serin and Daniel what we did, we're going to leave this part out."

She laughed a touch hysterically as Loki popped up, getting to his feet as if nothing had happened. "Let's hide them."

"How?" The original plan was to hide them out of sight, but they'd severely underestimated how heavy their adversaries would be.

Loki glanced around. "What if we assemble a crate over them instead?"

She hesitated. "Don't you think the real Armand would find it strange, a big box like this appearing suddenly in the middle of the walkway?"

Loki shrugged. "Good help is hard to find."

Her lips compressed.

"All right." He spun around. "Maybe there's a trolley or a cart around here."

In the end, the only thing they could find was a tarp. Loki pushed the bodies close together and Noomi threw it over them, wiping the oily residue from the canvas on her pants.

She turned around to meet two pairs of eyes. Armand—the real one—and his guard were watching them.

They'd been caught.

She smacked Loki on the arm, and he straightened up. His lips parted. For a second, he froze, but he didn't launch into his prepared spiel. He tugged on her arm, pulling her after him as he ran away.

Armand shouted something she didn't catch. Noomi made the mistake of glancing back as the hulking bodyguard put his head down to charge like a bull.

"Run!" They darted into the side lanes created by the crates, but their feet pounded on the concrete, the racket giving away their location.

Wood broke as their pursuer batted some of those massive crates aside, chasing them down like vermin.

"Why didn't you throw a spell vial or try another glamour?" she panted as they careened around another blind corner.

"Armand is not a goblin. He's some kind of high fae. I can feel it. He can see through any glamour."

"What?" How could a highborn fae be here? Most of the upper caste was so severely allergic to iron they couldn't even be in the same room as a gun, and this room was full of them.

If a high fae could tolerate being here, then he was warded-up beyond reason.

Wood splintered by their heads, and hands reached through a broken crate. Noomi screamed as the hand grabbed Loki, jerking him off his feet. He flew back as he was hauled bodily through the air.

She tried to follow, but the spill of guns and packing material blocked her way.

Crying, Noomi climbed over the weapons, praying they weren't loaded. Half-jumping, half-running, she managed to clear the spilled pile.

The man had Loki pinned against another crate. The monster was choking the life from him.

A broken cry escaped her throat. Noomi jumped on the man's back, trying to surprise him into letting go, but it was like tackling a brick wall. He didn't react at all, not even to bat her away.

Baffled, she hung on before gritting her teeth and climbing him like a tree.

Loki whimpered, his face going from white to beet red. His hands scrabbled at the bull's, trying to pry the beefy fingers away from his neck.

The vials.

Noomi clung to the beast with one hand, dumping out the contents of the little bottles directly over his mouth.

Nothing happened. She knew some of the liquid had entered the man's mouth, but he kept going, refusing to drop her friend.

How was that possible? The sleeping spell was strong enough to take down a war elephant.

Tears stung at her eyes as helplessness swamped her. Desperate, she fished out her small knife and plunged it into the back of the man's neck.

The short blade pierced the flesh, sinking in several inches...but the monster didn't react.

Loki was losing consciousness, his lashes fluttering as his eyes closed, maybe for the last time.

"Allow me," a woman's voice said.

Noomi jerked her head away as a spike with a wickedly sharp tip emerged from the monster's forehead. Gasping, she let go, falling to the floor with a crash right next to a raggedly breathing Loki.

"*Serin?*"

Noomi wanted to weep in relief. The Water Elemental had ridden to the rescue, her human mate at her side.

Serin had made good use of the Sai she'd recovered recently. It was running straight through the back of the man's head, the sharp point poking through his forehead. It was without a doubt the world's most terrible unicorn.

A corner of Serin's mouth pulled up, but it wasn't a smile. "Didn't you notice the mark on his forehead?" she asked Noomi.

"What mark?" She scrambled to her feet.

Daniel nodded at her, kneeling to check on Loki.

"How did you find us?" Loki asked, rubbing his neck. His voice was hoarse, but he still managed to sound disappointed.

"Alec had Diana send word out through the aether. He told us about the books Noomi had borrowed from the archive and what he suspected you were up to. Tracking you became a priority."

Serin hopped up, bracing herself against the man's buttocks. She pried her blade out of the corpse's head before jumping back down. The giant fell backward like a sequoia felled by a storm.

"If you're going to insist on going out in the field, you have to pay closer attention to the details," the Water Elemental scolded, pointing at the hulk's forehead.

There was a subtle tracing, a word that had been interrupted by the wound.

"It's a g-golem!" Noomi stammered.

The word Serin had punctured was in ancient Mesopotamian. When carved into a clay automaton, it could animate them— provided the complicated ritual was done correctly. Other variations of the spell included writing the holy words on a parchment and sealing them in the mouth of the golem, but either way, Noomi had never expected to see one in real life.

Golem were nearly invincible unless their sacred words were destroyed.

Noomi knelt, fascinated despite herself. "How in the world is he so lifelike?"

All the golems she'd read about were roughly hewn clay or mud creatures. This one had skin and hair. Every detail had been rendered with exquisite detail. The verisimilitude was astounding. Even the marking on the forehead was subtle. More like a brand than a tattoo, it could have been confused for a scar. Only close inspection would have revealed that it was a word.

"Someone has been making refinements to the original ritual," Serin said with a little shrug. Her lack of alarm made Noomi think she'd seen a lifelike golem before.

She shuddered delicately, but Serin had moved on. The Water Elemental turned to Daniel. "Did you see where the other one went?"

He nodded. "Out the back. I'll lead the way."

"Wait!" Noomi cried. "The other one is high fae."

Serin lifted a brow, but Daniel just raised his gun. "Then a plain old bullet should be all I need," he replied.

They all stared at him in surprise. He shrugged. "I've been

reading."

"That's true," Serin said. "But high fae—especially ones who move out in the world—are far too tricky for a simple bullet. I'll come with you."

She nodded at Noomi, gesturing at Loki. "Do you have him?"

Loki answered for her. "Yes, she does. But I'm all right. Let's go get him."

The fae struggled to his feet. Serin tapped her foot. "I'd tell you to stay put, but I know it won't do any good."

Loki beamed, grabbing Noomi's arm.

Serin glowered at him. "Keep your heads down till Armand is secure."

Noomi hung back as the others filed out of the rear entrance, the cowardly tail in a string of brave warriors.

They exited, fanning out with almost military precision.

The warehouse was part of a series of others just like it. A narrow asphalt road separated it from the identical building next door.

Noomi was ready to run, searching for the high fae, but he hadn't gotten far. The arms dealer was running toward them, his mouth open as he screamed.

Genuine terror was etched across Armand's face. She understood the reason seconds later.

A massive black wolf was running toward them. It had silver paws and jaws so wide she was reminded of the massive sharks that liked to breed off the waters of T'Kaieri.

When Armand saw them, he turned left, trying to escape down the alley, but the wind whipped up. Logan appeared, blocking his path. Armand turned right instead, running straight into Daniel's waiting fist. The fae sank to the ground, insensible.

Noomi came to an abrupt halt, panting from the exertion. There wasn't much call to run in the archives.

"Hey," Logan said as she struggled to calm her breathing. The Air Elemental waved cheerily at the rest of the group.

Smiling, Serin threw an arm up at her sister. "What are you doing here?"

Logan shrugged as her mate shifted. Connell appeared at her side, tugging on a pair of pants he'd gotten from the Mother only knew where. "We heard Noomi was out of the basement, and we figured this was an all-hands-on-deck situation," she replied with a grin.

Blushing, Noomi ducked her head.

"Not a bad idea actually," Serin said, touching Noomi's shoulder comfortingly. "We're going to need Diana. This entire warehouse needs to burn down to the foundation, with every gun and bullet inside."

Logan nodded. "She's not far. I'll go get her."

Noomi noticed Daniel hadn't moved. He was staring down at the unconscious man.

"What's wrong?" she asked.

He glanced up, his eyes darker than their normal hazel. "I know this man."

"Who is he?"

Daniel passed a hand over his face. "I know him as Dallas Munroe. In Washington D.C., he's a hotshot DEA agent. If I'd gone to work there as planned, he would have been one of my bosses."

Connell whistled. "I smell a conspiracy."

Serin picked the fae up. He didn't wake. "Well, if there is one, his part in it is over."

"He's still glamoured, even in this state," Noomi said, examining him closely. She could feel the disguise like an overlay over his core being. "He must be reinforcing it with a potion or physical charm."

Daniel clenched his fist, slight disgust on his face. "Do you think he was replaced, or has he been fae the whole time?"

"We may never know," Serin said. "But at least we have an idea of where to search for the artifacts."

Loki gestured to the warehouse with his thumb. "Back in there?"

"Yes, and whatever office he's been using as part of his DEA persona."

"I'm on it, chief," Logan said with a small salute. "I'll pop into his office in D.C. after bringing Diana here."

After taking Connell's hand, she disappeared with a gust of wind.

"I'll help Noomi start the search," Loki said after watching her go. "We have a big ass warehouse to search before Diana torches this place."

Daniel was still frowning at Armand. Serin put a hand on his shoulder. Noomi tugged at Loki's hand. The human needed a moment to come to terms with this latest discovery.

It was going to take her a lot longer...

EQUAL PARTS VINDICATION AND DISAPPOINTMENT FLOWED THROUGH him. Loki wanted to celebrate his first successful superhero mission with Noomi, but he understood her pressing need to take the artifacts they'd found in the warehouse back to the archive. T'Kaieri's underground chambers possessed potent natural wards that muted their power.

Even the amulet had given off a ghastly vibe, and all it did according to Noomi was create a squirrel flash mob.

"More like a rabid squirrel army," Serin corrected.

He'd immediately wanted to see that, but Noomi had taken the pieces away before he could put them together. That was probably for the best.

Whatever else was true, Loki had a newfound respect for librarians. Not only had Noomi kept a whole museum of evil artifacts from cross-reacting and destroying the world, but with a little push from him, she'd also jumped into the fray to kick some golem ass.

Damn. He should have asked Serin if he could tag along to T'Kaieri. She would have let him if he'd asked nicely. But Loki was a tiny bit ashamed at needing the last-minute save, so when the Elemental had rushed off and offered to drop the librarian off, he hadn't complained.

He'd take Noomi out for a celebration soon enough. She would love Dionysia.

Loki rounded the corner of the warehouse, intent on finding a car to hotwire.

The blow caught him on the back of the head. He groaned, stunned, but he managed to cover his head and spin around. The edges of his vision growing dark, he recognized Mayon, the personal bodyguard and occasional consort to the Queen of Air and Darkness.

Loki passed out with Mayon's name on his lips.

When he came to, he was in an iron cell. Despite never having seen it in person, Loki recognized his prison instantly. This hellhole was legendary among his kind. Fae from every caste knew what it looked like.

He was in the Seelie Court's dungeon.

"This is my worst nightmare." He clutched his aching head. Hell, this was every fae's worst nightmare.

Mayon smirked at him from the other side of the bars. But Loki knew something was off. The fire fae's smell was unmistakable. This guy reeked of the wildness of the forest, not fire and ash. The queen's favorite guard was a fire fae. This guy wasn't Mayon.

"Give it up. I know you're not him. You can't fool a Loki with that weak-ass glamour."

The imposter scowled. His face rippled, the striking features melting away to reveal a harsh and wild visage.

Fuck me. It was Thracian. The forest smell made sense now. The man in front of him was the head of the Great Hunt.

"I'd start preparing for my trial now," Thracian said, sneering down at him.

"Trial?" Loki was mystified. "What trial?"

It was true the Seelie Court had no love for Elementals, but they wouldn't actually punish him for consorting with one. Hell, Serin was his closest friend. If anything, they'd give him a pass to avoid pissing her off.

But if that were true, then why the hell was the head huntsman holding him prisoner? Had something changed?

"Are you here keeping that rabid mob you call the Great Hunt in check?" he asked.

Thracian sneered. "Don't worry about them. You'll be seeing them soon enough."

Loki did not want to know what the other fae meant by that. He got to his feet, holding his aching head gingerly so it wouldn't fall off his shoulders. The lightbulb finally went off. He swore. "You were in league with Armand. You wanted to buy his guns. Who were you going to shoot with them?"

Thracian laughed. "*Me*? I caught *you* trafficking in human arms."

Loki wanted to roll his eyes, but his head hurt too much. "I helped destroy the cache."

Thracian dropped the pretense. He squatted close to the bars, being careful not to touch them. "And in doing so, you ruined a year's worth of work. Those weapons were going to liberate us."

"Are you mad?" Loki scoffed. "You'd never be able to smuggle one of those guns into the court. There are way too many safeguards in place for such a simpleminded plan."

Thracian face darkened, his flat grey eyes promising death. "I assure you there was nothing simple about our plan."

"*Our* plan? So there are more conspirators?" Loki leaned back on his hands. "Don't you think it's a bit stupid to give me so many details?" The real Mayon would be very interested in learning he had a cabal intent on bringing down the monarchy right under his nose.

Thracian put his hands on his hips. "Why? I doubt anybody will bother to ask you anything. It's been a while since we had a good old-fashioned treason trial. But we've both been around long enough to know it's a formality. In fact, by the time they get around to the proceedings, I doubt you'll be able to walk, let alone speak."

Loki clenched his fists. "You know this won't work. I'm going to beat this if it's the last thing I do."

The hunter laughed. "It would have to be. The penalty for treason is death."

33

A WEEK LATER

The desert air was so dry it was sucking the moisture from Daniel's eyeballs. Every time he opened his mouth, he tasted sand, but he didn't dare spit it out. He needed what moisture was left in his body.

Their investigation had led them to a small but luxurious palace in the desert outskirts of Dubai. The arid atmosphere didn't seem to bother Serin at all, but her powers were bound to be affected.

This location made perfect sense. If Jordan wanted to hide from an all-powerful Water-wielding Elemental, where would the cowardly little traitor go? A seaside villa was out of the question. *Just ask the Reaper how well that had turned out for him...*

The palace had been built by a sheik in the sixties as a private retreat where he could indulge in his love of Western vices. He'd invited Hollywood movie stars and showgirls to entertain him, throwing lavish pool parties and decadent balls worthy of the *Great Gatsby.*

Today, the pools were empty. None of the fountains were operational and the elaborate gardens were bone dry. There were still splashes of color here and there—plants protected from the wind kept their blooms, but they were desiccated, almost as if they'd been pressed between the pages of a massive book.

Every time the Santa-Anna-like winds blew, he felt like the flowers were crumbling only to blow straight into his face.

Serin was busy doing the magical equivalent of reconnaissance. Water content let her count the number of people with ease, but she wanted a bit of recon in case there were booby traps she needed to deactivate.

The full moon lit the gardens better than a spotlight. Nighttime was also better for Serin. She drifted close to the ground like a fog. The vapor circled the building, listening. The image stirred a memory. Just before he'd noticed her at the farmhouse, he'd seen Serin rising out of the mist. At the time, he'd assumed it was mist from the rain, but he knew now that small intermediary step was part of her power—Water but a little bit of Air, too.

There had been that moment where she'd wielded Fire as well, helping Diana ignite the curse tentacles on T'Kaieri. Though Water was her primary gift, it must have taken ages to learn to control all three elements. She might be able to do Earth magic, too, for all he knew. Her skills would only grow over time.

Fuck retiring in ten years. If Serin wanted to keep working, Daniel was going to make sure no one stood in her way.

His heart swelled with pride, but he pushed it down, refocusing on his surroundings. He couldn't afford to be distracted. No matter what went down, tonight was going to be brutal.

Which was why despite all her gifts, Serin needed him. *Whether she realizes it or not.*

She materialized next to him as if he'd summoned her from a lamp. The look on her face reminded him of a Djinn as well, not the happy-jokey cartoon kind, but the dark and deadly interpretations that had started to grace the small screen in the last few years.

He gestured at the house. The lights were on. Loud music was playing. "Is he there?"

"Yes." She turned to him. "Listen. I want to do this alone. You should stay here."

Daniel pulled his gun out of his holster. "Hell no."

That asshole in there had nearly destroyed an entire civilization. Maybe things hadn't worked out for Jordan the way he'd wanted with Serin, but that was no reason to take it out on the rest of her community. Those people had embraced him, shared meals with him. They had made him a part of their lives, and the bastard had tried to destroy them.

The more Daniel thought about it, the angrier he got.

Serin ran her teeth over her lip. "*Please.* I want you to stay here."

His heart ached, but he shook his head.

She stared at him, her full lips parting. "I...I don't want you to watch."

"I know." He really did. Daniel put his hands on either side of her face. "Nothing you do in there will change how I feel about you."

Her head tilted as she studied him, weighing his words. "You think that now. But all you've seen me do is try to save people I love or defend myself. This is something else."

Aw, screw it. He was never going to have the right words to convince her. He was going to have to show her.

Daniel put his arms on her shoulder, gently turned her in the direction of the French doors. A light feminine giggle could be heard as a shadow passed on the other side of the gauzy curtain covering the interior of the glass.

"It's time to end this. I'll be right behind you," he said.

Daniel was still holding her when she let go. She didn't carry him with her this time, so he was able to feel that moment when Serin transformed from a strong and supple woman to her water form.

She was gone the next second, slipping through the crack under the door.

That better not be a fucking metaphor, he told the universe, raising his gun and following her inside.

THE INSIDE OF THE PALACE WAS RICHLY TILED. SOME EFFORT HAD GONE into its upkeep, but not the careful tending the intricate mosaic walls required. The plaster between them was cracked. Nothing a little tender loving care couldn't fix, of course, but Jordan had evidently not been concerned with home improvements.

He was too busy carousing.

The detritus of parties past littered the floor and the surface of every table. There were gilt plates and silver cutlery, some dirty, some clean. A few were piled with fresh fruit or delicate morsels of food next to partially filled champagne glasses.

She picked up a glass, noting the bright pink lipstick stain on the rim. So far, she'd been unnoticed by the three drunks dancing at the other end of the room. Jordan had always been partial to champagne. Personally, she couldn't abide the stuff.

Her former partner was swaying side to side with his eyes closed, a bottle in his hand. He took a swig as his dance partners, two silicone-enhanced blondes, rubbed against each other and him. It should have been sexy, but here, in the middle of nowhere, it just seemed...sad.

One of the blondes noticed her first. She pointed at Serin, but the sudden movement was too much for her drunken state. Off balance, she bumped into the others, laughing nonsensically as she slid to the floor.

"We have company," she said with a giggle, tugging on her short skirt—too late to keep her assets private. The woman wasn't wearing underwear.

Jordan spun around. His eyes flared when he saw Serin standing there. He stopped swaying, lowering the bottle to his side. His face was expressionless, but his eyes roiled. He didn't even glance at Daniel, who circled the room with his weapon aimed at the trio.

After a moment, Jordan laughed. It was effortlessly charming, the laugh of a carefree and caring man. She had never realized how good he'd been at lying to her.

"Welcome, my love," he said with an exaggerated bow. He held up the bottle. "Care for some champagne? It's your favorite."

Serin pinched the stem of the glass between her two fingers. "Actually, it's your favorite. I prefer a sweet red." She set down the glass, the clink of fine crystal resonating as it hit the wooden table. "You should tell your friends to leave."

Jordan's face twisted, and he pulled one of the blondes against him like a shield. The woman squealed, her stilettos sliding on the tile floor.

"Hey," she protested, confusion and a little fear flashing across her perfect features.

Serin's mouth turned down. "You know that won't help. Let her go."

Jordan huffed and shrugged, releasing the girl abruptly. Without his hold, she stumbled, nearly losing her balance.

"Sorry, Jess." He reached into his pocket, then tossed a set of keys at her. "You and Misty should take off."

Scowling, Jess caught the keys. Her eyes went from his to Serin, finally resting on Romero aiming his gun, his stance marking him as a professional.

"Yeah, okay. Call us later," she said, pulling the other lady off the floor.

"But we were just getting started," the one called Misty whined.

"Shut up," Jess snapped, yanking her toward the other side of the house and the exit nearest the garage.

Serin didn't bother watching them go. She kept her eyes on Jordan, making sure he didn't reach into a pocket for a spell bomb or an enhanced firearm.

Jordan turned his head, noticing Daniel for the first time. "Who the hell is this?" he asked, a mix of indignation and jealousy in his voice.

"You don't get to ask any questions," Serin said, picking her way across the room, stopping here and there to pick up an object.

She set down a jeweled letter opener before holding up a vaguely Elephantine statue carved out of cloudy blue crystal. "This is the memory stone. I recognize it from the list of items you stole before you faked your death. According to our records, a skilled practitioner can use it to read a person's memories...even change them."

Was this meant to be Jordan's get-out-of-jail-free card? If so, he shouldn't have left it out where it was so easy to recover.

"It was deadweight. It doesn't work." Scowling, Jordan took a swig of the bottle. He wiped his mouth with the sleeve of his silk robe before spitting on the floor. "It's just a chunk of crystal. I shouldn't have bothered taking it."

Serin inclined her head, acknowledging the fact he wasn't bothering with pointless denials. She held the elephant higher. The crystal grew clearer, lighting up like a beacon from within. "Or you just didn't try hard enough to master it."

Jordan huffed, looking down at the floor. "Of course," he muttered.

Serin put the crystal elephant down, continuing her circuit of the room, her fingers running over the objects that weren't visibly filthy.

She wiped her palms on her pants and waved, the gesture encompassing the room. "When I realized you were alive, I didn't expect you to be living like this, hiding like a coward."

Jordan rubbed his red eyes. "Did you miss me?"

Serin stopped a few yards away, her hands at her sides. "No."

Laughing, he took another drink. "That's my lovely bride. Honest to a fault."

She glanced at Romero. Daniel's lips were curled in disdain.

Something was off. When the others had suggested Jordan was the mastermind behind the thefts, she'd dismissed the idea. She had been with him for years. The willingness to do harm required something her bonded hadn't possessed. Ambition. But this—a man drinking and wallowing in self-pity, this was Jordan she knew.

The curse that had come out of the body on T'Kaieri had been some of the most advanced and complicated magic she had ever seen. By comparison, the memory stone was child's play.

Jordan was skilled in the craft, but he lacked direction. He was a dabbler. The poison could have easily been him. The glamour as well, but not the curse. At least, not *that* curse.

"This wasn't your idea, was it? Who helped you create the curse?" Jordan had a lot of friends on the island. His charm and attractive features had won people over so readily. Of course, none of them had to live with him....

Jordan lowered himself to the floor. "I did it all. The robbery, the poison bullets, the glamoured corpse, but it was all *your* fault."

His eyes streamed. "I did everything for you—followed you all over the world, bought you everything your heart could possibly desire. I did everything, and it was never enough."

"She didn't need *things*, you prick—just a partner who understood," Daniel fumed.

Jordan's lips parted. Comprehension flashed across his face. "And you're him." He pointed at Serin. "She's yours. It's why she brought you."

Daniel adjusted his grip on the gun. "Serin belongs to herself, asshole. I'm just along for the ride."

Jordan took another swig. Finding the bottle empty, he tossed it away. "It doesn't matter." He reached under his shirt, then drew out a pendant hanging from a silver chain. "I have this, so you can't touch me."

She raised a brow. "Where did you get that?"

"From the damn archive, of course. It nullifies your power."

"But *I* can still touch you," Daniel said, his weapon trained on Jordan's head.

Serin sighed heavily, finally convinced. Jordan wasn't the mastermind. He also wouldn't ever tell her who really did it, but he didn't have to anymore. "That won't be necessary," she told Daniel.

"And why is that?" Jordan asked, twirling the chain to make the pendant swing.

"Because that isn't an anti-Elemental amulet. There's no such thing. If I recall correctly, that charm lets you find things that are lost."

There was a beat of silence. "You still can't touch me." Jordan didn't sound as confident. "This place doesn't have working plumbing. There's not enough water to drown me."

"I don't have to drown you." She kept her eyes on him, calling his water to her.

Jordan doubled over. His mouth gaped as he stared down at his hands and body. The confusion on his face was swiftly followed by horror.

Out of the corner of her eye, Serin could see Romero put his gun down, but she didn't turn her head. If she saw his reaction, she might stop.

"Your body is mostly water," she reminded Jordan in a steady tone.

"But *you* can't. This is beyond your skill." Jordan's cheeks sank, pressing deep into his skull. He was starting to get the gaunt appearance of a starving man.

His mouth contorted, body falling forward. He lay on the floor as his body shuddered, shrinking before their eyes. "I would have loved you forever and look at you, you heartless bitch. This is so easy for you."

Guilt tore her heart to pieces, but Serin didn't release him.

A thin trickle of water was running from him to her. She forced her features to remain expressionless. "Actually, you have no idea what this is costing me..."

She didn't look at Daniel. She couldn't. *This will be over soon, all of it.*

More and more water ran toward her. Jordan's body was starting to disintegrate. Without the water to hold it together, parts of it were turning to dust. Soon, only bones remained. They were bleached white by magic, surrounded by a pile of pink and tan dust.

S ERIN HAD KILLED MANY TIMES OVER THE YEARS. S HE HAD FELT satisfaction, a sense of justice. This time, she felt nothing. She embraced the silence, holding as still as possible before she had to go on.

"You'll feel it later."

Her breath caught. Daniel was still there. Dumbfounded, she gaped at him with her mouth open. "What are you still doing here?"

Daniel holstered his gun. "Did you expect me to leave?"

On some level, she had.

He shook his head at her. "Well, that's not happening."

"But you did see me, right?" She waved at the bones. Had he turned away and covered his ears?

Daniel's head dipped. He appeared a little confused. "I did. And?"

"He was my ex. We were bonded for almost a decade."

"Yeah, and he betrayed you and tried to kill you and your entire island. The shithead deserved what he got."

"But *I* did that," she said, pointing at the bones in bewilderment.

Daniel scratched his head. "Um, babe—I mean, Serin—can I ask you something?"

"What is it?" she asked, an impending sense of doom engulfing her.

"How is making mummies all that different from drowning some-one?" He appeared genuinely perplexed.

"Because it is," she said slowly.

Water talents shouldn't be able to pull the moisture from a body. A person's aura, their chi, was too strong a barrier. Daniel shrugged. "Well, it isn't to me."

"As far as I know, only one Water Elemental has been able to do it. She lived thousands of years ago. According to their records, the only reason she was able to do it was because she'd given herself over to the black."

"As in evil?" Daniel scoffed. "You're not evil. Again, that asshole had it coming. And maybe more Water talents would have developed that skill if you didn't have that stupid arbitrary cutoff of a hundred years."

"I didn't say I was evil, but that is the only time one of us had the ability."

"That you know of."

He had a point. Serin had thought she knew everything about Water talents, but T'Kaieri held more secrets than she'd realized.

Daniel broke away, pointing at the bones. "About Jordan... I thought you would question him more."

Serin shook off her malaise, beginning to gather the stolen objects. "He wouldn't have named his accomplice."

"You're probably right," Daniel said, opening his pack so she could stow the artifacts.

"Wrap them first," she reminded him.

He nodded, taking out a small roll of silk. Magical artifacts in close proximity could interact. There were other more effective barriers, but this was the most lightweight. "So, about the accomplice... Are we back to square one?"

"No." As much as she wanted to deny it, there was really only one viable suspect. Serin paused, picking up the memory stone. Snatches of a conversation she'd had years ago came back.

It had been a few decades into her service. She'd been sharing a meal with Gia on the beach. When the Earth Elemental left, Serin went to the archives to research an upcoming job.

She'd found him handling the elephant-shaped stone, turning it over and over in his hands. When he saw her, he put it down, changing the subject when she offered to demonstrate how it worked.

I should have known then. A scholar of magic wouldn't have turned down a demonstration like that. Not unless he already knew how it worked.

Heart aching, she reached out and took Daniel's hand. "We need to go. I have a good idea of who the accomplice is."

34

Gia opened the door, then climbed down the winding stairs. The ancient stone steps were slippery. They'd been polished smooth with age, the center of every one so worn there was a dip in the middle of each.

The castle was on the coast of the Isle of Man. But Gia hadn't need to see the crumbling turrets or partially rebuilt bailey to know that its history was long. The stones were whispering their stories in her ear, but she shut them out. She was only interested in the castle's most recent occupant.

He hadn't been here long. Since leaving T'Kaieri, he'd been all over, Italy, Spain, Greece—anywhere there were repositories of ancient learning. That was in line with his interests. However, it hadn't been necessary to track him through all those places. When she decided to find him, it was simple, because he hadn't been hiding. Uncle John wanted to be found.

He was sitting on a far bench surrounded by glass vials filled with multicolored liquids, extracts of rare herbs and flowers. Bunsen burners warmed glass distillation equipment. She traced the line of condensation as a potent hallucinogen dripped into a collection flask. It was sitting next to a state-of-the-art compound microscope.

He'd even added a sprinkler system on the ceiling and drains on the linoleum-covered floor, just like a modern laboratory. The alchemist's lair had been updated, embracing the latest technologies as they were invented.

He'd even embraced new lighting technology. Sickly blue fluorescent lights highlighted every object in the room. It made Uncle John resemble like a living cadaver as he mixed his many vials and experiments.

She hadn't made a sound, but he knew she was there. A little smile played on his lips as he continued in his work, meticulously counting giant seeds with a pair of forceps. When he was finished, he glanced up from his workbench, his face bright and welcoming.

The expression was so warm that for a second, she almost convinced herself she'd made a mistake.

But Gia had finally remembered the lessons she'd learned as a child. The best liars always smiled. They hid what they were behind bright grins while trying to hug others, but only so they could bury the knife in their backs.

John stood, bowing at her. He beckoned her closer. "I was hoping it would be you."

Gia didn't move. She kept her eyes fixed on him, but her other senses were rapidly scanning the room, searching and identifying threats.

Gia didn't move until she was satisfied she'd cataloged them all. She walked the length of the bench nearest her, running her hand across the pitted surface along the edge.

"You're not even going to try to deny you were behind the theft, Puck?"

He shrugged, the hapless little gesture effortlessly charming. "Why bother? You're here. Obviously, you know that I was involved— although, I am curious. When did you realize I framed Jordan?"

"It's not a frame-up when the subject allows himself to be led into committing the crime," Gia muttered.

She stared at him, still in disbelief that John was the one behind this entire mess. "You played Jordan, didn't you? He actually thought you were helping him—being supportive. I saw you with him and the elders, playing the wise but reluctant counselor. Jordan had his pride. It wouldn't have been difficult to convince him to be dissatisfied with his life on the island."

She picked up a rusty scalpel with dried plant residue caked on the blade. "But now that I think about it, you were the one who brought him to the island in the first place. You were aware of the community's traditions, the steps they take to continue the bloodlines. Dalasini had already started quietly searching for candidates when you brought Jordan—a strong talent, fresh and young and just the right age to be bonded to Serin."

Gia narrowed her eyes. "What was he to you? I don't believe he was your nephew."

"Why don't you think we're related?" John seemed genuinely interested in her answer.

"Perhaps I'd like to think no one would screw over their own blood so badly. You know Serin executed him for what he did, right?"

It was as if a cloud passed over the sun—a momentary aberration. John's face cleared, and he shrugged. "A slight miscalculation. I underestimated her. I thought she'd feel too guilty for failing to return his affections."

He shuffled a few Petri dishes around, presumably to continue counting seeds.

"You didn't share a drop of blood." If there had been a chance for John's line to mingle with an Elemental one, he wouldn't have risked everything this way.

"No, those days are long over for me," John admitted. "Jordan was just a poor orphaned teen, very talented and personable. I took him under my wing."

"But your mentorship only went so far. You set him up, playing on his dissatisfaction until he joined you in betraying us."

John tsked. "Betrayal is such a strong word. I merely wanted to expand my horizons, test a few limits. But the archivists and you ladies are so protective of your powers."

Gia felt like screaming. "We freely shared our knowledge with you. You lied and stole from us. The worst part is *you didn't have to*. The archivists gave you carte blanche with our records. They would have let you borrow whatever you wanted, but that wasn't enough for you."

His eyes widened. "I appreciated that, but I came to the realization there was no point to it all."

"What the hell are you talking about? You had access to the most advanced magic repository in the world, yet you threw it away and for what?"

She waved to the sad basement laboratory. "So you can mix up poisons capable of killing all Supes or to continue that pathetic pursuit of all alchemists—searching for the philosopher's stone?"

John laughed. "My dear, I don't have to do *that*. I found the secret to eternal life long ago."

Her vaunted self-control was cracking under the strain. She expelled a frustrated breath. "So, you're just mad... Is it congenital or were you driven insane?"

"Neither, of course. But I don't pay the skeptics any mind. Not anymore. You see, all I have to do it wait...all the naysayers eventually die off. It's a numbers game. "

He waved dismissively, but there was an unwholesome excitement just below the surface. Joyful glee animated his features. "My child, I'm far older than you could ever imagine."

He leaned back as if they were enjoying a coffee in the sun. "I've had so many names I've forgotten some of them. But you've heard of a few of my more notable ones. Children learn them in school. Newton, for one. He's a great favorite. There are so many societies devoted to me under that name. Then there was the stint for her

Highness Queen Elizabeth when I first used the name John. It was so simple and utilitarian I decided to use it again and again over the years."

Gia resisted the urge to roll her eyes. Of course he was claiming to be John Dee. The occult astrologer was a go-to for mad megalomaniac practitioners. She couldn't count the number of times she'd stripped or killed a John Dee. It was like an insane human claiming to be Napoleon.

"Yes, yes," she said on a sigh. Gia had heard this kind of thing before, always from crazy, murderous practitioners just before she punished them.

"Anyone else in there?" she asked. "Archimedes, perhaps—*'give me a lever large enough and I will move the world'* and all that jazz?"

His mouth dropped open. "How astute of you to guess. You really are the brightest witch I've ever encountered. So noble, so gifted... Yes, Archimedes was my first name. I've grown quite fuzzy over the years about my own origins, but everyone remembers their first."

Gia sniffed. "No."

"Sorry, dear?" He leaned forward as if he'd suddenly grown hard of hearing, the weight of his many years pressing down on him.

It was a very good act. That or he really believed it.

"You are not old enough to be any of those men. You're a hundred and forty-three years old and not a year more. Younger than Caimen. More than Dalasini. And you're nowhere near as old as I am. Not to mention the fact I met Newton once. You're nothing like him."

Her heart was breaking in her chest. Part of her had hoped this was all a big mistake. But when she'd heard Jordan reading that recipe, she'd instantly known they weren't his words or his work. He'd been relaying orders for someone else.

The bored tone alone was tipoff enough. Jordan had been reluctantly performing a chore, and there were very few people he'd do actual work for. Her sister Serin was above suspicion. Jordan might have done work for one of her parents, but they would cut their own hearts out before betraying their community.

John, on the other hand, had lived among them, a trusted and benevolent presence. But for some reason, he'd acted like a visitor the entire time.

"I trusted you." There had been no reason not to. By the time she'd met him, he'd already been living on the island for a few years. To her, the fact he'd been embraced by that closed-off society meant he'd been thoroughly vetted. He was the only one Jordan would have done anything like this for.

Not to mention the fact Jordan would never send recordings to the gun manufacturer. He'd been a man of the modern age. He would have emailed the recipe. No, what had happened was that John had recorded him rattling off the poison's components. It had been John who sent them to Armand. She doubted Jordan had even known.

John had laid the trail of breadcrumbs to Jordan's door, but it was a half-hearted effort. In the end, he'd wanted the Elementals to know *he* was the one ultimately responsible.

"You wanted to get caught," Gia said, looking down her nose at him. "Like all sick criminals, you couldn't stand the idea of not getting the credit."

John's lips firmed into a thin line. "That is enough of that, young lady," he said sharply, a thread of an accent she'd never noted before rising to the forefront. "It's very rude. And the fact I don't resemble him is simple. It's a spell, dearie, one undetectable to even your admirable powers of perception."

He was so convincing she took a second gander at him. "Nice try. But of all my sisters, I'm the one you can't fool that way. Your bones don't lie. No spell can change them."

John paused, his face stiffening. "My bones?"

"Almost as good as stones. They're easier to read."

John snorted. "So it's like built-in carbon dating?"

She didn't answer.

The first hint of a sneer broke through the genial facade. "Well, if you insist on living in denial, far be it from me to try to correct you.

But I think you'll agree I've had quite a bit of luck with getting spells past you and yours."

Gia shifted her weight, hiding a clenched fist. The room grew colder as she thought back over recent events, connecting the dots.

"You were in touch with Stephanie Burgess, weren't you?" she said, replaying the details of the case that brought Alec and Diana together. "The masking spell was your work."

He affected modesty, waving his hand in a negative gesture. "Not all of it. I only made a small contribution. That Burgess girl was really quite a talent in her own right. I admired her moxy. It's really too bad Diana caught on to her so quickly. I was very interested in watching the girl's progress. So much potential up in flames..."

That witch had killed repeatedly to catalyze her spells. She'd broken the Covenant—had even murdered a child.

Gia refused to let her disgust and anger show. "And you were the one who gave the staff of Feng Po Po to the Colorado Basin pack traitor." Logan's mate had been shot by the man.

John held up his hands, flapping them like an amateur in a theater troop.

"Guilty again," he said in a slight singsong. "I've known Bishop Kane for years. Mutual interests and all that. Giving him the staff was strictly an experiment, of course. I made it work straight off. Handy little thing, the way it stripped the magic from a body, living or dead. But after realizing it wouldn't work on Elemental lines, there wasn't much point in keeping it around. I wanted to see how far Kane could go with it, if he would have more luck in retaining the magic it removed. He had the time, you see, and I had other irons in the fire."

"So was that your goal? To steal our power?" It was almost anti-climactic. Black magic practitioners had been trying to steal Elemental magic since the dawn of civilization—or very likely before. Even the archives didn't record their inception. But if there had been a first Elemental, then there had been a witch trying to take their magic as sure as the sun rose every day.

But John was shaking his head. "Nothing so plebeian," he insisted before coughing. "Well, not anymore. I've been studying the problem for decades. It was brutal at first. I didn't want to admit the truth, but I had to. You are Her chosen and Her chosen are always female. There's no changing that, believe me."

This time, John didn't try to hide his disdain. The choice of words and his emphasis on certain ones of them clicked.

No doubt he had hundreds of justifications for betraying them but in the end, the reason was simple misogyny. *Some things never change....*

"I understand now. You're not after Elemental magic because you want it. You're trying to take it because it lies exclusively in the hands of women."

She passed a hand over her eyes. "When did you convince yourself that you would be one of us if only males were chosen?"

"You don't know what you're talking about," he said, that clipped tone surfacing again.

It was British, but definitely not Newton or John Dee. The rhythm was too modern. A person's underlying speech pattern never changed, no matter how old they were. Even she could be dated by the way she spoke, not that anyone ever took the time to notice.

"Sorry, kiddo. As usual, you're way off." John set the dishes aside.

Gia twitched her wrist. A small throwing knife fell from the hidden holster strapped to her forearm into her hand. "Oh, I'm certain. This is all because you feel passed over."

There may have been more to it, but she wasn't interested in the minutiae of his reasoning. She was going to bury him. John's motives could rot with him.

John sprang out of his seat, striking like a cobra, faster than a man of his build should be able to move. He flung a thin-walled vial of glass at her, but her knife was already flying. She batted the container out of the air without touching it. It crashed to the floor, the noxious substance beginning to smoke on contact.

John clutched his shoulder, blood pouring from beneath his

fingers. Her knife had pierced down to the hilt. "That wasn't supposed to happen. I guess my deflection spell isn't working."

Gia withdrew her long blade from the holster at her back. "It's glass, and glass is made of sand."

"Of course," John winced, his round face sweating. "But it doesn't matter where the vial broke—just that it did."

Gia spun around, prepared to blow some poisonous fumes away, but there was nothing like that. The smoke was just smoke.

She faced John again as he was scrambling up, starting to run away. She sent her hands out, knocking him back to the ground with a little telekinetic push. A silent spell and the short blade materialized in her hand.

He turned around to face her. "Finally!" he sputtered.

Gia frowned as a drop hit her. The smoke bomb had drifted up and set off the sprinklers, but it wasn't water falling from the jets.

She knew the instant it hit her she'd miscalculated. The drop disappeared into her skin, instantly absorbed.

Her head began to swim and her ears dimmed, as if the sound in the room was coming from a great distance.

"Poison," she muttered, her stomach twisting painfully as the toxic rain saturated her hair and clothing. Gia fought to keep standing, but her legs felt like straw. She fell to her knees.

John was on his feet now. "I'm so glad that you're here to see this," he said, beaming. "I would have settled for Serin, too, of course, but your younger sisters wouldn't have appreciated what I've created here."

Bile rose in her throat, and she gasped aloud. Every drop that touched her sank through her skin and raced through her bloodstream, slowing it down as if were turning into tar.

"I made some refinements after the earlier version failed to kill Serin, but I think I've got it now. This is my *pièce de resistance*, my life's work," John exclaimed, holding his hands out like a parched man in the desert. "It is the ultimate poison and for good reason. I've been working on it for the last fifty years or so. It kills any Supernatural creature—every single one so far. None are immune."

"Can't...be...true." Her vision was darkening now. He couldn't have created something that worked on all of them. The species of the Otherkind were too varied and numerous. And he was standing there, hale and hearty. "It...would kill...you, too."

She rolled over on her back. Black threads appeared up and down her arms, thickening like tree roots.

He bent over her with a smirk. "That's right, it should kill me, too. After all, I'm a skilled practitioner of magic."

"Witches...can't..."

He held up his hands, rubbing the poison between his fingers. "No, they're not exempt. And no I haven't taken an antidote because there isn't one. It's a hundred-percent fatal. I've tested it extensively."

This was where she was supposed to ask how he'd done it, but Gia disappointed him by being unable to speak.

She tapped the floor weakly. By rights, she should have felt the stones and soil under the linoleum, but they weren't responding to her.

John was studying her avidly, but she gritted her teeth, refusing to writhe and show her pain when all she wanted to do was scream. It felt as if her insides were liquefying into toxic sludge.

"You really are a remarkable creature, Gia. No one else has lasted this long, and I soaked you in the stuff. The doses everyone else received were tiny by comparison. But this is very good news, very instructive. You were the strongest test case I could possibly conduct before the real thing."

Gia didn't answer. Her heartbeat was slowing. He'd won. She was dying.

Chingado.

She closed her eyes. Her only satisfaction was in knowing that her sisters would avenge her.

35

Was Gia still breathing? John couldn't tell, but it didn't matter. There was no coming back from his poison. It was only a matter of time.

I almost forgot. John picked up his video camera. Documentation was key. He needed to record every detail of this test. He wasn't going to be able to conduct another one. There wasn't a subject on earth that would be more informative.

He'd certainly gotten lucky. Serin and Gia were the Elementals who knew him best. Both trusted and cared for him. If it had been one of the others, this would have been far more difficult. The Fire Elemental would have set him on fire straight off. That one shot first and asked questions later. Of course, her flames would have set off the sprinklers as well, so perhaps that would have worked, but he wouldn't have been around to document the results.

He turned on the camera and grabbed a ruler, intent on capturing the thickness of the black veins running up and down Gia's body. He'd have to undress her to get the most precise measurements.

A little tremor ran through him. At first, he believed it was excitement, but the rattling of his many flasks and vials let him know that wasn't the case.

He frowned at the dust falling from the ceiling. They weren't on any fault-lines, but the tremors kept building and building until he could feel the earth rolling under his feet.

Damn. He should have known. A creature as powerful as the Earth Elemental would have had a fail-safe. Her death must have triggered it.

He huffed in annoyance, sucking in a shallow breath. The taste of the acrid poison hit his tongue. *Disgusting.* He spit, searching for something clean to wipe his mouth. Even though he was immune to the cocktail of toxins, ingesting it was a bad idea.

Rushing around, he grabbed his precious notebooks and a few of the choice items he'd kept from the Elementals' hoard. The data and those artifacts were the most important thing. He could recreate the poisons and set up a new lab elsewhere, but these were irreplaceable.

A hard jolt knocked him onto his rear end. John braced himself, using the bench to pull himself up. The entire room was rattling and shaking. A loud crack filled the room. The walls were starting to break up. He had to get out of here.

He cast a last longing glance at Gia. Unless he could carry her out, all that data would be lost.

John started for the body, determined to salvage his experiment, but the ground didn't cooperate. The linoleum parted, ripping apart as the earth rose. It swallowed Gia whole.

John swore and grabbed his bag, running for the stairs as the walls started coming down around him.

36

Serin fell, a stabbing pain in the vicinity of her heart.

"*Gia,*" she cried, putting her hands on her chest instinctively to keep herself from bursting open.

"Serin!" Daniel's arms hauled her up from the ground. Deep shudders racked her body, bone-deep jolts that made her entire body ache.

She cried out, her heart beat slowing in time with Gia's. Serin could feel her sister's essence being violently ripped away.

"*No,*" she moaned, cradling her knees.

Logan and Diana could feel it, too. They were screaming into the aether. Their voices drowned out Serin's cries.

Cars honked, and she could hear someone asking if she needed a doctor. "No, she's okay," Daniel lied, pulling her in close as he hurried them down the sidewalk.

"What's happening?" he asked, panic making his voice high and tight. "What do I do?"

"We need to go." Tears streamed down her cheeks and she could barely see, but they had to keep moving.

They had been tracking Uncle John for less than a day and she knew they were close. She was using one of his many discarded handkerchiefs to scry for him. It had led them to a little picturesque village on the Isle of Man.

She knew as soon as they were on the ground that John was there, but the signal immediately became confused. John had been prepared and had scattered spells and charms, laying false trails. Ignoring the beacons, she and Daniel scoured the town, turning around in circles when they had learned there was a famous ruin on the nearby cliffs.

Serin had known John most of her life. An atmospheric ruin on the coast? She hadn't needed the scrying spell to tell her that was where he was.

Forcing the pain to the back of her mind, Serin pushed out of Daniel's arms, determined to walk. She stumbled along the path to the castle when her mate hauled her to the side.

"Get on," he said, climbing on a motorcycle parked just outside a quaint pub.

It was stealing, but Serin didn't care. She swung her leg over the seat, then reached around him to put her hand on the ignition. A quick incantation and the motor roared to life. Daniel hit the gas and the bike jumped, flying down the street.

The castle was little more than a pile of fallen rocks near the cliff's edge.

"This is not what the townspeople described." Daniel spun in a bewildered circle. "There's supposed to be a standing structure here."

Serin examined the ground. There were fresh scars on the rocks. "This just happened."

A sob was carried on the wind. Serin turned to see Logan weeping openly from the cradle of Connell's arms.

The Were's face could have been carved from granite. "It's not true, is it?" he asked, his voice grim.

Diana appeared out of the corner of Serin's eye with Alec in tow. Daniel must have started a fire so the pair could travel here.

She tried to take a deep breath, but it was difficult with her chest muscles frozen. They didn't want to cooperate.

"Gia's here," Serin whispered, gesturing at the pile of stones that used to be a castle. "I can feel her."

But not her essence. Whatever circuit had connected them had been severed.

"But she's not dead.... She's just *not*." Diana's voice was shrill.

"She has to be. How else would we all be able to stand here, together? The Mother herself designed us so that would never happen."

Diana's face crumpled. She slid to the ground, hoarse jagged sounds coming from deep in her throat. Her vampire mate was holding her shoulders, squinting in the bright light. As a Daywalker, Alec could stand under the sun without bursting into flames, but he wasn't used to it.

Serin moved so they wouldn't see her wiping her eyes. Putting her hands together, she called on the Mother to return their sister, but deep down, she knew it was futile.

Their Mother slept on, undisturbed.

"We need to kill that fucker." Diana was furious.

Serin closed her eyes. "I will," she promised. "He can't hide from me now."

"Um, I hate to point out the obvious, but he just killed your strongest sister." Daniel's shoulders were tight, but his face was resolute. "You can't do this alone."

"No, Logan and I will hold that fucker down while you smash his face in. He's going to die screaming," Diana vowed.

"Hell yeah, he is." Logan wiped her eyes with the heels of her hand.

Daniel cleared his throat. "I actually meant me, but yeah, the more the fucking merrier."

"We're all going to help," Connell promised. "And once he's dead, we'll grind his bones and suck out the marrow."

Alec wrinkled his nose, but nodded sharply. "His head will hang in our hall for the rest of our days."

"You own a penthouse, not a medieval castle." Diana sighed as if this were a running argument, almost making Serin smile.

But she didn't. That wasn't going to happen for a long time.

The wind picked up, almost howling in their ears, and the air heated as if they were near a wildfire, but Diana had herself in hand. The disturbances weren't her or Logan. It was the earth, reacting.

The ground began to tremble. Connell's head whipped around, seemingly following something under the ground. "Uh, guys, we got trouble."

Daniel grabbed her hand. "We need to get out of here."

"No." Serin pulled away. She could feel it now, too. Nothing else could shift the earth like that except one of their own.

But the link was broken. Serin couldn't feel Gia. Whatever was coming toward them wasn't her.

No. It's too soon. The Mother couldn't have chosen another already. But the rumble in the earth continued.

Her hands flew up to her mouth. *No, no, no.* She had to stop this. Logan and Diana weren't ready. *She* wasn't ready.

Serin and her sisters spun around as the ground began to lift behind them a few steps away from where Alec was standing. He hopped to the side, scrambling away as the earth parted and a prone figure rose from the depths.

It was Gia. Her eyes were closed, disgusting thick black threads covering her arms and face.

"Oh my God," Daniel said, followed by a swear.

"It's Gia," Logan cried, running toward their sister.

Daniel ran in front of her, almost tackling her to make her stop.

"Hey!" Connell ran after them, growling. "Don't you fucking touch her."

"And she can't touch *her.*"

Serin pulled Connell off Daniel with a rough yank. "*Enough.*"

Her voice carried with supernatural power. Connell winced, his hands flying up to cover his sensitive ears. "He touched Logan," he growled.

"And he probably saved her life," Alec said, kneeling next to Gia. He scanned the mess on her skin. "She's soaked with toxins."

Diana stepped up to him. Quick as a flash, Alec was on his feet, his arms out to keep her from getting her any closer. "It's poison. Whatever killed her is a poison."

Connell's indignant expression melted away. "Fuck, he's right. I can smell it. There's everything there—nightshade, hemlock, and amanita just for starters. There's even garlic and wolfsbane."

Daniel fished something out of his pocket. It was a pair of rubber gloves. Kneeling, he reached out. Serin grabbed him before he touched the body. "I don't think you should touch it."

"It's okay," he said, nodding reassuringly. Very gently, he tilted Gia's head away from them, pulling her ponytail away from her neck.

"What are you doing?" she asked when he put two of his fingers on her skin.

"Checking for a pulse."

Connell sighed. "Daniel, I know you're new to this, but if the girls say she's gone, then she's gone. They're never wrong. It's actually super annoying."

Logan twisted at the hips, then punched her mate in the arm.

"Ow," he said, wincing and rubbing the spot.

"Daniel, we would be able to feel her," Serin explained, not wanting to prolong the torture. "Our connection has been severed. Her aura is gone—completely wiped away. That's what happens when you die."

Daniel tilted his head back. "Then why am I getting a pulse?"

Serin gasped, leaning down. He nudged her back with his shoulder so she wouldn't get too close, but she spotted it anyway—a telltale flutter at Gia's neck.

"It's weak, but it's steady. And her chest is moving. She's still breathing."

"How is that possible?" Diana asked. "Serin is right. Gia has no aura."

"Don't ask me," Daniel muttered, standing up and stripping off the gloves. He dug a little hole with the toe of his shoe, then dropped them inside. When he started to cover them up, the ground liquefied and swallowed them.

He straightened. "Okay. That was...interesting."

Serin shook her head, putting her hand on her mouth. "This shouldn't be possible."

"*Get it off her.*" Logan's red eyes were burning a hole into her.

She nodded hurried and backed up, gesturing for the others to do the same.

Closing her eyes, she pulled at the ocean. The water ran up the cliff face, working against gravity. It raced over the ground, running over Gia with churning force. Serin was determined to wash away every trace of the sticky poison.

When Gia was clean, Serin stopped, letting the water return, the venom diluting in the vastness of the ocean.

But the black threads hadn't disappeared. Gia didn't magically open her eyes.

Serin kneeled, resting her hands on the dirt. The earth responded by liquefying, pulling Gia down into its depths.

"What the hell?" Serin snatched her hands off the ground, and it stopped.

"Are...are you Earth now, too?" Logan's huge dark eyes blinked at her.

"No," Serin said automatically, gazing down at her hands.

"Are you sure?" Daniel asked.

"I—well, I don't think so, I don't feel any different."

Logan cocked her head and reached down, curiosity all over her expressive face. The same thing happened. "What the hell?"

Alec nudged Diana. Frowning, she crouched as well.

"Holy shit!" she cried when Gia began to sink. When she stopped, the body rose again.

"Is that the Mother? Are we supposed to share Gia's Earth talent now?" Logan asked.

Serin rubbed her forehead. "I don't think so. This isn't the Mother. I would feel that. I think She's still asleep. I...I believe this is the Earth itself. It swallowed Gia up to protect her. It's as if it's holding her in trust or something."

"Can you heal her?" Diana asked.

Serin took one more long look at their sister before shaking her head. "This is beyond my skill."

It would have been beyond Gia's as well. Elemental were soldiers, capable of triage and battlefield-level medicine. Anything more complicated and they were lost.

Logan hung her head. "Then there's no hope."

"Not necessarily," Daniel said. "It's bad, but there was to be someone in your world that might be able to help—the magic equivalent of a hotshot surgeon. A witch doctor or voodoo priest maybe?"

"We have healers in our community," Diana said. "There are two on T'Kaieri, but you'll remember they couldn't heal Serin. She did that on her own, with your help, and that was a lot less poison that this. Something tells me we won't be able to do the same here. Gia's aura is already gone."

Serin shook her head. "I don't know of any healer who could handle something like this. They'd have to be an expert on treating poisons *and* black magic. And anyone who was well-versed enough in the latter wouldn't be trustworthy."

"Why not?" Daniel asked.

"Because anyone with that knowledge would be a black witch—enemy number one...or at least they were until John revealed himself as an alchemist."

A hopeless silence descended on the group.

Alec cleared his throat. "Um, I might know someone."

His cheek was pulled up, a strange tension tightening his shoulders.

Diana scowled at him. "Who?"

"His name is Salvador," Alec said slowly. "He's a skilled healer, who has practiced on the fringe for years. He's very well versed on spells, curses, and poisons, but he's not a black witch."

"If he's not a practitioner, then how does he know so much about curses and poisons?"

"Well, that's the sticky part." His head drew back, and he turned to Serin. "You are not going to like this, but I've dealt with him twice before and he came through both times..."

"Just spit it out, Alec." Diana was done being patient.

"Salvador is an outcast. His father, Fulgencio Torre, disowned him over a decade ago."

"Fulgencio Torre as in Fulgencio Torre *Delavordo*?" Logan blanched.

Alec nodded. "Yes. The man you need was once the heir to the Delavordo throne."

Daniel scrubbed a hand over his face. "Fuck, I need a directory or something. Who are the Delavordos?"

Serin was getting a migraine. "They're one of the seven families— witch families so strong and rich they're a kingdom unto themselves. The Delavordos are the worst of the lot. More than half of all the black witches in history came from their family."

A short silence followed. "Do we have a choice?" Daniel asked Alec. "Is there no one else?"

Alec shrugged, shaking his head at the same time. "I can't think of anyone." He turned to Connell. "Can you?"

"No." The shifter grimaced as if smelling something foul. "But I think it's a bad idea."

"Well, unless someone thinks of a better one..." Alec trailed off.

Daniel put his hands on his hips. "It's up to you ladies. She's your sister."

"Gia calls the Delavordos public enemy number one," Diana said with a frown.

"She's also the one who always says there's an exception to every rule," Logan said. "I say we do it."

Both turned to Serin, waiting for her verdict. She blinked and swallowed before nodding. "Alec is right. We don't have a choice. Let's do it."

The second the words were out of her mouth, the ground rumbled. The soil liquified, wrapping around Gia like a blanket before she sank, disappearing from sight.

37

Salvador Francisco Delavordo unwound the bandage around the girl's chest, making sure his eyes stayed on the wound located over her heart. Thanks to the herbs he'd administered earlier, she was still insensible. She wouldn't have known if he saw her breasts, but he adjusted the sheet anyway if only to preserve her modesty in his own head.

The blackened center of the injury had faded to a sickly green. Some of the edges were still purple, but he was reassured by what he saw. The girl was going to make a full recovery.

He went to the doorway of his makeshift examination room, waving in the grief-stricken parents.

"The curse is responding to the poultice," he told them in Spanish. "She needs to rest for a few more weeks, but she will recover."

The girl's mother surprised him, jumping forward to burst into tears against his chest. He stiffened. When she didn't let go right away, he patted her awkwardly on the back.

"It's all right," her husband said, helping pry her hands off him.

The devoted mother and father had driven thousands of miles, selling tamales and homemade sweets along the way to pay for the gas they needed to make the journey.

Salvador nodded stiffly. On those occasions when he was able to help, he was frequently subjected to bouts of emotion from the families of his patients. Despite the number of times it happened, he still wasn't used to it. His parents hadn't been big touchers.

Salvador hid his discomfort with action, bustling around the room getting more ingredients together so they could take the medication they needed home.

"You'll have to reapply the poultice twice a day for the first week," he said, rattling off other instructions for bathing and a diet that would speed the healing process, which the father scribbled down on a worn paper pad.

Salvador caught himself halfway through his list of recommended fruits. "Do you want me to continue?" he asked.

More often than not, the families who came to him couldn't afford the long list of things he recommended.

The man waved him on. "Some in our village have promised to help, but..." He exchanged a loaded glance with his wife.

"Yes," Salvador prompted when the couple remained quiet.

The woman leaned forward, her eyes heating with anger. "The one who did this, the Brujo, he is still there. He was angry at Angelica for rejecting him, so he hexed her. He has done it before, years ago when his lover chose another. The Brujo is older than I am... Everyone is afraid of him."

"I understand," Salvador said, his lip curling.

Most of the women he saw had been struck down by a male witch or someone who could afford to employ one. Sometimes it was a jealous rival, but those cases were the minority. If was a woman was hexed, there was almost always a man behind it.

He bent at the waist, digging out a small wooden box from under his workbench. Flipping the lid, he dug through the various cards and small scraps of paper. Each bore the name of someone who he'd done business with, specifically those who owed him.

His healing business was strictly pro bono. Salvador paid the bills by crafting spells and charms for a highly curated group of members of the Otherkind. Most paid cash, but depending on the client, he sometimes bartered for a service in trade. These favors came in handy on occasions like this.

He riffled through the short stack of papers, pausing when he came across Alec Broussard's name.

Tempting. But he couldn't use that one. Though Alec shared his eye-for-an-eye philosophy, rumor had it he'd taken one of the Elementals as a mate.

Salvador had initially dismissed the rumor as utter rubbish, but the story kept spreading and spreading. More than one reliable source swore it was true. Alec could have handled the patient's problem with a flick of his pulse-less wrist, but Salvador couldn't risk drawing an Elemental's attention to himself or his operation. Sighing, he shifted the paper to the back of the pile.

He fished out two other pieces, debating the merits of each. The Loki wasn't all that reliable, but the shifter would make a bloody mess out of the culprit. While that would be satisfying, a bit of discretion was safer.

His ears almost missed the sound—a whispery susurration. He glanced up as the girl's mother went out to the cottage's waiting room. Had she invited one of his neighbors in?

Perhaps another client had arrived. He was expecting one of the locals to stop by with some herbs, which they were collecting for him as part of their payment.

The shifter will finish the job, Salvador decided. If things got a little bloody, it would only serve as a warning to others. He just had to impress on Canaan that he needed to make sure he kept the collateral damage down to the guilty party and any henchman he might have.

"Excuse me, señor."

Salvador turned around. The parents were staring at him with wide eyes. "You...you have a visitor."

He smiled reassuringly, wondering why they appeared so shocked. "It's fine. I was expecting her."

The father's mouth dropped open, and his wife gasped. "You *were?*"

Salvador frowned, deciding their reaction didn't fit with the arrival of a teenage girl with baskets of wildflowers and grasses.

His stomach dropped open when he saw the antechamber. The packed dirt floor had been raised into a makeshift platform—an altar. There was a woman lying on it. Her dark hair was braided, the long length of it wrapping around from the back of her head to fall at her side below her shoulders.

The woman's luminescent cocoa skin was marred by thick black spidering veins that covered all of her visible body. Underneath, the face was a work of art. Full lips and cheekbones that spoke of both European and a Native American heritage.

His stomach fluttered, a sense of awe filling him. This person was important. He didn't know how he knew that, but the certainty was there. What the hell had happened to her? Salvador put on a glove before reaching out to touch one of the thick raised strands. It was rock hard. He'd never seen anything like it.

Salvador turned back to his guests, pressing the shifter's name and number into the father's hand. "Call this man. He can help you with Angelica's attacker. She can go home now, but you better take her out the back way."

He turned back to the body, his heart beating too fast. "It seems I have another patient."

THE END

The end is just the beginning!

A MADMAN IS TRYING TO KILL OFF MOTHER EARTH.

Earth Elemental Gia has been poisoned, and the only man who can heal her is the scion of the most evil witch family in history, Salvador. If she fails to trust him—or if putting her trust in him fails her—Mother Earth will die.

After a madman ingratiated himself to the Water Elementals, only to later betray them, Gia's trust is shaken. But the same misogynist man who infected her with poison threatens to infect Mother Earth as well—an act that could change life on earth irrevocably...or end it forever.

A dangerous journey to the Mother is only half the battle. The real challenge comes in the form of what Gia must agree to once she arrives: wipe out the human race she's spent her whole life protecting...or wipe out the supernatural race she belongs to herself.

Available Now

Thank you for reading Water! Reviews are an author's bread and butter. If you liked the story please consider leaving a review.

Subscribe to the L.B. Gilbert or Lucy Leroux Newsletter for a *free* full-length novel!
www.elementalauthor.com/newsletter/
www.authorlucyleroux.com/newsletter

ABOUT THE AUTHOR

L.B. Gilbert is another name for USA Today Bestselling Author Lucy Leroux.

L.B. spent years getting degrees from the most prestigious universities in America, including a PhD that she is not using at all. She moved to France for work and found love. She's married now and has a polyglot 4 year old. The family moved back to California a few years ago.

She has always enjoyed reading books as far from her reality as possible but eventually the voices in her head told her to write her own. So far the voices are enjoying them. And judging by the awards, a few other people are as well. You can check out the geeky things she likes on Twitter or Facebook.

If you like a little more steam with your Fire, check out the author's award-winning Lucy Leroux titles, FREE to read on Kindle Unlimited.

www.elementalauthor.com

or

www.authorlucyleroux.com